MAGIC IN THE RAIN

A CLEAN, SMALL TOWN ROMANCE

MCKENNA FAMILY ROMANCE
BOOK SIX

LUCINDA RACE

MC TWO PRESS

Copyright © 2017 by Lucinda Race
Published by MC Two Press

Edited by Kimberly Dawn
Cover Design by Meet Cute Creative
Manufactured in the United States of America First Edition
December 2017

ISBN 978-0-9986647-2-9
ISBN Paperback 978-0-9986647-3-6

Thank you for purchasing Magic in the Rain. I hope you enjoy reading Dani and Paul's story. I love writing characters who are a bit older and deserve a second chance at happiness. So, turn the page and fall in love in with the McKenna Family.

If you'd like to stay in touch, consider joining my

newsletter. I release it twice per month with tidbits, recipes, and an occasional a special gift just for my readers.

https://lucindarace.com/newsletter/ and there is a free book when you join! Happy reading…

For Rick
Thank you for your never-ending support and love.
I love you…

Starting over is easy when you find love

PROLOGUE

QUICK NOTE: If you enjoy Magic in the Rain, be sure to check out my offer for a FREE novella at the end. With that, happy reading!

***

Dani jiggled the knob. Satisfied the café door was secured, she paused to check her reflection in the window. *Being a brunette suits me.* She ran her fingers through her shoulder-length curls. *I guess that's why I was born one.*

I'll keep this color for a while. I'm tired of not recognizing myself in the mirror.

After taking the stairs two at a time, she pushed open her apartment door. Stepping out of her clogs, she left them by the door. She flopped onto the sofa and propped her feet up on the coffee table. Sorting through the mail, she said, "Junk, bill, junk…" She turned the cream-colored square envelope over. There was no return address. She lifted the envelope to her nose. The distinct musk smell was faint but unmistakable. Dani's heart quickened.

"It can't be."

She dropped the envelope onto the table as if it burned her fingers, staring at it.

"I'm not going to open it. It's going in the trash."

She dropped it on top of the garbage and grabbed a bottle of water from the fridge. Taking a long drink, she watched the envelope out of the corner of her eye, as if expecting it to come to life.

Curiosity got the best of her. She retrieved

it from the trash. She ripped open the envelope. A strangled laugh filled the small room. Why was she afraid of a silly puppy card? She flipped it open.

Looking forward to seeing you again. It was unsigned. But the handwriting… "Derek."

She ripped the card and envelope into tiny pieces and buried it at the bottom of the can.

1

ani surveyed the contents of the
farm stand basket, thrilled to see
apples and a couple of sweet pumpkins to
spice up the baking case. She loved the fall
season with the comforts of stews and soups
simmering and a reason to bake lots of pies
and cookies. Not that Dani needed an excuse
to bake. Since becoming the primary cook at
What's Perkin', she thought she had died and
gone to career heaven. Peeling, slicing, and
dicing the pumpkin and contemplating a new
muffin flavor, Dani heard the bell on the front

door jingle. Wiping her hands on a towel, she peered through the window to see who had arrived.

"Morning, Luke. When you're ready, come on back and we can go over today's specials."

She really liked working with Luke Ford. He handled the front with ease while she filled all the orders he sent her way. It was a perfect working relationship.

"Give me five. I want to get the lights on and coffee brewing."

Dani glanced at the wall clock, wondering what time Cari would be in, when the back door slammed with a bang. Cari entered, shaking off her coat.

"My gosh it's windy out there and raining buckets." She glanced at Dani. "Did you happen to hear the long-range forecast?"

"I did. Damp and rainy. It's a good day for a new beef stew and your signature buttermilk biscuits."

Cari smiled. "That's why you're perfect for this job; you read me like a book."

"The one thing I've learned since working here, comfort food is always on the menu."

Cari's smile was genuine and lit up her deep-green eyes. "What's it been, almost two years since you started working for me? We need to talk about a raise."

"Cari, that isn't necessary. You've been more than generous with my pay, and the rent on the apartment upstairs isn't really the market rate. I'm perfectly content with how things are."

Cari's eyebrow arched. "I've never heard of anyone saying, don't give me a raise. You're a rare breed, Ms. Danielle Michaels."

Dani was pleased with the opportunity to take over the kitchen for Cari's daughter, Kate. It was the highest compliment Dani could have received. Then, to top it all off, when Dani asked for some ideas on where she could find a decent place to live, Cari and her husband, Ray, showed her the upstairs apartment and said it was hers if she wanted it. Dani had been bowled over.

"Right back at ya, Cari. I don't know of many people who would give a stranger a job and apartment with zero references."

"You underestimate yourself, Dani. We put you through a week-long screening process. It might not seem like it was a long time, but you stepped up and showed us your talent. You deserve to stand in front of this stove."

Luke popped his head inside the swinging door. "Dani, are you ready to fill me in? It's almost showtime."

Dani rattled off the breakfast and lunch specials with Luke taking notes. He would transfer it to the blackboard out front. She returned to the baking list, finishing the house specialty, blueberry muffins, cookies, and breads until the front cases were overflowing with tempting treats. Later, she was going to whip up a batch of pumpkin caramel cupcakes. On weekdays, with the exception of holidays, all breakfast platters were some type of sandwich combo or burrito, and then on the weekends, Dani would whip up eggs and pancakes. The bakery portion of the café was in higher demand Monday thru Friday, as many customers were on the commuting trek.

Dani smiled when Cari wandered into the kitchen and broke off a piece of a fresh oatmeal cookie. She perched on the stool.

"Dani, I'd like to talk to you about something. If you think I'm sticking my nose into your private business, I'll drop the subject."

Dani didn't look up from the batter she was stirring. "What's up?"

"You're a hard worker, whether it's in the shop, babysitting for Jake and Sara's triplets, or lending a hand at Ellie's gallery, but I don't see you dating. You're not obligated to the McKenna-Davis clan. You can say no to us anytime we infringe on your personal time."

Dani laughed. "You don't have to worry, Cari. I love feeling like I'm an honorary member of the family. As far as The Looking Glass, I never had much time to appreciate art in any form. This has opened a whole new world for me, and Ellie and I have become great friends."

"I know Ellie feels the same way. She's always had trouble letting people in, but I think Pad Stone has helped Ellie blossom."

"It certainly doesn't hurt to have a handsome man in your life." Dani slid a tray of cupcakes into the oven and avoided Cari's gaze.

"And what about a handsome man for you, Dani?" Cari spoke softly so Luke wouldn't overhear the conversation.

"Boyfriends and me aren't a good combo. I'm better off alone." Dani dropped the bowl in the sink and was grateful when Luke announced an order and put it on the pass-through shelf.

Dani picked up the order. "I need to get this ready."

"All right." Cari stood. "Well, if you need a hand, let me know."

Dani steadied her racing heart. If Cari only knew the truth, would she want Dani working for What's Perkin'? Fearing she knew what the answer would be, she reminded herself she had to keep the past in the past. Reinventing herself was the right move at the time and keeping it a secret was her only choice.

***

*E*llie bopped in the door of the shop. "Hey, Mom, Luke. How goes the morning?" She mopped her forehead with a napkin. "Any idea what Dani is whipping up for today's specialty cupcake? I was hoping to pick up a few. Pad's coming for dinner tonight."

"And what makes tonight different?" Luke teased. "I thought you two were stuck like glue. He spends more time with you than at work."

Ellie grinned. "Tonight it's Pad's turn to cook, and my job is dessert."

Cari smiled at her youngest daughter. "Been for a run already?"

"Of course. Can't you tell by the rain running off my face?" Ellie took the glass of water Cari handed her.

"Breakfast, Ellie?" Luke paused at the kitchen door.

"Um, yeah, I guess I could suffer with a little something."

Laughing, Luke went into the kitchen and told Dani that Ellie was out front.

Dani set a plate in front of her friend sitting at the counter. "Just the way you like it with extra cheese and hot sauce."

"A burrito." Ellie picked it up and took a huge bite, sauce dribbling down her chin. She closed her eyes. "This is so good." Ellie winked at Dani. "Don't ever tell Kate, but this is better than hers."

Dani made a cross over her heart. "Your secret is safe with me." Dani poured herself a cup of hot water and dropped a tea bag in. "Care if I sit?"

Ellie twirled on the stool to face Dani. "Sure. We haven't talked in what eight hours?"

The girls chatted and laughed, happy to

have found a kindred spirit in the other. Ellie had been through some rough patches, losing her dad when she was barely five, pushing herself to get through college early, and then opening up a gallery only to have it threatened by her former boss. In the process, she allowed herself to open her heart to find love and friends. She often wondered how Dani had found her way to Loudon alone and lived out of a tent. It didn't matter, Dani had found her place at What's Perkin' and as an extended member of the family. However, nothing was ever as simple as it appeared.

2

"I've got news about Pad." Ellie leaned in. "But don't say anything. We want to tell the family over the weekend."

"Are you engaged?" Dani whispered.

Ellie giggled. "No, nothing like that, although the thought has crossed my mind a few times. I might be ready to take the plunge. But no. Hank Booth, the chief of police, offered him a permanent job on the force and Pad accepted."

"Does that mean he won't be doing photography anymore?" Dani wondered aloud.

"No, but he wants to be home more, and he loved being a cop. He just didn't want to do undercover work anymore. He still doesn't talk about what he went through before we met. It must have been pretty awful."

"It'll be nice to have him around all the time." Dani winked. "Maybe this means wedding bells are in your future?"

Ellie grinned. "Maybe. But keep our secret until Mom says something. I'm going to have the family over on Sunday, and of course, I expect you there too."

"Jeez, El. I don't want to intrude on a family thing," Dani protested.

"You're an honorary McKenna, and besides, I won't take no for an answer, but there is one small caveat."

"I think I know what's coming…"

"Can you fix something for dessert? Nothing fancy, but I do love your chocolate cream pie."

"You got it." Dani beamed. It was a good feeling to be, in some small way, a part of a family. She had some place to go for holidays, and they had even given her a birthday party the first year she moved to Loudon. Last year, they surprised Dani again on her birthday when there was another dinner party for her. "What time?"

"I'll close the shop at four, so come over about five." Ellie glanced at her watch. "I gotta fly, but remember, mum's the word until Sunday."

Dani crossed her hand over her heart. "I won't tell a soul."

Ellie called out goodbye to her mother and Luke. "Oh." She stopped short. "Any cupcakes today?"

"I'll have something before lunch. Should I save you a few?"

"You know me too well. I'll stop back if you can put six aside?"

"When we close, I'll swing over. It will be good to stretch my legs."

"Sounds good. See ya." Ellie left through the back door and Dani went back to baking.

She needed to whip up the promised cupcakes. She was already looking forward to hanging out with Ellie.

*D*ani was strolling up the sidewalk when she noticed a cop car sitting outside Ellie's. Concerned, she walked faster.

Almost jogging up the driveway, Dani relaxed when she heard deep male laughter. Ellie wasn't alone. Ever since Ellie had been attacked last year, Dani had been on edge, despite the fact that the person responsible was locked up.

Giving a sharp rap on the door, Dani called out hello and walked in. This was the norm after Ellie had admonished Dani about standing on formality when dropping by.

"Come on in, we're in the family room," Dani heard Ellie call out.

She set the cupcake box on the counter and went down the hallway toward the back of the house. She was taken aback when she discovered a police officer in uniform sitting in the chair.

"Am I interrupting anything?" Dani asked.

"Not at all," Pad said. "My new partner, Paul, stopped over." Ellie looked from Dani to Paul. "Have you two met?"

Dani shook her head. "No."

Paul stood up. "Yes, we met last year when Ellie was attacked and I've been in What's Perkin' many times." Extending his hand, he said, "Paul Greene, at your service, Miss?"

"Dani Michaels." Dani withdrew her small hand from his firm handshake. "I work at What's Perkin'."

"So, you're the one responsible," Paul teased.

Dani's heart raced. "I'm sorry. Responsible?"

"The extra miles I've had to run. Your cupcakes are fantastic, and I'm a huge fan. Pad has brought some to the station from time to time.

I think it's when he feels sorry for the boys in blue, to be honest."

Dani reminded herself to breathe. Paul Greene, despite his slender frame, dirty-blond hair, and his boyish good looks, was Ellie and Pad's friend. He must be a good guy.

"That's me, the baker." Dani forced herself to smile. "Ellie, I'm going to run since you have company. I put the cupcakes on the counter."

Ellie jumped up. "Stay. I was waiting for you. We're going to have coffee."

"Don't let me scare you away. I just stopped by to check on my buddy and they coerced me into coffee too."

Dani would have had to be blind to not see the deep dimples when Paul smiled. "Well, you've talked me into it. But I can't stay long."

"It's all settled, then. Paul just finished his shift so there's no reason for anyone to rush off." Ellie went toward the kitchen with Dani trailing.

"Why didn't you tell me you were having company?" Dani murmured.

"Paul's become a great friend. He really helped me get through the worst time in my life." Ellie glanced at Dani while she got water from the tap. "He's a sweet guy. You don't need to look at him like he's a wolf that's going to eat you alive."

"It's not like that, Ellie. You know I'm shy." Dani pushed her oversized glasses up her pert nose and brushed back her bangs.

"Did you see how cute he is? Of course, not as tall as Pad, but still, some girls would go weak in the knees for his crystal-blue eyes."

"I didn't notice," Dani lied.

Ellie gave her a knowing smile and set out mugs on a tray along with the cupcakes and napkins. "Would you grab the cream from the fridge and the sugar bowl?"

Dani did as requested. "How well does Pad know Paul?"

"He's tagged along a few times when we've gone fishing, and I know he and Pad have been running together quite a bit. I'm glad he's making friends in Loudon."

Pad and Paul came into the kitchen. "What's taking you two so long? Did you send Dani back to the shop for more cupcakes?" Pad laughed. "I don't know if six will be enough."

Dani blushed with the implied compliment. "I can run back to the café. I think there were a few left unless Cari took them home."

"No need. I'll be good and share with everyone." Pad picked up the tray. "Deck or family room?"

Ellie glanced at the thermometer outside. "The rain's stopped and it's warmed up. Let's go out back."

Paul held the door open for the group and waited until Dani stepped outside before closing it.

The conversation never slowed, and with the sun almost kissing the horizon, Pad's stomach rumbled.

Dani teased, "Ellie, I think your man is starving."

Pad asked, "Instead of me cooking, who wants to have pizza? Paul, Dani, are you interested in hanging out a little longer?" Pad grinned at his girl. "Ellie does great takeout."

"Hey, are you saying I can't cook?" Ellie tried to look irritated but laughed instead.

"Not at all. You're good at everything you touch when it comes to food, but I'm in the mood for pizza from Slices."

Paul looked around the trio. "Well, you can count me in. Pizza is a major food group in my book."

Dani hated to be a wet blanket but didn't relish the idea of walking home after dark, and she didn't want to ask Pad for a ride. "I think I'm going to head out. I didn't bring a flashlight and critters are coming out after dark. I don't think Cari would appreciate her kitchen smelling like Pepé Le Pew. It would be a business killer."

"No, stay. We'll walk you home," Ellie pleaded.

"Dani, I can drop you off. It's not out of my way at all." Paul's voice was like warm honey to Dani. "I'm going with Pad to drop off the cruiser and pick up my truck. The neighbors won't think you're in trouble with the law."

Dani tamped down her instinct to flee. She wanted to continue being with friends, as her apartment got lonely at night. "You talked me into it."

Pad and Paul took off while Ellie called in their order and then texted the pickup number to Pad. "I ordered some wings and salad too. We'll have more than enough for four, but pizza is tasty for breakfast, don't you think, Dani?" Ellie touched her arm. "Earth to Dani?"

"Sorry, I was thinking about the next cupcake special and didn't hear what you were saying."

"Is everything all right? You seem distracted." The girls had settled into overstuffed chairs in the family room. "I hope you're not upset we sort of pressured you into staying for dinner."

"No, I'm happy to be included. I'm not a fan of walking in the dark." Dani choked back the fear in her voice.

"Dani, what's really going on? You got nervous when you saw Paul in uniform, and I would never think you were afraid of anything, much less the dark. You lived in the state forest when you first came to town."

Dani struggled with her inner self, desperately wanting to confide in Ellie but worried about what she might think.

"In a nutshell, before I came to Loudon, I was in a really bad relationship with a fireman. He wasn't the guy I thought he was. On the outside, he was all charming and sweet, but out of the public eye, he was nasty. Finally, I reached my breaking point and broke up with him. Unfortunately, he didn't take it well and had one of his buddies stop by the bakery I worked at, saying I had taken money from his wallet." Anguished, she continued. "I swear I didn't take it. I think he did it to harass me, and it didn't stop at just the one time. He was unrelenting. I had to get out. When my old boss decided to retire and move away, I took off. For a long time, I didn't even tell my parents where I was living. I was afraid all men in uniform would stick together, and he'd send someone else after me. About a month ago, I got a letter. It wasn't signed, but I know it was from him."

"Dani." Ellie took her ice-cold hands and rubbed them. "Why didn't you tell me or at least Mom? She and Ray would have made sure to have an auto floodlight installed at the very least. We wouldn't want you to feel uneasy in your home."

"I'm not going to burden any of you with my problems." Dani pulled away and looked out the back window. "It's my problem, and I'll take care of it, even if it means I have to move again."

"Pardon me for being selfish, but I finally have a good friend, and I'm not going to let some jerk drive you out of town. Besides, he doesn't even live around here." Ellie put her arms around Dani. "Let me help you. Let us help you."

"El, help with what?" Pad stood in the doorway with a huge pizza box, and Paul was right behind him, holding a large paper bag.

"It's nothing, Pad," Dani interjected. "Ellie is going to help me pick out a new pair of boots." Dani tried to brush aside the conversation.

Ellie looked at Pad. His brow creased. "Dani, I think you should tell Pad. He'll know what to do. He's one of the good guys."

"It's nothing, really. I'm overreacting is all." Dani looked from Ellie to Pad and then Paul. "Really."

Paul crossed the room. "Is someone bothering you around the shop, Dani?"

"No, I haven't seen anyone." Dani wrung her hands and cried, "This is what I wanted to avoid, having people know the truth." Dani tried to flee, and Ellie stepped between her and the door.

"It's time to stop running, Dani, and between the four of us, we can come up with a plan. I promise, no one will blame you for someone else's actions."

Pad gestured to the chair. "I've always believed the best place to start over is to revisit the beginning, get a new perspective, and then the solution will follow."

Dani sat down, dropping her head into her hands. After taking a few deep, ragged breaths, she looked up. "You have to promise me you won't tell Cari and Ray. I don't want them to worry."

"Dani, I can't promise you. If there's something Mom should know, we have to tell her." Ellie perched on the chair. "But Mom won't be angry with you. She's been through enough in her lifetime to know when a friend needs help. You need help."

Pad and Paul both sat on the edge of the couch, waiting for Dani to begin.

"About five years ago, I worked at a bakery in Chester. I started there when I was in high school and knew most of the regulars. It was a popular spot for cops and firemen, and Angelo encouraged them to stop by for coffee. You know, if the cops are in and out, it keeps the riffraff down."

Paul nodded. "It's a great perk to get hot coffee at various locations."

"After I graduated from high school, my parents moved out west, but I wanted to stay on at the bakery. I found a small apartment and kept working with the Hassetts. Helen was an amazing cake baker, and I loved working with her. The way she combined flavors was light years beyond what I can do. Anyway, Angelo, Helen's husband, taught me about breads, and I planned to buy them out when it was time for them to retire. And then he walked into the bakery, and I was a goner. I think it was love at first sight. Derek is a fireman. He's a big guy, strong and always joking. He was off duty, and it was his turn to pick up muffins for the next shift. After that first day, he volunteered to pick up breads and anything else he thought the guys would eat. The first time he asked me out, I thought, why did this guy want to go out with a little mouse like me? I accepted before he could change his mind."

Dani stopped and took a sip of cold coffee. "We spent a lot of our free time together, and I was awestruck. All the girls drooled over him when we were out, but he only had eyes for me."

She exhaled. "After about six months, we started staying together at his place several nights a week, and a couple months afterward, I gave up my apartment and we lived together full-time. He would bring home flowers and little gifts on a regular basis, and then things slowly started to change. He started to criticize what I wore, how I cooked, how I cleaned. Nothing I did was good enough."

Ellie grasped Dani's hand. "Sweetie, you know he was verbally abusing you, and it sounds like nothing you could have done would have made him happy."

"At the time, I thought I was a failure and it was my fault. Somehow, I was flawed. And then Maureen, an old friend of my mother's, stopped at the bakery. It was like she could see right through me, right to my soul and my bleeding heart. She asked if I would meet her after work to talk. We met at a fast-food joint and, over French fries, I told her everything but begged her not to tell my mother. I was sure she wouldn't understand, and they loved Derek. He was the perfect boyfriend in my parents' eyes."

Pad spoke gently. "Dani, this is often the case with men who abuse women. They can be very charming to everyone, but behind closed doors, they want to control the women they claim to love. You could have done everything he asked, and it still wouldn't have been good enough."

"I know that now. After talking to Maureen, I started to understand. She gave me her number and told me to call anytime. We talked a few more times. After each time, I got stronger and more in control of my emotions. I planned on leaving, and I never said anything to Derek. After the bakery closed and he went to work, I packed everything I could into my car and took off, and I've never looked back."

"Is that how you ended up in Loudon?" Ellie asked.

Dani nodded. "It wasn't a direct route. I drifted around for almost a year."

Paul had been listening quietly until he asked, "Have you heard from this guy since you've been here?"

"My parents know where I'm living. I've asked them not to say anything to Derek if he calls or give him my address. But then I got a card, but it was unsigned. I don't know for sure if it was from Derek."

Paul looked at Pad, his lips in a thin, hard line.

"What did it say?" Ellie asked.

"Dear Danielle. I hope you're doing well. Looking forward to seeing you."

"Do your parents know why you broke off the relationship?" Paul asked.

"I told them it was a bad breakup and nothing more."

"Were you ever afraid for your safety?" Pad jumped in.

Dani chewed on her lower lip before answering. "There were a couple of times I thought he wanted to hit me, but the most he did was grab my arm once."

Paul and Pad glanced at each other. "Dani, did he leave any bruises on your arm?"

Dani nodded. Tears hovered in her eyes. "I never told anyone. He said it was my fault. I made him angry."

"You know that's a lie, right?" Ellie's voice cracked.

Dani looked at her hands in her lap. "Yes."

Paul pulled a card out of his shirt pocket. "Dani, take this. If you hear from him or if, for any reason, you think you're not safe, call me, day or night. My cell number is listed."

"Do you think he found me?" Dani's voice quivered.

"I don't have any reason to think he'll go out of his way to come here, but I'd feel better if you had my number. Actually, program it into your phone."

Ellie grabbed Dani's handbag. "I think you should put Pad's cell number in there too. Strength in numbers." Ellie's voice was calm and soothing.

With hands shaking, Dani did as they asked. When she was done, she looked up. "I'm sorry I was such a downer, and now the pizza's cold."

Pad smiled. "I've eaten a lot of cold pizza in my day, and as far as I'm concerned, that's the way it tastes best."

Dani looked at her friends. "Then I guess we should eat."

3

Dani peered into the shadows. An involuntary shiver raced down her spine. Steeling herself for the walk home, she jumped as she felt someone's hand on her shoulder.

"There's nothing to worry about, Dani. I'm here."

"Paul. I'm fine. I should have grabbed a jacket."

He cocked one eyebrow. "You're not a good liar."

Relieved to have company, she said

goodbye to Ellie and Pad. The pair walked down the back steps and headed down Main Street.

"This is very nice of you, to walk me home. Are you sure I'm not out of your way?" Dani said. "And what about your truck?"

"It's not a big deal. I'll walk back and get it. It's a nice night to walk."

After the short stroll, Dani stopped at the base of the stairs to her apartment. "Here we are."

"It's pretty dark up there. Do you want me to come up and take a look around?"

Dani shook her head. "I'll be fine. Thanks." She stepped onto the bottom stair and turned. "Paul, thanks again for everything."

"No need to thank me. I didn't do anything yet. But you need to tell Cari and Luke. If you have a picture, show them and Ellie too. This way, if someone comes poking around, they'll be in the loop."

"I'll give it some thought." She ran up the steps lightly, and Paul waited until she was safely inside and heard the lock click into place. Dani hovered near an open window. She heard Paul on his cell phone.

"Hey, it's Paul. Can you ask the patrol guys to keep an eye open for anyone loitering around What's Perkin'? I'll swing by and fill you in. We may have a situation brewing."

Dani pulled back the curtain and watched as Paul walked away. What had possessed her to confide her deepest, darkest secret to Ellie, Pad, and his new partner? She turned the teakettle on and waited for the water to boil. The small task helped calm her down. The phone ringing shattered the silence. Dani jumped. She glanced at the caller ID.

"Hi, Mom. I didn't expect you to call tonight. It's not Wednesday or Sunday."

Dani heard her mother laugh. "Hello, Danielle. I had to tell you, Derek called tonight. He's anxious to get in touch with you. Can I give him your number?"

"Absolutely not. Mom, please. We've been over this time and time again."

"Sweetheart, he says he's heartbroken and wants to make amends."

Dani held her temper in check. "Mom, I'm not ready to face him, and until I am, please don't give him my number or tell him where I work or live."

"All right, if you insist. If it makes a difference, he sounds like he misses you."

If only Dani's mother could see her pacing the floor, she wouldn't be pressing the point. "Did you call to plead Derek's case?"

Mom ignored the question. "Well, I'd love to chat, but your dad and I are on our way out for dinner, but I did promise Derek to get in touch with you right away. I'll call you Sunday when we both have time to talk."

Dani sighed. "Sounds good, Mom. Have fun with Dad."

After the typical good nights and love yous, Dani sank down onto the hard kitchen chair, oblivious to the screeching kettle.

"How can I convince her to stop talking to Derek?"

Dani turned over several ideas in her head until the realization dawned on her. The only way for this to end was to tell her mother the truth. Deciding Sunday was a good day for a tough conversation, Dani turned off the kettle and dropped in a tea bag. *Hopefully, this will calm my frazzled nerves.*

Sunday evening approached, and Dani had prepared a couple of sweet treats for Ellie's cookout. She glanced out the window and noticed ominous clouds gathering, hoping it would hold off until later tonight. She was looking forward to getting together with Ellie's family. The triplets were always a hoot, and no one made her feel like an outsider.

Dani parked next to the curb and began to unload her truck, when a deep male voice said, "Here, I'll take the tray."

Dani twirled around, pleasantly surprised to see Paul Greene walking toward her.

"I didn't know you were invited too."

"I think Pad and Ellie took pity on me. You know, the single cop friend needs a place to go on Sunday night." Paul fell in step with Dani. "I think they invited Judy Bell too." He pulled open the door. "Have you met her yet?"

Dani nodded. "She's been in the café frequently and seems really nice."

"Yeah, we've been partners for a few years now. Best there is."

"I see." Dani surmised they were more than friends and looked around the room to see where they could set the trays of cupcakes and pumpkin whoopie pies.

Three little voices shrieking caught her attention. She caught a glimpse of them running toward her.

"Dani, what did you bring us? Mommy said we have to wait to try them." Kaylee, the only girl, was the most talkative. She looked up at Dani with large crystal-blue eyes, which she inherited from her grandfather, Ray. Her brothers, Brad and Zach, stood behind their sister, keeping a close eye on the trays.

"Mommy's right. We all have to eat our dinner first before filling up on goodies." Dani winked. "But I packed a few extra in a box for Mommy to take home, and you each can have one tomorrow too."

"You did? Oh, thanks, Dani," The triplets all clung to her legs, each one trying to squeeze harder than the other, causing Dani to laugh.

Sara pried them off Dani. "Sorry about the mass assault. The kids have been waiting all day to see what you brought."

"They're great, and I just told them there are a few tucked away for tomorrow."

"You didn't need to, but they won't go to waste." Sara's attention was diverted toward the sound of tears. "Gotta go."

Dani hoped it was nothing serious when Ellie walked over and gave her a welcoming hug.

"I thought you were coming early to hang out?"

"Sorry. I got caught up in an Agatha Christie book and lost track of time, but I'm here now. Can I help?"

Ellie gave her a little shove out the back

door. "Nope, go enjoy yourself. Mom and Ray are out back with Shane and Abby."

Dani stepped into chaos as the triplets came flying out the back door in search of their cousin Devin, Abby and Shane's little guy. Soon, the four kids were tussling in the grass over a ball.

"Hey, Dani." Shane waved as he jogged backward to the kids.

Abby watched her husband divert the kids' attention away from the solitary ball and shepherd them to the swing set.

"He's a natural with them," Dani said.

Abby smiled. "He is, isn't he?" Abby held up a bottle of wine. "Would you like some?"

Dani shook her head. "No, thanks. Water's good for me."

Abby set the bottle down. "Do you want to sit? We haven't had a chance to chat in a while, and after working in the office and spending time with Devin and Shane, I could use some female conversation."

Dani was a little uncomfortable. She and

Abby had never had a conversation without others involved. But she followed Abby to a small table with two chairs.

"Ah, now this is nice." Abby's smile lit up her eyes. "I see you whipped up some whoopie pies for today. What flavor are they?"

"Um, pumpkin. I thought with fall coming, it was a good choice."

"Pumpkin is my absolute favorite. Well, after chocolate, of course." Grinning, Abby glanced over to where Shane tossed Kaylee a ball. "Isn't he amazing?"

Dani followed her gaze. "He certainly is. Everyone in this family is wonderful."

"How long have you been in Loudon?"

"Just about two years." Dani wondered where this conversation was headed.

"You've done great things at What's Perkin', and I know Cari is very happy with how you've handled the added responsibility as she's begun to move into semiretirement."

"Truthfully, Cari makes everything easy. She's the best boss I've had."

"She's the best mother-in-law too." Abby grinned and then grew serious. "You know, when I moved back to Loudon, I had no family, and Devin and I were a little lost. The McKennas took me into the fold and stood by me when I didn't have anyone else to turn to."

Dani figured Ellie had spilled the beans on her story. "Did Ellie say something to you about me?"

Abby shook her head. "No, of course not. I just get the feeling something is troubling you and has been since you arrived in town. I wanted you to know, we care about you and consider you a part of our big, goofy extended family, and if you ever need someone to talk to, I've been through a lot, and I'm a good listener."

Dani's head dropped. "I'm sorry. I told Ellie some stuff about my past, and she's encouraged me to talk to Cari. I don't know how, and I don't want her to regret hiring me."

"Dani, Cari would never have kept you around if she didn't believe you were an asset to her business as well as all our lives. She is a true blue, loyal to a fault woman."

Dani looked across the yard and saw Cari sharing a laugh with Ray. "Do you think there is ever a good time to tell someone some tough news?"

Abby reached over and squeezed her hand. "Rip the Band-Aid off. March over there before you lose your nerve and ask her for a few minutes. Then you can relax and enjoy the party."

"You think that's a good idea, to talk to her now, at a picnic?"

"I do. Now go, and remember, I'm here for you too." Abby's smile sparkled in her eyes.

Dani stood up, straightened her shoulders, walked over to Cari, then turned back to look at Abby, who gave her a thumbs-up. "Cari?"

"Hello, Danielle." Cari gave her a hug. "Did you just decide to say hi to your favorite boss?" Cari teased.

"I'm sorry, I didn't mean to offend you."

"Oh, Dani, it's fine. I was joking."

"Oh. Um. Well, do you have a minute? I mean, can we talk?"

Ray started to step away. "Ray, please stay."

Cari said, "Let's go out front where we can have some privacy."

"Look. I think Dani's going to tell Mom about her ex-boyfriend. Do you think I should follow them? Or maybe we should go out there."

"El, if Dani needed backup, she'd have asked. She can handle this." Pad kissed Ellie's temple and handed her a tray of wings. "Let's get these on the grill before the family starves."

Ellie looked back over her shoulder at Dani. "Right behind you."

Dani picked at her fingernail and took a deep breath. "Cari, Ray, I haven't wanted to burden you, but after talking with Ellie and Pad, I've decided you deserve to know the truth. If you decide you would like me to move on, I completely understand, and there will be no hard feelings."

"Dani, I don't think anything could be as awful as you think. Just tell us what's going on." Cari spoke in a soft, soothing voice.

"I wasn't completely honest when you hired me. I'm on the run."

Ray took Cari's hand. "From…"

Dani swallowed hard. "I was in a bad relationship, and after things got pretty intense, I packed my bags and didn't look back. Until recently, my mom didn't even know specifically where I was living and working."

"Dani, what do you mean by a bad relationship?" Concern flooded Cari's eyes.

"Derek was verbally abusive. One night, he grabbed my arm and left a huge bruise." Tears choked her throat. "That scared me, and you know with everything in the media about domestic violence, I thought things would continue to escalate. One day, when he was at work, I packed everything I could fit in my car and left."

"Where do things stand now?" Cari prodded. "Has this man been in contact with you?"

Dani shook her head. "No, although my mother called and told me he wants to make amends and get back together."

"He's been in touch with her?" Cari asked.

"Yes, a few days ago, he called my mom telling her he missed me. I never told her specifically why I left him. I was mortified, and my parents still think he's a great guy." Dani shrugged. "It was easier."

"What do you want now?" Cari said.

"I never want to see him again, but I'm afraid it's only a matter of time until he finds me. I don't think he'll come to Loudon, but I wanted you to know in case someone comes around. Maybe you can say I've moved on or something."

"First off, you're done running. You've become a part of our family." Cari's voice was stern. She had a glint in her eye like when she was formulating a plan. "Do you have a picture of him? I think we should show the family and Luke too. He needs to know."

"Cari, there's just one small thing."

Cari glanced at Ray and then Dani. "What?"

"He's a fireman in New York, and he's very charming and handsome."

Ray interjected. "Men who are abusers think they can fool people. It's their inflated ego. You have nothing to be afraid of. We'll be on the lookout."

Cari put her hands on Dani's shoulders to face her. "You need to remember, we have a lot of friends on the police force, and Ray and the boys are a formidable force."

"Thanks, Cari, and you too, Ray. There is one small thing Pad suggested I ask you."

"Fire away."

"He thinks there should be additional exterior lighting in back of the shop and maybe something on a motion detector too. This way, if someone is out there, I'd be able to see them before leaving the café or coming down from my apartment."

Ray said, "I'll call the electrician tomorrow."

"I'm happy to pay for the lights and installation," Dani quickly said.

"I appreciate the offer, Dani, but we're the landlords, and it's our obligation to make sure you're safe. I'm only sorry I didn't think of it when you moved into the apartment." Cari looked at Ray. "How quickly do you think we can get it done?"

"Hopefully, sometime this week." Ray looked at the young girl. "You've been through some tough times, Dani. In the future, don't hesitate to come to Cari or me for anything. We want you to feel safe in your home and in the café."

Dani breathed a sigh of relief. "Thank you for being so understanding. Ellie and Pad were right."

Cari chuckled. "Well, if you ask Ellie, she's usually right about lots of things. But what specifically?"

"She said you wouldn't let me leave. I don't want to be a burden to anyone."

"Dani, running away never solves a problem. It will follow you. But with the support of good friends, there isn't anything we can't deal with, including an ex." Cari gave Dani a warm, motherly hug. "If you ever feel uncomfortable, call one of us, or you can always call nine-one-one."

"I will. Thanks again for being so great about all of this."

Cari looked toward the back. "Oh, there's Ellie calling us for dinner."

Ray said, "Dani, do you know what's up with Ellie tonight? She said she has some good news."

"Don't ask me to divulge any secrets. She plans to tell you over dessert." Dani winked at Ellie as she stepped onto the back deck.

"You've got the best parents."

Ellie grinned. "You're not telling me anything I don't already know."

*E*veryone gathered around the large table and devoured every morsel on the platters. Ellie looked at Pad, and she winked at him.

"I'm glad everyone could come over tonight," she began. "Pad has some exciting news."

"I hope everyone will think this is good news. As you all know, Ellie and I have been doing a long-distance romance as I've traveled around the world, taking pictures and preparing for a new gallery opening. But what you may not know is, last year, Hank Booth gave me a standing job offer. I guess he liked my style of police work during the problems at The Looking Glass. After giving it careful thought, Ellie and I have decided it's time for me to put down some deeper roots. I took the job. You're looking at the newest member of the Loudon Police Department."

Shane hopped up and thumped Pad on the

back, pumping his hand up and down. "That's fantastic news!"

With an enthusiastic response from the family, Pad appeared to relax. "I've told Aunt Winnie, who, by the way, sends her regrets she couldn't be here tonight. She's in New York getting ready for a new show."

"Pad." Cari's eyes sparkled. "Should we expect any other announcements tonight?"

"No. I think that just about does it from me." He glanced around the group. "Does anyone else have news to share?"

With everyone looking at Abby and Shane, Abby quickly murmured, "Nothing from our house."

Ellie chimed in. "Dessert?"

Dani jumped up. "I'll help."

The two girls were giggling in the kitchen when Judy came in. "Need a hand? I'm feeling a little overwhelmed out there on my own. Paul and Pad are talking shop, which I refuse to do when I'm not working. Abby and Sara are talking babies, and everyone else is playing with the kids. I think the adults are going to overwhelm the little guys."

"Sure, the more the merrier," Dani chirped. "Does this mean Pad will work with you or Paul, or does he get a new partner?"

"There's a rookie starting in a couple of weeks, and I've volunteered to take him on, show him the ropes, so to speak. Pad and Paul will be riding together."

Ellie carefully measured coffee into the pot and glanced at Judy. "Does it bother you that Pad's taken your partner?"

"Not at all. Paul and I work well together, but change is good. It keeps us fresh. Besides, training someone will look good on my resume." Judy picked up a tray of mugs. "Does anything else need to go outside?"

"I'm right behind you with the cupcakes." Dani followed Judy out the door as Cari came in.

"Pixie." Cari placed a hand on Ellie's arm as she called her by her childhood nickname.

"How do you really feel about Pad officially moving to town?"

"I'm thrilled. It will give us a chance to spend time together without dreading the time he has to pack his suitcase again. Why?"

"You seem, I don't know, upset about something?"

"A little." Ellie wiped the spotless counter. "How could you put Pad on the spot? I knew what you were getting at. We're not ready to announce an engagement." Ellie's eyes sparked. "You know Pad is my first serious boyfriend, and I'm moving at a snail's pace compared to everyone else around here. I want to enjoy getting to know him and all his quirks."

"And you should." Cari sighed. "All I want is for you to be happy. Out of my three children, I think you were hurt the most growing up without your dad."

"Mom, I don't want you to worry about me. I'm better now. Dad coming to me when I got attacked helped me realize he didn't abandon me or leave because he wanted to leave us. If anything, I understand more than ever he wanted to be there for us, watching us grow up. Otherwise, why would he have been able to stay around?"

Cari nodded. "I've always felt he had unfinished business with us all. That's why he used to come and talk to us."

"Don't worry about me. Let's focus our energy on helping Dani. She needs us more than she realizes."

Cari hugged her daughter tightly. "I'm glad you convinced her to share her secret. Hopefully, in time, she'll forgive herself."

"What do you mean? She didn't do anything wrong."

"I know that, and you know that, but she needs to come to terms with what happened. It's common for women to blame themselves for being abused."

"Maybe she'll talk to someone, like a counselor." Ellie's face perked up. "I'll ask Pad if he can find out if there is someone the police department uses for victims of domestic violence."

"Dani's lucky she has you in her corner."

"Nah, it's no big deal."

Dani popped her head in the door. "Are you bringing out the coffee or should I grab the pot?"

"I've got it and we're right behind you." Ellie and Cari followed Dani out to the deck.

4

*D*ani flipped the covers off her head when the phone started to ring. She glanced at caller ID and didn't recognize the number. She let it go to voicemail and waited for the little red light; someone left a message.

"Hello, Danielle."

At the sound of the familiar, deep voice, Dani's blood froze.

"Baby, when are you going to stop this foolishness and come home? It's just a matter of time until I see you again."

She threw the phone on the bed and flew to the front door. Jangling the lock, she exhaled. It was secure. She peeked from behind the curtain. Was someone lurking in the parking lot? Satisfied all was quiet, she climbed back in the bed and turned off the ringer before putting it on the nightstand. *Should I call Ellie? It's just a voicemail. Derek's not beating down my door.*

Dani waited until a weak stream of sun appeared on the windowsill before flying through the shower. Hurriedly, she dressed for work and peered out the window that overlooked the back parking lot. Satisfied it was empty, she dashed down the steps, jammed the key in the lock, and slammed the door behind her, grateful no one had arrived yet to witness her abrupt arrival. The silence in the shop steadied Dani's nerves. She flicked on the overhead lights and started the coffee pot. Nothing was better than work to get her mind off Derek.

Cari came in and startled her.

Dani dropped a muffin tin on the floor and dropped to her knees, using a towel to wipe up spilled batter. "Oh, Cari. It's you."

"My goodness, Dani. Is everything alright?" She grabbed a wet towel and knelt down to help.

"Sure. You know, just making muffins." Dani tried to steady her voice.

"Dani, what happened? You're like a cat on a hot tin roof."

"Nothing."

"I've never seen you drop a tin full of batter." Cari waited.

Dani couldn't stand the silence. "This morning, Derek left me a voicemail."

"What did he say? Did he threaten you?"

"No, he didn't threaten me specifically. He asked when I was coming home, and he said he'd find me."

"Did you call Pad or Paul and report it?"

Dani noticed Cari casually peeking out front. "No. I didn't want to get anyone wound up. I made sure my door was locked and checked the parking lot before I came down. I was a few minutes late, as I waited for the sun to come up."

Cari paled. "Wait. How did he get your number?"

"I think he wheedled it out of my mother. I never told her about the abuse. She still thinks he's a stand-up kind of guy. You know, being a fireman and all." Dani sank onto a stool, dropping her head in her hands. "Do you think I should report it to the police?"

Cari handed her the phone. "It's ringing."

Dani bumbled the receiver and held it to her ear.

"Officer Greene, how can I help you?"

"Paul, it's Dani Michaels."

"Hey, Dani. Is everything okay?"

Paul's rich voice was comforting to her ears. "I might be overreacting, but I got a call from Derek."

"How about I swing by, and you can fill me

in on the details? I can be there in ten minutes."

"All right, but can you make it look like you're coming for coffee? I don't want to upset Cari's customers." Dani glanced at Cari. "You can come back to the kitchen."

"You're not alone, are you?"

"No, Cari and Luke are here."

"Pad and I will be right over."

Dani handed Cari the phone. "It sounds like Pad and Paul are coming over. I'm sorry to cause you any trouble."

"I'm the one who's sorry, Dani. I don't like the fact that this guy probably knows where you live and that leaves you vulnerable. I'm going to call Ray and have him get the electrician here today. We're going to make sure there are no blind spots out back."

"Cari, really, there's no need. I'll be fine."

Cari stopped dead in her tracks, turned, and put her hands on the girl's shoulders and then gently pushed her chin up. "Danielle, if you were my daughter, I can promise you this is the least I would be doing. You've made some good friends in Loudon. Lean on us, and let us help you through a difficult time."

Despite the lingering fear, Dani let herself be pulled into a warm hug. "Cari, thanks for everything. I have a feeling this is a long ways from over."

"Unfortunately, I think you're right, but this is the beginning of the end. Mark my words, your ex-boyfriend will be sorry he tangled with your adoptive Loudon family."

Dani laughed halfheartedly. "I hope you're right. But he always gets what he wants."

With green eyes glinting, Cari said, "Not this time."

The swinging door burst open. Two men, one in uniform and the other in plain clothes, swooped inside. With a nod of his head, Pad said, "Morning, Cari, Dani."

"I'm glad you're here. Dani, go with Pad and Paul out front and grab a table. There aren't many people eating in, and you can fill them in. I'll take care of the grill."

"Cari, no. I can work and talk," Dani protested.

"You don't need to be distracted when giving them all the details." Cari's look said it all, and Dani didn't dare argue with her. "Grab some coffee for the guys."

With a cop on either side of her, Dani had no choice. Once they were seated, Paul pulled out a notebook and pen and said, "Start at the beginning and tell us everything. No detail is too small."

Taking a deep breath, Dani told them about the voicemail. "I'll play it for you."

"It would be helpful to hear exactly what he said."

Pad nodded in agreement. "You don't have to listen to it again, Dani."

She shook her head. "I'm fine. But I'm not gonna lie; I'm sure Derek knows exactly where I work and live."

Cari checked to see if they needed refills and slipped away.

After Dani laid the phone on the table, Paul

said, "Dani, you're not going to like what I want you to do, but here's your first step. Call your mother and ask if she's told him where you live. Unfortunately, you're going to need to tell her exactly what happened, both in the distant past and last night."

"Are you kidding? When I talked to her on Sunday, I chickened out. I can't tell her the truth. She thinks the sun rises and sets on him."

"You're her daughter, and she loves you more than anything else. Your mother will protect you, and the best way she can is to tell you if Derek knows where you are."

Dani's lip quivered. "All right, I'll call her tonight."

For the first time, Pad spoke. "Dani, don't put this off. The more we know what Derek knows, the better."

"I know we talked about this the other night, but do you have any pictures of him?" Paul asked.

Dani shook her head. "I didn't take any

photos with me. But he shouldn't be hard to find. He's a lieutenant on the Chester Fire Department."

"I'll track him down," Pad's voice rumbled.

Dani looked at the two. "Where do I go from here?"

"Call your mother and keep a watchful eye. Do you carry pepper spray?"

"I have some upstairs."

"It's not going to help you in your apartment. From now on, where you go, it goes." Paul's voice was firm but gentle.

"Yes, got it."

"Better yet," Pad said, "Paul, go with Dani. He can do a little scouting and you can put the spray in your pocket."

Paul's chair scraped over the wooden floor. "I like the way you think, partner."

Dani called out to Cari, "We're going upstairs for a minute, and then I'll take over."

"No rush," Cari called after them.

Pad walked into the kitchen. "Hey, Cari, any idea when the electrician is coming?"

"I called Ray. He'll get someone here today to get started."

"Good, make sure he gets motion sensors on all the lights. I have a bad feeling this guy is gonna come calling before long. It was a pretty bold move, calling her cell."

"I'm glad she told you and Paul. It's better for the boys in blue to know of a potential problem before we find ourselves in a really bad situation."

"Agreed. Make sure Dani fills in Luke or at the very least you should. He needs to be aware of this situation, and as soon as I get a picture of Derek, I'll bring it by. You need to be able to recognize him if he does show up."

Cari handed Pad an oatmeal cookie. "Do you think you're going to like carrying a badge again?"

Pad took a bite. "Absolutely. It keeps me close to your daughter, and I've grown fond of this little town."

"Might be a little tame for a world traveler such as yourself," Cari prodded.

"It's time for me to come home. Winnie isn't getting any younger and neither am I." Pad glanced around. "Cari, now that we're alone, I wanted to tell you, I intend on marrying your daughter."

"Are you asking my permission?" Cari teased.

"Not yet. I'm stating my intentions. Be prepared. At some point soon, I will be stopping by to talk to you and Ray."

"We'll look forward to it." Impulsively, Cari threw her arms around Pad's neck and kissed his cheek. "Treat my baby girl well or you're cut off from cookies."

"You have nothing to worry about. She's my home."

Dani's eyes darted left and right, despite having a cop right behind her on the stairs. Every noise made her heart skip a beat.

Paul's gaze took in the area. "I'm going to talk with Cari about the overgrown trees and some bushes. Currently, they make great camouflage."

Dani stepped over the threshold. "Here we are."

"Was the door unlocked?"

"Well, yes. I-I never lock it. I'm just downstairs." Her hand flew to her mouth. "Wait, I did lock it this morning."

Paul thrust her behind him and stepped into the room. "Wait here."

Dani watched Paul move about the tiny apartment, opening the bathroom door, looking behind the shower curtain, and then checking the bedroom closet, even under the bed. "All clear," he stated.

"Maybe I didn't lock it." Dani shuddered. "All this is making me crazy."

Dani walked into the bedroom and pulled open the drawer on the nightstand. She pulled out a small can of pepper spray. "Here it is."

Paul turned it over in his hand. "This will

do for a quick getaway, but I think you need something a little bigger to have in your nightstand and in your handbag. I'll pick something up and drop it off later today."

"Paul, you don't need to go to all that trouble."

"Dani, it's no trouble," he growled. "I like to think we're friends."

Dani sank onto the small couch and tilted her head back. "Thanks, Paul. It's been a long time since I've had good friends I can count on." She pushed her bangs out of her eyes. "Do you really think all this is necessary? Maybe Derek just called to scare me."

"Do you think he is the type of guy to mess with your head, especially after all this time?"

Dani dropped her head. "I don't know. I tried to convince myself I was being paranoid when I left him and went into hiding. Things weren't good between us, and they were getting worse. After he grabbed me, I figured it was just a matter of time until he really lost his temper."

Paul sat down next to Dani and remained silent.

"I guess time and distance caused my memory to get a little fuzzy, like I didn't want to believe he was all bad. Especially with my mom telling me he was a great catch. I wondered if I had misjudged him."

"Dani." Paul's voice was gentle. "Good guys don't ever lay a hand on a woman to cause pain or want to control her. Most guys respect their woman and would lay down their life to protect her. She shouldn't need protection from the man in her life."

Dani's ice-blue eyes filled with tears. "I guess I just wanted him to be, you know, that guy."

"Of course, but men like him don't come with a neon sign telling you to be wary."

"I can't imagine what you must think of me."

Paul's finger tapped the top of her hand. "Stop. It doesn't matter what I think. But for the record, I happen to think you're strong, smart, and resilient."

"Well, thanks." Dani wiped her damp cheeks with a tissue. "I should get back downstairs."

"Dani, before you do, maybe you should give your mom a quick call. I can hang around and be here for moral support."

"I'm not ready."

"What will be the difference if we do it now or later today?"

Dani shrugged her shoulders. "I don't know."

Paul glanced around the room. "Where's your cell?"

"Downstairs."

"All right, let's get it and give her a call."

Paul stood on the second step and waited while Dani jiggled the doorknob.

"You really don't need to hang around."

"If you don't want me around, call Ellie or ask Cari. You've kept this bottled up for a long time. I'm sure it's going to be tough talking to your mother."

"You have no idea," Dani said quietly. "I can ask Cari."

"Good. You'll feel better once everything is out in the open, and if Derek tries to get any more information out of her, she'll tell you first."

Dani's smile tugged at the corners of her mouth. "Are you always right, Officer Greene?"

"Most of the time." Paul chuckled. "But don't worry, you'll get used to me."

Dani felt almost lighthearted going back into the kitchen. Cari looked up as they entered.

"Hold on a sec." She flipped over the pancakes and picked up a floral plate. She placed bacon and then a short stack on it, turned, and added a few slices of orange, and then handed it to Luke through the window.

"I can tell something's on your mind, Dani." Cari leaned against the counter.

"I was wondering if, and you can say no, you'd mind being with me when I call Mom. You know, and tell her about the past."

"Of course, I will. Just say when."

"I was thinking when we close up today. It'll give me time to get my thoughts together." Dani looked at Paul. "Okay?"

"It's a start. I know you'll feel better, Dani, with Cari's support."

"I should have told her a long time ago."

Cari nodded. "Speaking as a mom, we want to know the good and bad stuff so we can help our children."

Paul glanced at the clock. "I need to roll, but if you need me, just call. I'm always around."

"Thanks for everything, Paul. I really appreciate it."

Pad held up two cups of coffee in to-go mugs. "Are we good?"

Dani nodded. "Thanks again, Pad, and you can tell Ellie what happened. I don't want to have to talk about it again." She glanced at Cari. "Except for Mom."

"I'm sure Ellie will check in later."

The two officers left the kitchen, and Dani could hear them asking Luke about filling a bag with some stuff for the squad room.

"Luke, it's on me," Dani called out.

Cari finished filling another order and asked, "Are you sure you want to wait until this afternoon, Dani? Sometimes, it's better to just rip off the bandage and let the wound get some air, if you know what I mean."

Dani pretended to study the order Luke handed her. "Cari, I need to prepare myself for this conversation. How would you feel if the man you thought was perfect for Ellie or Kate turned out to be a bully, and they kept the truth from you for several years? I'm sure it would be difficult to hear. When Mom realizes I didn't turn to her for help, she's going to be upset and wonder why."

Cari said softly, "I do understand how hard it's going to be for you and your mom, and I'm here for you when you're ready." Cari flipped open her recipe book. "Today's a good day for some wonderfully decadent brownies."

Dani breathed a sigh of relief and directed her focus to cooking instead of watching the hands on the clock fly around the dial.

5

ani twisted a strand of hair and watched Cari lock the front door after Luke left for the day. She knew Luke would have to be told what was going on. Just one more person who'd hear this embarrassing story. But that was tomorrow. There was a phone call to make, and she couldn't stall another minute.

"Cari, are you ready?"

Cari pulled out two chairs at a small table and placed a pot of tea in the center with two pink floral cups. "Chamomile."

Dani sat and hit the speed dial and then the speakerphone button. While it rang, Cari patted Dani's hand.

"Just breathe."

"Hello."

"Hi, Mom."

"Hi, Dani. This is a nice surprise. Are you working today?"

"We just closed up. Mom, my boss Cari is with me. Do you have a few minutes?"

"Is everything all right, Danielle?" Concern emanated from the tiny speaker.

"Yeah, I'm fine, but I need to tell you something, and I don't want you to interrupt or get mad."

"All right." Dani could hear her mother exhaling.

"Cari, it's a pleasure to, sort of, meet you. I'm Olivia."

"Hello, Olivia. Likewise."

Dani took a deep calming breath and dove in. "Mom, you know I spent a couple of years in a relationship with Derek. But what you don't know is that during that time, he was verbally abusive to me and before I left, it escalated, and he grabbed me, leaving a bruise on my arm."

"What are you talking about? Derek is always a gentleman. Holding doors, putting what you wanted to do first. He told me you might try and spin a story about him being a little angry with you occasionally."

"Mom." Dani squirmed in her chair. "You need to listen to me. It wasn't simply a lover's spat. He would yell at me, tell me I was worthless and that I needed to be told what to do, where to go, who to be friends with, and even how I should wear my hair and clothes. Nothing I did was good enough for him."

"Um, but when we saw the two of you together, well, frankly, you always seemed happy."

"I was faking it. If I didn't put on the happy face, we'd get into a fight when we got home. It was easier to just ride his moods than face the truth."

Cari said, "Olivia, if I may. My youngest daughter, Ellie, and Dani have become good friends. When Dani opened up to Ellie and her boyfriend, who's a police officer, about what had happened, they encouraged her to tell you. She also shared with us that Derek is still in contact with you."

"Dani, I just don't understand. Why would you tell strangers before me?"

"Mother, Cari and Ellie aren't strangers. We've become very close. And remember, you've spent the last couple of years saying how great Derek is and how I had lost my chance at happiness when I broke it off with him. Don't you see? I remained silent and disappeared because I was afraid of him!"

After what seemed like several minutes, Dani said, "Mom, are you still there?"

"I'm here. I don't understand why you couldn't be honest with me. You're my little girl. I want you to be happy and safe. If you told me Derek was hurting you, then I would believe you."

"Oh, Mom," Dani's voice cracked. "I'm sorry. I was ashamed, and it was my fault I got into that mess."

"Oh, no, Dani. I've done something terrible." Dani could hear the anguish in her mother's voice. "Derek called last night. He said he has a surprise for you, and I wasn't to tell you, but he plans on seeing you."

"Mom." Dani's throat went dry and her heart pounded. "What did you tell him?"

"He has your address and where you work." Mom's voice was barely audible. "What can you do? Will you move?"

"Dani isn't going anywhere, Olivia. She's done running," Cari stated.

"Dani needs to be safe. Now that Derek knows where she lives and works…"

"Mom, he left me a voicemail last night. I've talked to the police this morning, and they're aware of the situation."

"Olivia, my husband and I are installing motion sensor lights, and my son is cutting down and trimming hedges and trees to eliminate any potential hiding places. We're going to do everything we can to ensure Dani's safety."

"I've got pepper spray, and my friends' numbers are programmed into my cell."

"I don't think that's good enough, Dani. Derek was devastated when you left him."

"Mom." Dani's voice sounded harsh, even to her ears. "His pride was bruised, not his heart."

"Maybe, but you need to be careful. I think he's coming to Loudon in an attempt to convince you he's a changed man. He even confessed he has a problem with his temper, and he went to anger management classes."

"That's rich," Dani said. "Bottom line, I was the first girl to leave him and it hurt his pride. He's feeding you a line of crap in the hopes you'll convince me to cave. But I'm not buying what he's selling."

"Dani, what can I do to help? I feel awful."

"Do you have any old pictures of Derek you could email to me? It would be helpful for

Cari and Luke, who works here, to know what he looks like—the police too."

"I'm sure I have something. If not digital, I'll send them by overnight mail. I know I have printed photos." The line held a moment of silence. "Danielle? I'm sorry. I should have trusted your judgment. Derek was a charmer."

"Mom, it's how he lured me in too, but it doesn't matter now. If he comes to town, I'll be ready." Dani smiled at Cari. "Or, I should say, we'll be ready."

"Do you want your dad and me to come out there?"

"No, I've got great people in my corner. Besides, you didn't raise a wimpy chick." Dani laughed softly. "Derek would be stupid to show his face in this town and he doesn't know the new me. I can be one tough cookie."

"If you're sure. But promise me you'll call me every day, just to check in."

"Don't worry, Mom. But I'll call you when I'm home and tucked in for the night."

"It doesn't have to be at night; call anytime."

Dani could hear her mom crying.

"Dani, I'm really very sorry I didn't make it easy for you to come to me. I've never had someone I know or love deal with something of this magnitude. I feel just awful."

"Mom, if you were here right now, I could give you a big hug, and you could see my face. I don't want you to blame yourself. This thing crept up on me, and it took a while to see who Derek really was."

"Ladies, playing the blame game doesn't change the past. You need to move forward and promise to talk and listen to each other. I'm confident if you do, you'll find you can get through anything, together. You two need to talk, so I'm going to leave."

"Cari? Please watch over my girl."

"As if she were my own daughter."

Dani took the phone off speaker. "Mommy, I let you down." Tears rolled down Dani's cheeks and dripped from her chin.

"Honey, never. I let you down, always going on and on about how great Derek was. I never gave you an opportunity to open up. At times, I'm not the best listener, but I'll work on it."

Dani dried her glasses with a napkin. "Cari's right, we shouldn't be heaping blame on ourselves. Will you tell Dad for me and reassure him I'm okay? These are really great people, Mom. They truly care about me and I them. It's like having a second family."

"I'll talk to Dad, and he'll understand. But he's going to want to talk to you."

"I'll call tonight." Dani glanced over her shoulder. Cari was talking with Pad in the kitchen.

"Mom, I need to go. Send the picture as soon as you can."

"As soon as we hang up. Dani?"

"Yeah?"

"I love you very much. Stay safe."

"I love you too, Mom, and don't worry. Cari and Ray have electricians putting up all kinds of floodlights. The back will light up like a Christmas tree, and it'll spot any movement in the parking lot."

"If you're sure…"

"I am." Dani wiped tears from her cheeks. "I gotta go, Mom. I love you."

Dani went into the kitchen. "Hey, Pad. What's going on?"

"Cari was filling me in on the conversation with your mom. I'm glad she's in the loop."

"Yeah, but did Cari tell you Derek knows exactly where I live and work?"

"She did and I shot Paul a text. There will be patrol cars making the rounds more frequently, especially after hours."

"Sounds like you have everything covered." Dani rubbed her hand over her throat. "Do you think he's coming?"

"Yeah, Dani, he'll show up eventually." Pad's voice held a trace of something Dani could understand.

"Pad, I'm sorry I pulled you and Ellie into this mess. I still think it might be easier to just move. My parents will never tell him where I live again."

"Dani, running never solves problems like this, and I'm confident we can sever his unhealthy attachment to you."

A sharp rapping came from the back door. "It's Paul. He picked up a can of spray for you."

Pad flipped the lock and Paul strode in. "Cari, Dani." With a curt nod, he handed Dani a brown paper bag. "You have a can for your bedside table and one for the kitchen. Remember, this gives you time to get away. It will incapacitate him until one of us can get here."

Dani peeked inside. "It looks like there are enough cans for more than just two places."

"I got some for Cari and Ellie too."

Dani pulled out a small can and passed it to Cari. "I'll give one to Ellie later, unless you want to give it to her, Pad?"

"No, you can. I'm going to be working tonight. I've got an idea. Why don't you two have dinner together? I'm sure she'd love the company."

"I can see through your thinly disguised attempt to keep my mind off my problems."

Pad laughed. "My devious plan has been foiled. Seriously, I think you could use the company, and you ladies seem to have unlimited things to talk about."

Cari chirped in. "Ellie can talk to a wrong number for an hour."

Dani threw up her hands in mock exasperation and dialed the phone. "I'll call her."

"Hey, Ellie." Voicemail, she mouthed. "I'm cooking tonight. Want to have dinner at my place? Your boyfriend and mom think we need some girl time. Give me a call."

Dani slipped the phone into her apron pocket. "Are you three satisfied?"

"Actually"—Paul grinned at Pad—"depending on what you're having for dinner, maybe we could swing by and get a to-go bag?"

"You're assuming I'm cooking enough for four?" Dani teased.

"Well, a guy can hope, right? I can guarantee you're a much better cook than we are."

"Speak for yourself, Greene. I know my way around a kitchen; just ask Ellie."

Paul held up his hands. "I give up, dude. I was just trying to score us something good to eat."

"All right, I'll make sure there's enough for you guys." Dani gave Paul a gentle push. "Now, take off."

Dani's phone vibrated in her pocket. She glanced down. "I got an email from Mom. Here's a picture of Derek." She turned her phone around so everyone could take a look.

"Forward it to me?" Paul rattled off his email address. "I'll make sure copies are distributed at shift change."

Cari studied the picture. Her brow furrowed.

"Cari, does he look familiar?"

"No, I don't think so, but if I see him, I'll remember."

Dani's phone vibrated again. "Looks like dinner's on me tonight. Ellie's coming over after she closes The Looking Glass."

"Looking forward to it." Pad and Paul left the way they came.

Cari announced, "I'm going to head home. Are you going up to your apartment or do you need to go to the grocery store?"

"I'm going upstairs, throw together a pot of chili, soak in a hot bubble bath, and relax."

"Sounds like a great idea. If you need something, don't hesitate to call. Ray and I can be here in flash."

"Cari, please don't be a helicopter friend. I'll be fine. I've been dealing with the threat of Derek showing up for the last two years. Today isn't really much different." A shiver raced down her spine.

"Okay, then I'll see you in the morning."

Dani turned around in the kitchen, wishing her safe haven didn't have a dark cloud hovering over it. Straightening her shoulders, Dani turned off the last of the overhead lights and pulled open the door. Looking left and then right, she dashed up the stairs, unlocked the door, and secured it behind her.

Dani glanced out the window and thought she saw someone step behind the dumpster. Chiding herself on seeing things, she did exactly what she had told Cari she planned. Before long, chili was simmering, and Dani had slipped into the deep claw-foot tub filled with steaming hot water and fragrant bath salts with bubbles.

Baths were Dani's one true indulgence. She bought thick, luxurious towels and an array of salts and bubbles, depending on her mood. Candlelight pushed back the creeping shadows. She had about an hour before Ellie would be over, so it was time to let the worries of the day slip away.

*P*ad parked the squad car at the bottom of the stairs and glanced around. He was pleased to see the new lights working.

"I'm glad to see the new lights were installed so quickly."

"You know when Mom and Ray decide to get something done, it happens fast. You didn't need to drive me over." Ellie grabbed her bag. "I could have walked."

"Well, it's nice stealing a couple of minutes with my beautiful girl." He tweaked her nose. "Keep your eyes open. Cari called me when she got home. She didn't tell Dani, but after she saw Derek's picture, she's pretty sure he was hanging around last week." Pad lightly kissed Ellie's lips. "When you're ready to leave, give me a call. It will be my excuse to run over with Paul and pick up you and dinner. I'll take you home and leave Paul here for a bit. If someone is watching her, I'm hoping seeing a couple of cops coming and going might make him think twice."

"Do you think that will stop him?"

"No. But I want to slow him down a little. Just until I can get some information from the Chester PD. I've made, what I hope, is a discreet inquiry."

"What are you trying to find out?"

"If there have been any women who have filed any charges against him."

Ellie glanced at the stairs. "Well, I hope this doesn't take long. Dani's a good friend, and I don't want her to feel like she has to look over her shoulder, or worse, run."

Pad cupped her face in his hand. His heart thumped in his chest. "You need to keep your eyes open at all times."

"Don't worry, I'm old hat at playing Nancy Drew, remember?"

"You remember to be careful, and I love you."

Ellie smiled and pushed open the car door. "See you later."

Pad watched Ellie jog up the steps and stop to wave before opening the door and slipping inside. Pad started to back out when he put the car in park. He got out and walked over to the dumpster. Sitting on top of the trash pile was yesterday's copy of the Chester News. On the front page was a report of a fire. The text below stated it could have swept out of control if it wasn't for the bravery of Company Two.

Pad strode back to the car, waiting for the cell line to connect.

"Paul, he's in town."

Pad shot Ellie a text.

Be extra careful and don't leave the apartment - I'll explain later and DON'T tell Dani.

Pad didn't wait for an answer before pulling back onto the street. If this guy wanted to play cat and mouse, he'd just turned into the mouse. His phone beeped.

Will do - xxoo E

After arriving back at the station, Pad thrust the newspaper across the desk for Paul to see. "This wasn't left behind accidentally.

I'm sure this guy was hoping Dani would find it and send her into a tailspin."

"If he's been watching her, he's got to know there are a lot of people coming and going at all hours. Delivery people, customers, and the family. It's not an easy place to stake out." Paul studied the picture Dani had emailed him. "He's a big guy."

"The bigger they are, the harder they fall," Pad stated flatly.

"What's the plan for tonight?"

"I told Ellie to hang out, have some fun, and we'll swing by on the pretext I'm taking her home. Then you can stay, and when I get back, we'll do a little stakeout of our own."

"I can stay after we go off duty."

Pad nodded. "What we do on our personal time is up to us, and there's nothing like a little stakeout over leftovers."

Paul grinned. "Any idea what Dani's making?"

"Nah, and I've seen what you eat. Dani

could make shoe leather, and you'd think it was delicious. You have an iron stomach."

"Doesn't mean I don't appreciate good food. As a cop, sometimes we get used to whatever. Things aren't always quite as appetizing as a meal from What's Perkin' or the White House."

Pad glanced up, surprised Paul would reference the best restaurant in the area. "Have you eaten there before?"

"No, everyone at the station raves about it and Luke used to work there, so it must be good."

"Maybe I should take Ellie there for a romantic night out," Pad mused.

"Hey, maybe we could have a double date?" Paul suggested.

Pad squinted. "Who might you want to take?"

"Well, maybe Dani would consider going out to dinner with me if it was a double date. I think she might not be ready to have it be a date for two."

"Do you fancy the young lady?" Pad teased.

"She's cute and funny and wicked smart. I guess you could say I'm intrigued."

Pad folded his arms across his chest and watched his new friend squirm under his gaze. "Let me see what Ellie thinks and I'll get back to you."

"Thanks, Pad." Paul glanced at the time. "How long do we need to wait before we make our appearance?"

"A couple of hours anyway. Want to hit the streets?"

"That's one way to kill some time, and Dani deserves to have a little fun."

*D*ani pulled corn bread from the oven and ladled thick steaming chili into bowls. "I like to serve chili in a bread bowl, but I just didn't have time to make any. We'll have to make do with corn bread."

"I love corn bread and chili; it's the perfect combo. In my humble opinion, bread bowls are better with stew anyway." Ellie picked up the plate of bread and carried it to the small kitchen table.

"Are we eating at the table?"

"No, let's eat in the living room." Dani giggled. "It's not like there's much difference since this is one large room."

"You've done a great job decorating. When Shane lived here, it was definitely a bachelor pad."

"I was lucky your parents gave me free rein with paint colors, and of course, over time, I've added the area rugs and a few more pieces of furniture. It's homey and all mine." Dani smiled. "Well, for now anyway."

"Are you seriously thinking of leaving Loudon?" A frown flitted over Ellie's face.

"I don't want to leave. I like it here. I'm saving to buy a small house. There's one I like. It's been on the market for a few months, on Middle Road, the little gray house with maroon shutters."

"I know the house. You know, Jake's wife, Sara, is the real estate agent. I'm sure she'd be happy to show you around if you're really interested." Ellie wiped dribbles of sauce from her chin.

"I'm sure I couldn't afford it anyway."

"Hey, you never know. Besides, it's an estate sale, and it might go for a great price. Never hurts to look. I'll go with you."

"I'll think about it. Thanks, Ellie. If I was a betting kind of girl, I'd think you're encouraging me to stay around."

Ellie laughed. "You've discovered my ulterior motive."

"When's Pad stopping back to pick you up?" Dani asked.

"I have to give him a call. Are you ready for me to leave?"

"No, but since he's never driven you before, I'm going to assume Paul will be with him."

Ellie smiled. "You're a pretty smart chick.

Guess we're not very good at the cloak and dagger stuff."

"I don't need a babysitter, Ellie."

Ellie laughed harder. "I've said those same exact words. Trust me. It's easier to let these men do what they need to do. I swear, their blood flows blue, not red, once they become a cop."

"It's not necessary. I am perfectly safe in my apartment."

"I'm sure they have their reasons."

Dani noticed that Ellie hesitated. Something clicked. "What haven't you told me?"

"I don't know anything."

"Ellie, you're not a good liar. You know something."

Ellie shook her head and handed Dani her phone.

Dani stared at the cryptic message. "What does this mean?" A knock on the door caused them both to jump.

"Should I answer the door?"

Ellie jumped up. "I've got this."

Dani didn't want to cower on the couch and went with Ellie to the door.

"Who is it?" Ellie asked.

There was no answer.

Ellie shot Pad a text. "Someone is at the door. Hurry!"

"What do we do now?" she whispered.

"We wait." Ellie eased from the door. "Pad will be here soon."

Just as the words left Ellie's lips, she heard feet thundering up the stairs.

"Ellie, open up," Pad shouted.

Ellie unbolted the door and flung it open. Pad pulled her into his arms, holding her tightly. Dani peeked around the couple, surprised to see Paul was holding a bouquet of flowers in his hands.

"You… I don't understand. You brought flowers?" Dani asked.

Pad and Paul stepped over the threshold and closed the door.

"These were on the bottom step." Paul

looked for a card or note. "Do you think you heard the delivery guy?"

Ellie shook her head. "Whoever it was didn't answer. A regular delivery guy would have said something. If nothing else, they hope for a tip."

Dani took the flowers and handed them back to Paul. "Get rid of them. Now!"

"Dani, what's going on?" Pad asked.

She squeezed her eyes tight. "They're from Derek."

"How do you know?" Ellie asked.

"Whenever he sent me flowers, he always had one white rose directly in the center of the bouquet." She pointed. "There is a single white rose."

ani's knees buckled and she sank to the floor. "He was here."

Ellie knelt down and put her arms around her. "We don't know if it was Derek. It might have been a delivery man or someone."

"Nice try. A real delivery person would have answered you. Derek heard an unfamiliar voice and took off. I'm sure he thought I'd be alone."

"Dani," Paul said gently. "Pad and I are going downstairs to look around. Keep the door locked and don't open it until we get back."

Dani covered her face. "He's long gone. I'm sure he was hanging around, and when you pulled in, he took off."

"You might be right, but we need to check."

Pad opened the door and turned to look at Ellie. "Are you okay?"

"We're good."

Ellie tugged on Dani's arm. "Let's get off the floor and get comfortable. The guys might be a while."

Dani allowed herself to be pulled up, and instead of sitting, she began to pace. "Just who does he think he is? Coming around here and bringing me flowers. Doesn't he get the point? I don't want to see him. If I did, I would have told him where I had moved to."

"Anger is good, Dani. Let it all out," Ellie encouraged.

Dani fumed. "Just let him show up. He'll find out I'm not the shell of a woman who disappeared from his life!"

Ellie picked up a pillow and handed it to Dani, who promptly threw it across the room.

"I have a good mind to call and tell him to back off!"

"Whoa, tiger, I think you should talk to Pad first. That might only encourage him."

Dani stopped dead in her tracks. "Maybe that would be a good thing. Draw him out on my terms and turf. Ya know, reel him in to smack him down."

Ellie burst out laughing. Holding her belly, she said, "I like this side of you."

"You ain't seen nothing yet. I'm done being afraid. It's time I take back my life. I've let Derek Ryan control my life for far too long, and it ends, now."

Exhausted, Dani flopped onto the couch. "Do you think I'm crazy?"

"Not at all. I think everyone who's been battered gets to the point of getting mad and lets go of the fear."

Paul walking through the door interrupted Ellie. "Good news. There's no one hiding anywhere around the property. Bad news, it looks like he's been here before. We found empty water bottles and a fast-food bag."

Dani slammed her hand on the coffee table. "I knew it!"

Paul handed her the newspaper. "Can you tell me which guy he is in the picture?"

Dani studied the grainy image. "Unfortunately, with their helmets on, it's too hard to tell. They all look the same."

Ellie glanced at the article. "This says the department battled a heck of a blaze just a few days ago. Pad, I wonder if you gave the reporter a call if they'd tell you who is who."

"That's a good idea. I'll call first thing tomorrow."

Dani studied the small group. "Well, thanks, you guys, for being here."

"It sounds like you're kicking us out," Ellie said.

"I don't want to keep you. It's been a stressful night, and I could use some rest."

Ellie announced, "Well I'm not going anywhere. I'm sleeping over and I'm not taking no for an answer."

Shaking her head, Dani said, "No, absolutely not."

Ellie held up her hand. "No use. I'm staying. Pad and Paul can take off, and I'll walk home in the morning."

Pad said, "I have a better idea. How about we all hang out and see who stays where tonight?"

"Guys, have you taken a good look around? This isn't a big place, with only one tiny bedroom," Dani sputtered.

"Pad, I'm good with the floor; are you? Ellie, can take the couch. Dani, where do you keep the extra blankets?"

"Seriously?" Dani said. "You guys don't need to stay. I'll keep the door locked."

"You're going to be a killjoy, Dani. I had a great idea. We could all start the day with a nice breakfast. You can cook, and then Pad and I can save Loudon from jaywalkers and speeders."

Dani knew when it was time to give in. "All right, but we're not making a habit out of this. I know why you're doing this, so I'm not alone for tonight, but when you scare the heck out of that idiot"—Dani looked from Pad to Paul—"we're back to business as usual."

Paul chuckled. "You've got us all figured out."

"Let me finish, Officer." She gave him a half-serious look. "Breakfast will be served next door. I don't have time to cook here and get to work on time too."

Ellie jumped in. "This hasn't been about our lack of faith in you. We just want to make sure all necessary precautions have been taken." She glanced between the two men. "Right?"

Paul nodded. "Got it. Now, about those blankets and do you have something to snack on?"

"We can make some popcorn. Ellie, if you want to go into the bedroom, there are a couple extra blankets and pillows."

Pad followed Ellie into the bedroom and pulled her into his arms. "How do you think Dani is doing, really?"

Ellie encircled Pad's waist with her arms. "You know, she got really mad when you were outside poking around. I think it was good for her. This has finally given her the strength to push beyond any guilt she may have felt for staying as long as she did."

Ellie stood on her tiptoes and lightly kissed Pad's mouth. She batted her long, blond eyelashes. "If you hadn't noticed, we're alone, and you want to talk about Dani?"

"I had planned to be snuggled up on the couch with you tonight, watching some old movie, but considering the circumstances, I think we'll have to settle for a few stolen kisses." Pad's full lips brushed hers.

Ellie sank deeper into his arms.

Dani cleared her throat. "I thought you were getting blankets. With the heat you've created, I don't think you're going to need them tonight."

Ellie tried to pull away, but Pad held her tightly against his chest. "Just a boy kissing his girl and thoroughly enjoying it."

Dani giggled. "I can see Ellie seems to have enjoyed it. She's blushing." She turned away. "Carry on, you two."

"Right behind you." Ellie grinned. "We need to be better guests and not get caught sucking face again."

Pad followed the two girls into the living room, and Paul grinned. "Did you two get lost?"

Pad threw a pillow at his head and laughed. "It was sure worth it."

Pretending to be oblivious, Ellie set the blankets on the edge of the couch. "It's a little early for bed. Who wants to play cards or a board game?"

"Well, I don't have either," Dani confessed. "I haven't had people over since I moved here, except for Ellie."

"All right then, talking it is." Ellie looked

up. "This is a little awkward. Now that we need a conversation, I'm at a loss for words."

Dani smiled. "Ellie, how's the shop been doing? Your mom said Pad's exhibit on Scotland was a huge success."

With the ice broken, Ellie launched into stories of customers' reactions to the highlands. "One customer in particular fell in love with a sunset of the bay of Dail Mor on the Isle of Lewis. The colors of the water range from blue to rich lavender and deep purple with the cliff jutting toward the gold and purples of the setting sun." She beamed with pride. "I could almost taste the salt on my tongue and feel the stiff, cool breeze caress my cheeks as it rolled off the cliffs."

"It was beautiful, rustic, and rich with history. I stayed in a restored thatched blackhouse in the village of Gearrannan. Scotland makes our history seem like yesterday. The houses date back three hundred and fifty years, but it has been settled for more than two thousand years."

"Do you miss it, Pad?" Dani asked. "The adventure of traveling the world, stopping anywhere, taking pictures of whatever piques your interest?"

"Ellie and I plan to travel, and I'll always take photos, but being here and putting down roots holds more appeal to me now than traipsing around the world alone." He shot a look to Ellie. "Travel filled a need at the time. I'd been hurt in the line of duty and decided I needed a change before I got killed."

Paul gave him a sharp look. "Let's face it, you weren't just a cop."

With a wave of his hand, Pad dismissed the implication. "I was an undercover agent. It's not something I'm at liberty to talk about, but no, I wasn't a cop like I am today."

Paul nodded. "I bet you're happy to have an eight-hour shift and go home."

"Based on tonight, I don't think two of Loudon's finest are doing a typical shift since you're sitting in my apartment," Dani joked.

Paul touched his forehead in a mock salute. "We're here to protect and serve, ma'am."

Dani broke out in laughter. "I do like having you around, Officer Greene." She hopped up from the floor and went over to the fridge.

Pad jerked his head as Paul got up to follow her.

"Um, Dani?" he spoke quietly.

"What's up, Paul? Do you want some water or something?"

"No, I'm fine. Pad is taking Ellie to the White House for dinner next week, and I was wondering if you'd like to go and we could all have dinner together."

"Like a double date?"

"Well, we don't have to call it a date if you don't want to. It's just, I'd like to take you out to dinner, and we can have some fun and get to know each other better."

"Sure."

Paul beamed. "Great. We can sort out the details once Pad and Ellie talk."

"We should have a good meal. Luke is always talking about how it's the best restaurant in the area."

"I've never been. This will be a first for both of us."

"And Paul?"

"Yeah."

"I think we should call it a date." Dani smiled. "It's been a long time since I've been out, and it'll be fun to spend time with Ellie and Pad."

Paul grinned from ear to ear. "I'm glad I asked."

Dani touched his arm. "Thanks for not thinking I'm damaged goods or something."

"Dani, what happened is not your fault, and you never need to worry what I think about you."

"Thank you. It means a lot to me." Dani glanced at the other couple in the room.

"Hey, Ellie, wanna go shopping? Paul's asked me to join you and Pad for dinner at the White House next week."

Ellie didn't miss a beat. "Dinner out is always a reason to shop, and I always love to buy a new dress."

The two girls put their heads together to see what day would work best for some retail therapy, ignoring the men until Ellie looked at Pad. "What night did we choose?"

Pad ignored the smirk on Ellie's face. "Whatever night you'd like, my sweetness."

"Thursday it is, then. I'll make a reservation for four." Ellie put a note in her phone and then put it into her handbag.

Paul tossed Pad the report he had been scanning. "Derek Ryan is not a member of the Chester Fire Department. I don't know what he told Dani, but there is zero record of him ever joining the department."

"We need to make a few phone calls. Something's fishy. I'm sure he lied to her all the time. We need to run him for priors. Dani might not be the first woman he abused."

"One step ahead of you. I'm pulling up police records to see what I can find."

"I'm going to call the fire chief." Pad punched in a phone number on the desk phone and waited.

"Put that on speaker so you won't need to fill me in."

A deep voice answered, "Chester Fire Department."

"Hello, is Chief Rodgers available? This is Padraic Stone from Loudon PD."

"Hold, please."

The hold message was about fire safety, reminding people to check smoke detectors semiannually and chimney safety with the approaching winter months just around the corner.

"Chief Rodgers."

"Good morning, Chief. My name is Padraic Stone from the Loudon Police Department. I have you on speakerphone, and my partner Paul Greene is with me."

"How can I help you, Officers?"

"We're checking on a member of your department, a Derek Ryan."

"Derek Ryan? You're mistaken. He isn't a member of the department. He's a newspaper photographer."

"Oh, I must have incorrect information."

"May I ask why you're asking questions about Derek?"

"Someone thought they saw a man fitting Mr. Ryan's description in Loudon, harassing a woman, and we're just being thorough."

"Hmm. I guess I can tell you. It's not like it's a secret. He wanted to join the ranks, but something to do with his physical or something. Well, let's just say, he didn't make it into the academy."

"Good to know. I'm sure we must have a case of mistaken identity."

"Yeah, I'm sure that's all it is. Derek is a good friend to all the firemen in our house. Always hanging out when he has time. Heck, he even takes his turn cooking for the guys."

"Sounds like he's quite an asset." Pad was making notes as the chief talked. "When was the last time he was at the firehouse?"

"Um, let's see. I think he was here a couple of days ago. Thankfully, we've been slow. I'm not sure if you follow our news, but we had quite a fire a few days ago."

"We heard something about that," Paul said.

Pad cut in. "It's always good when the fire and police departments are slow. Thanks for your time, Chief."

"If you're ever in Chester, swing by and introduce yourself."

"Thanks, we will." Pad leaned back in his chair.

"What do you make of that?"

"It's crazy that Derek Ryan is pretending to be a fireman. He didn't make it through the academy. He's a newspaper photographer following the smoke."

Pad pushed back his chair. "I need to swing by What's Perkin'. Wanna come?"

"I got your six." Paul looked over and saw his old partner, Judy Bell, coming in from the parking lot with her new partner.

"Hey, Bell, how are things going?" Paul asked.

Judy stopped and said something to the other officer before walking over. "Hey, guys, how's it going?"

"Not too shabby. We're headed over to WP. Want anything from the bakery case? I know how much you love Dani's cupcakes."

"Aren't you nice. It's not every day your former partner remembers the little things." Judy laughed. "But, yeah, if there are any cupcakes, pick up one for me and Walker."

"Sure thing, Jude. How are things going with him?"

"Pretty good. He's easy to ride with, and I get to drive all the time." She laughed. "But you'll always be my favorite, Greene. If you get tired of riding with Pad, just holler. I'm sure we can get the captain to switch us up and you can take the rookie and I'll ride with Pad."

"Nah, I'm done breaking in rookies."

Pad rolled up in the squad car. "Bro, get in the car; we'll catch you later, JB."

Judy waved as the car pulled away.

"How's Judy doing with the new guy?"

"She says it's going good. Judy's a good cop and a better trainer than I am. He couldn't be in better hands."

"Do I detect a note of pride in your voice, Greene?"

"I guess you do. When Judy joined the force, I wasn't sure if she'd make it. Here was this pretty, petite, blue-eyed redhead who didn't look like she had a tough bone in her body, but let me tell you, she can hold her own against the best of them. She is smart, tough, and wicked strong. She can kick just about anyone's butt."

"I would guess she had a good mentor," Pad surmised.

Paul decided to let the line of conversation go. "What's your plan when we see Dani?"

"First off, we need a clear picture. I'm hoping her mother got it out in the mail. I want to get copies made for Cari's family members. With everyone coming in and out, we'll have lots of eyes open. I'm interested to see if Dani had any idea Ryan was a photographer."

"Yeah, considering he's been pretending to be a fireman." Pad threw the car in park.

"Obviously, he's someone who isn't happy he flunked out, for whatever reason."

The men started to cross the street. Paul rested his hand on his belt. He did a three-sixty turn in the middle of the street. "Do you think he might be in town?"

"Yeah, he's close and my instincts are usually right."

"I was hoping you weren't going to confirm what I was thinking."

Paul let Pad go in first, taking one last look up and down the street.

"Hey, Cari, Luke." Pad greeted them upon entering. "Is it okay if we talk to Dani?"

"Sure, go on back," Cari said.

Pad pushed through the swinging door. "Wow, something sure smells good in here today."

Dani set a tray of cookies, fresh from the oven, on the stainless-steel worktable. "I'm baking Cari's famous Romeo cookies, triple chocolate, and in my opinion, to die for."

Pad reached for one until Dani slapped his hand with a towel. "Let them cool, and then I'll give you a couple to go."

Pad withdrew his hand and smirked. "Only until they're cool, Ms. Chef."

"Oh, I'm not a chef, Pad. Just the baker."

Cari shouted from the front, "I heard that. You're not just anything; you're a great cook."

"What can I do for you two fine men in blue?"

Paul glanced out the back door. "Anything going on today?"

"No, business as usual." Dani's eyes narrowed. "Why, do you know something?"

"Dani, why don't you have a seat." Paul pulled out a stool. "We have a couple of questions."

"Okay." Dani perched on the edge of the stool, twisting the towel in her hands.

"There's nothing to be nervous about." Paul took the towel from her hands. "And the towel's never done anything to you."

Dani gave a weak laugh. "Ask your questions."

"Did you get the picture from your mother yet?" Paul began.

Dani shook her head. "I don't think we got the mail yet. But I know she got it out yesterday."

"Good." Paul pulled up the extra stool and sat down next to her. "Did you know Ryan is a photographer?"

"I know he had a lot of equipment. He loved taking pictures, mostly outdoor stuff, nothing like portraits. He said it was his way to relax."

Paul said, "Dani, we talked to the fire chief today. Ryan isn't on the Chester Fire Department. He's a newspaper photographer."

7

"What if your information is wrong?" Dani's eyes darted between Paul and Pad. "All his friends were the guys at the station. He stayed at the firehouse overnight several times a week. When he brought home laundry, the smoky smell clung to his clothes. I used to open the windows just to get rid of the odor."

"Dani," Paul spoke quietly. "He might have stayed there to be true and easy to explain if the department was part of his responsibility for the paper. But we spoke to the fire chief. He confirmed Ryan didn't make it through the academy."

"Are you kidding? He lied to me? What else did you find out?"

"At this moment, you know what we know. You said he likes photography and it fits together." Paul reached out and took her hand. "Don't worry, Dani. He's never going to hurt you again."

"I'm not afraid of him. Not anymore." A glint flashed in Dani's eyes. It hadn't been there yesterday.

"Good girl," Paul exclaimed. "There's just one more thing…"

Dani stated, "He's still here in Loudon, isn't he?"

"We don't have confirmation, but we think so," Pad said, "But yeah. He's not ready to leave yet."

"What's our next step?" Dani asked.

Cari popped her head in. "Mail for you, Dani."

Dani glanced at the return address. "It's

from Mom." She tore open the envelope and pulled out a photograph. She passed it to Paul, who took a long, hard look and in turn gave it to Pad.

"It's Derek."

"How old is this picture, Dani?" Paul asked.

"It was taken three years ago. But in all the time I knew him, he never changed. Always wore his hair in a buzz cut and worked out every day. He said he needed to stay in shape for the job." She snorted. "Another lie."

"I agree, it looks like it's all been part of an elaborate scheme to play the part."

"After I show this to Cari and Luke, I'm going to make copies and send it over to the station and leave one here."

Pad left the room, giving Paul a chance to talk to Dani.

"Dani, I think a lot is going on behind those eyes of yours. Mind sharing?"

"I'm furious. I thought I left this behind

and he was done with me and had moved on. Once I knew Mom gave him my address, it was just a matter of time until he came knocking on my door."

"This isn't typical behavior of a man who is verbally abusive. Usually, once the woman leaves, they find a new person to wine and dine and reel in. I've seen this type of behavior before, and in my experience, this is a man who is unbalanced, and you need to be prepared for him to show up at any minute."

"You know, Paul, I didn't want to believe he would show up. However, after the flowers, I know you're right."

"We're on the same page. Dani, you need a plan to defend yourself if Ryan catches you off guard."

"What do you propose?"

"My old partner, Judy Bell, teaches self-defense to women at the high school every couple of months. If you want, I'll see if she can give you a couple of lessons."

"Do you think she would? She doesn't even know me other than being the cupcake girl."

"I know she'd do it in a heartbeat. Judy's a good friend. If you'd feel more comfortable, ask Ellie if she wants to join you."

Dani grew quiet. After a few moments, she looked Paul square in the eye. "Call her and ask if she'd help me out. I'll keep her in cupcakes for life."

Paul said, "You don't need to ask me twice." He pulled out his phone and dialed.

"Hey, Jude. I need a favor. Would you mind teaching some self-defense to my friends Dani Michaels and Ellie McKenna?"

Dani couldn't hear what she was saying but hoped Judy would agree. This would be one more step in being prepared when Derek showed up.

Paul wrapped up the short conversation. "Great, I'll tell her to call you to set up a time. Thanks again, Judy."

"She said yes?"

Paul jotted down a number and handed the

paper to Dani. "Call Ellie, and then call Judy. She's ready whenever you two ladies are available."

Impulsively, Dani threw her arms around Paul's neck and squeezed. "I don't know how to thank you for everything."

"I haven't really done anything, Dani, other than my job."

"You've done more than your job, and you know it."

"Well, if you want to reward me, how about a couple of those cookies for the road?"

Dani packed a dozen in a white waxed bag. "Don't forget to share with Pad."

"I won't and please, be careful when you go upstairs. Look around and if you need any-thing at all, call me right away." Paul gave her a hard look. "Dani," he said, his voice holding a warning tone, "promise me you'll be careful."

"I will. But we both know I'm going to see him at some point soon."

"Try not to dwell. For now, let's get some

more information and get you a self-defense class or two."

Dani gave a mock salute. "Yes, sir, Officer Greene."

Paul couldn't help but laugh and tweaked her nose. "You're incorrigible, Ms. Michaels."

"I wouldn't have it any other way. Now, out of my kitchen. I have work to do."

Paul allowed himself to be nudged from the kitchen and found Pad pouring coffee in two to-go mugs.

"Are you finally ready to go?" Pad joked.

"As soon as you get the coffee poured." Paul held up a bag. "I've got the cookies."

"About time you bought some food for us."

"I didn't. Dani gave them to me, and if you don't stop poking at me, I'm not going to share." Paul tucked the bag under his arm. "After all, she did give them to me."

Pad shoved toward the door. "Let's get out there and see what we can find."

Dani watched the guys leave and sighed. "It's a good thing they come and go all the time. Makes people stay on the straight and narrow, but I do wish they'd eat more than cookies."

Luke leaned in the pass-through window. "You know, Cari likes to take care of everyone, even if we're all adults."

Cari grinned. "I do love to try." She tossed a cloth at him. "We should get ready for the lunch crowd."

Luke hummed while he did organizing of the bussing station before he found his way into the kitchen and discovered Dani smiling to herself.

"Hey, kiddo, what's going on?" Luke walked over to the stove and grabbed a teaspoon. "Mmm, chili." He took a generous spoonful and devoured it and then grabbed a glass of water. "Hot!"

"It's too spicy?" Dani's brow wrinkled as she started to dip a spoon into the pot.

"No," Luke managed to say. "Temperature."

Dani smiled. "Well, it is bubbling, Luke.

You should have figured it was hot."

Luke downed the glass and turned to his co-worker. "'Fess up, what's the smile all about?"

She batted her long eyelashes. "Nothing."

"I've never seen you grin like this, young lady. Do tell," Luke coaxed. "You know you're dying to tell someone."

"Well, I did want to ask you about the White House. Do you have any recommendations for dinner?" Dani tried to be super casual.

"Do you have plans to dine at the best restaurant in the county?"

"As a matter of fact, I'm going with Ellie and Pad."

"And maybe a good-looking cop who just left the shop?"

"Why would you make that leap? I'm perfectly content to have dinner with my friends. I don't need a man."

"Of course, you don't, but it is very romantic and an ideal place for a date." Dani knew Luke could play this banter game all day.

"Well, maybe there is someone who's the fourth person." Dani's shy side was apparent now.

Luke grinned. "Anyone I know?"

"Luke, can I ask you a serious question? Where you won't make fun of me? I could use an unbiased point of view."

"Sure, you can. We're friends. Bounce away."

"Do you think, given the current circumstances, I'm crazy to go on a date?" Dani paused. "It's been a long time, and I'm really over Derek, but maybe I should settle the past before I think about having a future."

"Are you nuts? You don't owe that jerk a single thing. What's happening now is his issue, and you'll deal with it as it comes, but you deserve to have some fun, and if going out to dinner with friends is the start of something amazing, then go. Enjoy and take a tip from me—the crème brûlée is the best dessert on the menu."

Dani moved on autopilot, filling trays for the front display. She stated simply, "I'm going out to dinner with Paul Greene."

"He's a good guy, Dani. I got to know him when Ellie was going through the break-in and vandalism at The Looking Glass. He's a stand-up guy."

"I don't think Pad and Ellie would be friends with him if he wasn't."

"Ellie's shrewd and I firmly believe, if she didn't like Paul, he wouldn't be hanging around."

Dani grinned. "It's weird. I've already got first date jitters or something." She laughed. "I'm sorry, Luke. I talk to you like you're my brother. You don't want to hear me prattle on and on."

"You're the sister I never knew I was missing, Dani. You can tell me anything, but please don't ask me for fashion advice. Guys yes, dresses no."

Dani crossed her hand over her heart. "Promise."

"When's the big date?"

"The guys left it up to me and Ellie, so we're going next Thursday. It'll seem less date-ish, if you know what I mean."

"Does the day of the week matter?" Luke asked.

"For a girl, Saturday is a big date night, and it comes with all kinds of pressure. Friday is meet for a drink night; during the week, it's more a quick bite thing and Sunday, well, Sunday is low-key and no pressure. The weekend is over; you're thinking about your next work week, and I think it's an easy-breezy kind of day. Oh, we should have chosen Sunday."

"It really doesn't matter, Dani, but good to know for future reference." Luke tapped his forehead.

"Luke," Cari called out. "Can you come out here, please?"

"Duty calls." Luke went through the swinging door. The man standing at the counter made him stop in his tracks. He looked back over his shoulder to see if Dani could see the customer.

"I've got this, Cari. Why don't you run out back and finish the cake you started."

"Thanks, Luke. If you need something, just holler."

Luke turned to the tall, hulking man perusing the menu above the counter.

"What can I get for you?" Luke pasted a smile on his face, praying Cari called Pad.

"Um, well, I know your cook, so I'm sure everything is good. But do you have something you'd recommend?"

"Today's special is chili and corn bread. Shall I get you some to go?"

"No, I think I'll eat here." The man glanced around at the tables. "Can I sit anywhere?"

"Of course. I'll be right back." Luke kept one eye on the customer and walked to the window.

"Cari, one chili and a side of corn bread, please?"

Luke could see Dani was deathly pale. One question answered—it was Derek Ryan.

Cari passed him a bowl filled to the rim and a small side plate with a generous serving of bread. She gave him a nod, and he turned to serve their customer.

"Here you go." Luke set the plate on the table. "Can I get you something else?"

"Is it possible for Danielle to come out and say hello?" Derek looked at Luke. His smile didn't warm his eyes. They were hard and cold.

"She's tied up at the moment, but I can check. Can I tell her who's asking for her?"

"Ah, just tell her it's an old friend from

Chester." Derek dug into the chili. "Just as good as always." He focused his attention on his meal and ignored Luke.

Luke returned to the counter and waited. He had no intention of telling Dani her presence had been requested.

The bell on the door gave a jingle, and the two men walked in—one in plain clothes and one in uniform.

"Hey, Luke. We thought we'd stop by for lunch. Can you fix us up with today's special?" Luke noticed Pad's banter was accompanied with his slow survey of the tables.

Derek looked up and grinned. "Hey, fellas. I highly recommend the chili. It's good."

Paul crossed the room. "Hi. I'm Paul Greene. Are you new in town?"

"Nah, I'm just passing through, and I wanted to stop and look up an old friend." Derek partially stood and stuck out his hand. "Derek Ryan, Chester Fire Department."

Paul hesitated and then returned the gesture. "Always good to meet a fellow public servant."

"Who are you here to see?"

"An old friend."

Paul cocked an eyebrow. "Well then, I'll let you get back to waiting." He adjusted his belt in an attempt to draw attention to his night-stick hanging by his side.

Derek paid zero attention to the gesture "Hey, dude, any idea when she might be free?"

Luke glanced at Paul and Pad. "Let me check." He walked into the kitchen.

"Dani, the guys are here, are you ready?"

Cari stopped at the swinging door. "Let me go out first. Take a minute to get ready, and I'll stall by clearing the dishes."

Dani rolled her shoulders and took some deep breaths, mimicking how a boxer gets ready for a prize fight.

Cari placed the dishes in a bus tray before returning to the counter. She struck up a light conversation with the guys, who were pre-tending they were studying the cookie choices.

Cari gave a slight nod as Dani walked into the room. She went directly to Derek's table.

"Derek, what are you doing here?" Her voice was strong and clear.

"I came to see you, baby. I thought it was time you stopped running and come home." His voice was low and smooth.

"Derek, I left you a letter explaining how I felt about things, and we should both move on with our lives, as individuals. What made you think coming here was a good idea?"

"Your mother and I have been talking, and she knows I love you and it's time I make an honest woman out of you." Derek pulled something from his pocket. "I want you to marry me, Danielle, and I'm ready to do anything to set things right between us."

Dani snorted. "You think popping a ring out of your pocket changes what happened between us?"

Derek's chair grated over the floor.

Dani saw Paul and Pad poised to intercede.

"Danielle, we had a misunderstanding. I lost my temper with you a couple of times. Let's not make a bigger deal out of it."

"Derek, you grabbed me and left bruises on my arm."

Derek reached out for her, and Dani backed into a chair. Oblivious to it hitting the floor, she said, "It's time for you to leave. Nothing has changed for me except I've moved on, and my life is pretty darn good."

"Did you get the flowers I left last night?" He glanced at Paul. "I knocked on the door but discovered you had company. I didn't want to intrude."

"Yeah. I tossed them in the garbage. Don't you get it? I don't want anything from you, not now, not ever, with the exception of you walking out the door and never contacting me again."

"I'm not leaving and your mother agrees that we're made for each other."

"She might have at one time, but I've told

her everything. The way you scrutinized every detail of my life. You drove away my friends; you got angry if I went anywhere without you, and you expected me to be sitting at home, alone, until you walked back in the door. I won't live that way."

"I don't know what you're talking about. You were free to have the friends you wanted. But it's not a crime to want your girlfriend around when you get home from a shift."

Dani laughed without mirth. "Tell me again, what exactly do you do for work?"

Derek's eyes shot daggers. "You know what I do. I don't have to listen to your smart mouth about my job. You should have been proud someone who fights fires wanted to be with you!"

Dani shouted, "Get out!"

Derek grabbed her arm. "Don't you walk away from me."

He whirled her around. They stood face-to-face. Dani didn't shrink away from his penetrating stare.

Paul stepped in. "Take your hands off the lady."

Derek dropped his hand. "No disrespect, Officer, but this doesn't concern you."

"From where I was standing, it sounded like you were asked to leave."

"Dani, tell them this is all a minor disagreement between lovers." Derek's glare said much more than words.

"This is not a minor disagreement. We haven't been in a relationship in a long time and I don't know why you were at my apartment last night or here today, but go back to Chester; we're through, Derek."

"I've never seen you like this, Danielle. What has gotten into you since you've been living in this little Podunk town? You've never spoken to me like this."

"I should have stood up for myself in the beginning of our relationship, but I can't change the past. Do us both a favor—leave now."

"I'm not going without you, Danielle. I

promised myself I would take you home as my wife or I wasn't going."

"I'm not going anywhere with you." Dani's heart hammered in her chest. She longed to run into the kitchen and hide but knew in her heart this was not going to be the last time she'd come face-to-face with this man. Being surrounded by friends gave her the strength to stand her ground.

"Mr. Ryan, Dani has made it clear you're not welcome here. I would ask you to get in your car and head to Chester." Paul maintained his professional demeanor.

Derek sneered. "I saw the both of you last night, skulking around outside Dani's apartment, and I know you spent the night, leaving bright and early this morning."

Paul's suspicions were confirmed. "Cari, would you like me to arrest this man as he just admitted to trespassing on your private property?"

"Not this time, Paul."

"Mr. Ryan, if you come on my property again, I will have you arrested," Cari stated. "Are you getting the picture? You're not welcome here."

Derek looked around the room. "Dani, they're not going to be hovering around you twenty-four seven. I'll find you, and then we'll see what you say."

Derek stormed out of the shop, and at the door, he turned. "Officer, keep your hands off my Danielle."

Paul stepped onto the sidewalk and yelled after Derek, "I don't take kindly to threats." He waited to take down the make and model of Derek's car. He jotted down the license plate number as the car roared past. He took a moment to call in the information and ask the patrol cops to keep their eyes open.

Dani had followed Paul outside, and he pulled her in for a comforting embrace. "He's gone."

Dani shivered. "You heard him. He'll be

back. He knows there is a lot of time when I'm alone. He doesn't make idle comments. He's going to be watching me and waiting. Then what happens?"

"Always be aware of your surroundings, and after you take some self-defense classes with Judy, you'll be able to break his hold if he grabs you, buying time to get help."

"You saw him. He's a big guy."

"Every mighty tree can be toppled by a small, powerful force," Paul spoke softly. "Have you talked to Judy yet?"

"Not yet."

Paul handed her his phone. "It's ringing. Set it up for tonight."

"I don't know if Ellie can make it too."

"Not to worry, I'm sure Ellie will be there."

"Hello?" Dani said. "Hi, Judy. It's Dani Michaels." She paused. "I'm using Paul's phone. Is there a possibility you could meet me tonight and give me the first lesson in self-defense? My ex showed up today."

Dani passed the phone to Paul. "She wants to ask you something."

"I know where this is going."

Dani listened as Paul said, "Yup, we'll all meet you at six."

"Pad, looks like we get to be the bad guys tonight. Judy needs some guys with some heft to toss to the ground."

Pad chuckled. "It's one way for us to spend time with the girls."

Dani looked shocked. "How am I ever going to throw either of you to the ground? I wouldn't want you to get hurt."

"Not to worry, ma'am," Paul teased. "We're happy to be of assistance, and remember our motto is to protect and serve."

"Well, if you say so. Want to pick me up at half past five?"

"Hey, Luke, can you do me a small favor?"

"Sure, what do you need?"

"Wait until Dani is safely in her apartment before you leave this afternoon? Then I'll be by to pick you up at five, and we'll swing over to Ellie's."

"Sure, I'll make sure she's safe."

Paul looked at Dani, who had irritation written all over her face. "Humor me until we get a better handle on this guy, okay?"

"All right, but this better not take too long. I'm done living my life according to Derek."

8

For the umpteenth time, Dani looked at the clock. Five minutes until Paul would be there to pick her up. She wasn't sure what to wear to a self-defense class, and after speaking with Ellie, they both agreed on yoga pants and a comfortable T-shirt and a fleece.

She heard a car door slam. Pulling the curtain aside, she was happy to see Paul ascending the stairs.

Before he reached the top, she yanked the door open. "Am I dressed okay?"

Paul's gaze traveled from the tips of her sneakers to her eyes. "You look like you're ready to kick butt and not bother to take any names."

Dani giggled. "I don't know about that, but I'm as ready as I can be." She rattled the knob. "All set."

"Uneventful rest of the day?"

"Yeah, I think Derek may have left town."

"Might be wishful thinking."

Dani's heart skipped a beat. "Why?"

"Just a hunch, but I think he's biding his time."

The couple drove in silence.

Paul pulled into Ellie's driveway. "Are you ready to toss me to the floor?"

"I'll be gentle." Dani chuckled. "Do you think this will be fun too?"

"If I know Judy, she'll make it fun while learning the moves."

Ellie came bouncing out with Pad on her heels. "Hey, guys!"

"Want to carpool?"

"Sure, hop in." He looked over his shoulder. "Do you have enough room back there, partner?"

Pad grimaced. "Sure."

Dani watched Pad struggle to get his feet under the seat. "Hold on a sec. Let me pull my seat up." Dani gave Pad some much-needed leg room.

Paul said, "Judy's waiting at the community center. She'll have the mats set up by the time we get there. She's hoping the girls don't hurt us."

Pad grinned. "She's a good teacher, but I don't know if Ellie or Dani will be able to cause physical damage."

"Watch out, Officer." Dani's eyes twinkled. "You might end up with a few bruises tonight."

Paul parked in the center's lot. "Dani, I know I've been making light of tonight, but you'll have a basic understanding of what you can do to protect yourself."

Dani noticed Paul's brow was creased. His

eyes had a spark of something she couldn't define.

"I'm taking this very seriously, Paul. I'll be ready for Derek the next time."

Ellie said, "Kids, let's get going. Judy's waiting."

⁂

Dani entered the large open room. The floor was covered with protective mats, carefully arranged in a large square. Judy stood on the far side. Her smile lit up her lightly freckled face, her ginger-red hair secured with a bandana.

"Welcome to Ring Their Bell self-defense course."

Paul snorted. "What's up with the name, Jude?"

Judy's hands sat on her slim hips, her feet planted apart. "I'm going to show Dani and Ellie how to ring some jerk's bell. And who says self-defense can't be fun, don't you think?"

The girls dropped their bags and fleeces against the wall and walked onto the mat.

Dani grinned. "We're putty. Shape us into petite, lean, kick-butt, self-defense machines."

Ellie's head bobbed. "And if you can show me how to keep my man in line, all the better."

Pad and Paul stood on the sidelines, shaking their heads.

Paul clapped Pad on the shoulder. "Ready to see how we fit into her scheme?"

"Yeah, how bad can this be?" Pad wandered over. "Judy, where should I stand?"

Judy pointed to a spot mid mat. "If you can face me, we'll simulate an attack and show the girls a quick way to escape."

Pad did as requested and Paul took his turn. Time after time, Judy had the girls practice techniques until they seemed comfortable. Amid the nervous laughter, Dani and Ellie caught on quickly.

"Now, ladies, remember, the object isn't to go looking for trouble. You don't need to be Supergirl, but remember, in four short steps, you can get away."

Judy held up her first finger. "One, forearm to the throat and put all your force behind it."

She held up her second and third fingers.

"Two, use your elbow and drive it into the attacker's midsection; three, follow it up with a shin to the groin, again using every ounce of force you can muster."

Judy put up the fourth finger. "The final step, one more shot to either the groin or the middle. At this point, the attacker will be off-balance, and you can get away."

Dani and Ellie looked at each other as Judy demonstrated on Paul. To Paul's credit, he looked menacing and played the part of a bad guy to perfection.

A shiver ran down Dani's spine. "I don't know if I'd really be able to do this, for real, I mean. It looks easy here while we're joking around but"—she shrugged her shoulders—"I just don't know. If it were Derek, he's a big guy and towers over me."

Dani's voice trembled. Paul grasped her hand. "All you need is time to get away and scream your head off." At the top of his lungs, he yelled, "Fire! People will come running."

Dani nodded, her eyes wide. "All right."

Ellie said, "I've seen you in action. You're a tough cupcake."

Dani smiled. "Well, at least one of us thinks so."

Pad's gaze swept the group. "I think we should go out for Chinese or something. I'm buying."

Paul was quick to say, "I'll be the DD." He looked at his former partner. "Coming, Judy?"

Judy looked at the couples. "I'd hate to be a fifth wheel."

Dani grabbed her arm. "Come with us. This isn't a double date, Judy." She winked at Pad. "Dinner's on the rookie."

"Hey, I'm hardly a rookie," Pad feigned a protest.

"You are on this force, bro." Paul scooped up the girls' bags. "Let's hit the road."

Talk turned to where they should eat while Dani froze in her tracks.

Paul said, "What is it?"

"I'm not sure, but I just had a feeling. You know the kind that makes the hair stand up on the back of your neck?"

Pad and Judy switched into cop mode. Back to back, they turned, surveying the vacant parking lot.

Paul put his body between Dani and the darkness, on alert.

Pad shook his head. "We're clear."

"I think all this action has put us all on guard. Food in our bellies will help." Paul took Dani's hand. "Hop in."

Dani peered into the darkness, her heart pounding. "He's out there."

Judy was going to follow them in her car.

Paul pulled out of the parking lot, keeping track of her headlights in his rearview mirror.

Paul caught Pad's eye in the mirror. "Give Judy a call and tell her we're headed to Slices."

Pad nodded and dialed. "Instead of Chinese, we're grabbing a pizza."

Dani studied Paul's profile. "What's really going on?"

"Just in case our conversation was overheard, I want to change where we're going. Judy will take a different route. If someone is following us, it will be easier for me to see."

Paul drove at a steady speed. "Judy just turned off."

Pad and Ellie didn't turn around. Any movement in the car was sure to be seen by any driver trailing them.

Paul took a right onto Main Street and parked the car behind the restaurant. He hopped out. Staying close to the building, he watched the street from the shadows.

Pad stayed with Ellie and Dani. A few minutes elapsed and Judy came strolling up the alley.

"We're clear." She pulled open Dani's door.

Dani stammered. "I hate all the cloak and dagger nonsense. I feel like you're protecting the president or something."

Dani stalked onto the brightly illuminated sidewalk. With hands on her hips, she stood tall. Ellie followed her.

"I'm not afraid of him, you know."

"I know." Ellie smiled. "And soon, he'll know it too."

"I'm gonna kick his sorry butt all the way back to Chester if he shows up again." Fire flashed in Dani's eyes.

The three off-duty cops hung back, scanning the street.

Dani swung around. "I'm starving; anyone else hungry?"

Concealed in the shadows, Derek sat, his hands fingering a delicate locket. "Enjoy dinner with your new friends, Danielle."

***

Dani groaned into her pillow. "What the heck?" Gingerly, she got out of bed. "I feel like I was in a fight last night, the way these muscles ache."

Dani stood under a hot shower, rolling her shoulders as the water washed over her. Lifting trays is going to be tough today. She wiped away the steam from the mirror with the palm of her hand. "Suck it up, buttercup."

Dani dressed in a purple What's Perkin' tee and jeans. She hesitated at the top of the stairs, listening to the predawn. She dashed down the stairs. Fumbling with the key, she thrust open the kitchen door and locked it behind her.

In silence, she flipped on the overhead lights but didn't turn on the radio.

With a shake of her head, she said, "Dani Michaels, if you keep jumping at every little noise, you're not going to be ready to open." With practiced motions, she went about her routine, mixing batter, and sliding trays of muffins and cookies into the oven.

Dani jumped as the back door burst open. Her hand flew to her chest, her heart hammering deep inside.

"Good morning, Dani," Cari called out. "How did everything go last night?"

Dani sagged against the counter. "Pretty good. Ellie and I learned four simple, but effective techniques to slow an attacker down. We should be able to get away and call for help."

"Did you toss the guys to the floor?" Cari grinned.

"Judy tossed them both, but we learned how to attack a few sensitive spots, if you catch my drift?"

"I do."

Cari noticed the cooling racks. "You've been busy. What time did you get in?"

"My usual time, but the day is humming along. Before I left yesterday, I put the breakfast and lunch specials on the chalkboard."

"I'm sure they'll be tasty and hot sellers as usual." Cari dropped her handbag in the tiny office. "I'm going out front." She pointed at Dani's empty mug. "Refill?"

"You don't need to wait on me. I'll fill the case and get it then."

Cari laid a hand on Dani's arm. "You don't need to worry. You're safe."

A crease wrinkled Dani's brow. "Who says I'm worried about anything?"

"It's the first morning since you started that there's no music." Without further comment, Cari left the room.

Dani stood, her mouth slack, at a loss for words. She pushed open the swinging door.

"Cari?"

"Yes, Dani?"

Dani shifted from one foot to the other. "Um. Thanks."

"You still don't understand, do you?"

"What?"

"You're one of us. If Derek messes with you, he found a heap of trouble. It won't take long before he hits the road and doesn't come back."

Dani returned to the kitchen. *How did I get so lucky as to find this place?* For the first time, Dani felt her relationship with Derek would be in the past, and she might have a future, a normal life.

The shop was its usual hustle and bustle when a couple of Loudon's finest walked in. Cari greeted them with a wink and jerked her head toward the kitchen. Paul and Pad walked through the swinging door into a flurry of activity.

Pad grabbed a cookie from the cooling rack and went back into the dining room.

ad waited for Cari to finish with her customer.

"Cari, do you have a minute?"

Cari swiped a damp cloth over the counter. "Sure."

"Can we talk somewhere a little more private?" Pad licked his lips and swallowed hard. "I wanted to ask you something."

Cari dropped the towel and walked to a corner table. "Is this okay?"

Pad nodded. The legs scraping the wooden floor sounded like nails on a chalkboard. He wondered how he was going to get through this conversation.

Pad leaned forward in the chair, his fingertips tapping on the smooth wooden top.

"Pad?"

His face flushed crimson to the tips of his ears. "I wanted to talk to you and Ray, but before I lose my nerve, I'll ask you. I hope you don't think I'm out of line or I'm rushing things since it was a few days ago we talked, but I want to ask for your permission to marry Ellie."

"You want to marry Ellie?" Cari hid a small smile behind her hand.

"More than anything. I love your daughter with all my heart."

The simplicity of Pad's statement melted Cari's heart. "What does Ellie think?"

"She doesn't know. I wanted to ask you first. You know, in case you had, well, objections." Pad grasped his hands. "I'm financially stable. I'll always do my best to love and protect her, and someday if we're lucky enough to have kids, I'll be the best dad possible."

"That's quite a statement, Pad."

Pad's heart pounded in his chest. It felt like Cari would never answer the question.

"If you want to marry Ellie, then you have my blessing."

Pad's shoulders sagged and he let go of the breath he'd been holding. "Oh, thank you. Now, there's just one other thing."

Pad pulled a small velvet drawstring bag

from his shirt pocket. "It was my grandmother's. Do you think she'll like it?"

Cari gasped. "This is the most beautiful ring I've ever seen."

Pad took the tiny ring in his hands. Turning it over to point out the specifics, he said, "It's an art deco style, a one-point-two karat diamond set in platinum, and see the diamond bezel inserts that make the ring pop."

Cari beamed. "You know she's going to cry."

Pad took one last look before tucking it back into his chest pocket and buttoning it. His eyes sparkled. "I'll have a handkerchief ready."

"Any idea when you're going to do it? I'd like to have champagne on ice."

"Soon." Pad saw Paul tapping his watch. "I gotta go, but mum's the word."

Cari ran her fingers over her lips. "They're sealed."

"See you soon."

Pad followed Paul to the street.

"What were you talking about with Cari?"

"Nothing. Just shooting the breeze." Pad's hand rested on the squad car door. "How'd you make out with Dani?"

"She's definitely getting more relaxed around me. We talked about dinner at the White House with you guys."

Pad buckled up. "And do I hear more in your voice?"

Paul chuckled. "Once Dani sees I'm a good guy with manners, I'm going to ask her to the movies or something, just the two of us."

"You really like this girl, don't you?"

Paul glanced over his shoulder before pulling out. "I do. There's something strong yet delicate about her all at the same time. Don't get me wrong, I don't feel sorry for her. I'm not a knight charging in to save the damsel in distress. She's beautiful, smart, sassy, and brave. In my book, an irresistible combination."

"Oh, man, you've been bit." Pad popped him in the shoulder.

"What do you mean?"

"The lovebug took a hunk out of you. Now all you have left to do is hope the same bug finds Dani."

Paul laughed. "I'm not worried. How can she resist a tall, muscular cop?" Paul glanced at his partner. "Especially since you're already spoken for."

"What do you mean?" Pad patted his chest pocket. "Who am I kidding? I'm over the moon about Ellie McKenna, and I've wasted more time than I'd like to admit."

"When are you asking her?"

"It's that obvious?"

"I've got eyes. You were talking to Cari way in the back and for crying out loud, you keep touching your pocket. I'm going to assume there's a ring in there."

"Guess I can't get anything past you, partner." Pad unbuttoned the pocket. "Want to see it?"

Paul pulled over. "Of course. I thought you

were gonna hold out on me." Paul let out a low whistle. "Wow."

"Yeah, it was my gram's. Do you think Ellie will say yes?"

"With this ring and your face, it's a sure bet." Paul handed him the ring. "But, if for any reason she doesn't love it," he teased, "I'll take it off your hands for a cheap price."

Pad tucked it away. "In your dreams."

9

The reflection in the small bathroom mirror begged for a touch more lipstick. Dani pressed her lips together and then smiled. "Well, I don't look like a clown." The doorbell interrupted her self-assessment.

"Coming," she called out. She paused, smoothed down the front of her dress, and then turned the doorknob when she paused again.

"Who is it?"

"Paul."

Dani swung the door wide and smiled. "Well, don't you look handsome."

Paul beamed. "I wanted to look nice for tonight, with Pad and Ellie." His eyes roamed. A slight shiver zipped over her skin.

Dani had swept her hair up, leaving the graceful curve of her neck exposed. She wore a short, dark-navy dress with short sleeves.

"You look gorgeous. The sparkly stuff makes you look like you're twinkling."

Dani tried to peek around Paul. "Are you hiding something?"

With a grand flourish, he presented a small square vase of apricot tea roses, sunflowers, and heather.

"These are for you."

"Paul, they're beautiful."

Dani held the flowers to her nose. She breathed in the sweet scent. With a tear hovering, she said, "It's been a long time since anyone's given me flowers."

"I'm glad you like them." Paul wiped away

the tears on her cheeks. "I'm sorry you haven't had someone who appreciates you."

Dani shook her head. "I'm fine, but now I'm starving."

Paul chuckled. "Then we'd better get going." He looked around. "Are you wearing a coat?"

Dani grabbed the pashmina from the chair. "Do you think I'll be warm enough with this?" She tossed it around her shoulders and flipped one side up and over the opposite side.

"If not, you can wear my coat."

Dani picked up a small sparkly clutch. "I'm ready."

Paul held the door open and took her hand. They walked down the stairs with Dani enjoying the simple pleasure.

"Are we meeting Pad and Ellie at the restaurant?"

"Ellie and I agreed to meet at six thirty."

Paul held open the car door, and Dani slid inside, tucking the hem of her dress under one leg.

He jogged around the front and hopped in. Gunning the engine, he pulled into light traffic.

Paul's gaze roamed all points around the car. "Luke used to work at the White House Inn. Did you ask him what he would recommend?"

"I did. He said someone must order the mushrooms beignet to share, and the oysters are amazing." She giggled. "I think we'll leave those for Ellie and Pad." She lowered her gaze and looked at her hands in her lap.

"I've heard they are one of the most notorious aphrodisiacs."

"I've never eaten them, so I couldn't say from personal experience." Dani continued to avoid his eyes.

"What about dessert? Anything special or should we just fill up on bread?"

Dani exhaled. Thankfully, Paul had changed the subject. "Luke said the crème brûlée should not be missed. I guess the pastry chef is one of the best. Someone who went to school with Ellie's sister Kate."

"Then I'll save room." Paul pulled into the parking lot and turned off the ignition.

"Do you see Pad's SUV?" Dani asked.

"Yup, he's right over there." As soon as Paul pointed out the vehicle, the doors opened and Ellie and Pad got out.

Pad whistled when he saw the couple. "Dani, you look very pretty."

Dani blushed and said, "Thanks, Pad, but well, Ellie is much prettier."

Pad pulled Ellie into his arms and grinned. "Paul, we're having dinner with the two best-looking women in the county, heck, maybe even the state."

Ellie looked up. "Why stop there? If you're looking to flatter us, I think you should just admit we're the most beautiful girls in the hemisphere."

Dani flushed a new shade of crimson when Paul hooked his arm through hers.

"Pad, if you aren't going to say it, I will. Our girls are the best-looking in the world."

Laughter rang out as the foursome walked up three wide stairs to the front door.

Dani's eyes caught Ellie's, and she winked. After worrying about this night for the last several days, she was having a great time.

Seated in a quiet corner, they had the suggested appetizers and had moved on to entrées before leaning back in their chairs.

"This was the best meal I can remember having," Paul said.

"I have to agree," Dani said.

"You guys need to take a trip out to Crescent Lake. Kate's restaurant is open, and it's the best food anywhere."

Pad winked at Ellie. "Not that Ellie's biased in any way."

"We could all take a day trip out. It would be a lot of driving, but the winery's beautiful, and Kate has a great brunch on Sundays."

Paul looked at Dani. "Would you like to go sometime?"

"Sounds like fun. But I'll need to check with Cari and see if she could spare me. Sunday breakfast is pretty busy." Dani took a sip of her tea. "I can't leave her in the lurch."

Ellie said, "She has reinforcements, and if we pick a historically slow weekend, Grace can help out along with Ray and Abby. Heck, at one time or another, everyone in our family has worked at What's Perkin'."

"Well, I know," Dani said slowly. "Your mom has been really kind, taking me on without a real resume and giving me a place to live. I owe her a lot."

"Dani, you work your butt off every day at the café. You've given her the chance to move into semiretirement. Stop fretting and re-member Luke works Sundays. She'll have plenty of coverage."

Dani's smile traveled to her eyes. "Then count me in. I'd love to go. I've never been to a winery."

"That makes two of us," Paul smiled.

Pad signaled for the check. "Where to

next?" He looked at his watch. "It's early. Do you want to come over to Ellie's, and we can play cards or something?"

Ellie kicked him under the table, and he looked at her, shocked. "What did…" She leaned her head in Paul and Dani's direction.

"Or we can hang out another time," Pad continued.

"Dani, what would you like to do?" Paul asked.

"We could go for a drive out by Green Lake, and then if you're interested, I have a couple of new comedies on DVD or watch a different movie." Dani's voice was soft.

"Sure, sounds nice." Paul looked at Pad. "If you don't mind, we'll take a rain check on game night."

Ellie grinned. "Of course."

With the check paid and the tip on the table, the couples walked outside into the cool night air. Dani and Ellie exchanged hugs.

"Call me tomorrow and tell me everything," Ellie whispered.

Dani nodded and laid a hand on her stomach. "I wish these butterflies would stop fluttering."

Ellie whispered, "Paul's a good man. Relax and have fun."

"I will." Dani giggled. "Have fun too."

Ellie glanced at Pad over her shoulder and sighed. "I love him. I can't believe how much my life has changed since he came home. I feel, well, I can't find the right words. Happy just doesn't begin to describe it."

"I'm happy for you. Pad's a great guy, and everyone can see by how he looks at you, he's totally hooked."

"Ellie, are you ready?" Pad called.

"Coming." Ellie squeezed Dani's hand before skipping over to where Pad waited.

*P*ad watched Paul and Dani drive away before starting the car. "How about we take a little drive out to the lake before we go home?"

Ellie shook her head. "We can't follow them. We need to go in a different direction."

"Are you dressed warm enough for a short stroll in the park?" Pad held his breath.

"We haven't done that in quite some time." Ellie flashed a sweet smile. "It'll be good to walk off some dinner. I'm stuffed."

"You look beautiful tonight, Ellie." Pad stroked her hand as they drove to the park. He turned off the ignition. "Hold on a minute."

Ellie watched Pad hurry around the car. "What's got him flustered?"

Pad held out his hand as she got out of the vehicle. With her hand tucked into the crook of his arm, the couple strolled down the flower-lined walkway.

Ellie tilted her head back. "Look at those

stars. Have you ever seen anything more beautiful?"

Watching her, Pad murmured, "Never."

Ellie bumped his arm with hers. "You didn't even look up."

"Everything I want to see is right in front of me."

She teased, "Did you have too much wine at dinner?"

"Nope, one glass. Let's sit down."

Ellie tucked her dress under her legs and snuggled next to his chest. They sat there for a few minutes, drenched in moonlight.

Pad pulled his hand from hers.

Ellie leaned forward. "Do you need something?"

Pad slipped to one knee.

Her breath caught. Ellie's fingertips flew to her lips.

"Eleanor McKenna. My heart started beating the moment I saw you standing behind the counter in your gallery. Every day I'm with you, it beats stronger. I thought I could live without you. I tried to walk away, but my heart and mind wouldn't allow me to forget your smile. You were there, around every corner. At night, you were in my dreams."

He popped open the box, and nestled in velvet was a ring.

"This was my grandmother's. If you say yes and agree to marry me, I will be the luckiest man alive."

He took Ellie's hand, resting the ring on her fingertip. "Ellie, say yes. Will you marry me?"

Pad's eyes glowed brighter than the moonlight.

"Padraic Stone, I'm honored to wear your grandmother's ring and yes," she cried, "I'll marry you."

He slipped the ring on her finger.

Ellie placed her hands on the sides of his face and pulled him in close. "Yes. Yes. Yes." After each word, she kissed his lips.

Headlights swept across the kitchen windows.

"Who do you think is here?" Cari peered outside.

"Ray," Cari shouted. "It's Ellie and Pad."

She pulled the door open.

Cari noticed Ellie's cheeks were flushed.

"Hi, kids. What brings you by tonight?"

"Hey, I hope you don't mind us just dropping in." Ellie glanced at Pad. "But we have some news."

Ellie extended her left hand, wiggling her fingers. "Pad proposed." The words tumbled out.

Cari pulled Ellie into her arms. Tears trickled down her cheeks. "Ellie, I'm so happy for you."

Ray entered the kitchen and saw his wife and Ellie crying. "What's with the tears?"

"Ray, look." Ellie flashed her hand. "Pad and I are engaged!"

Ray stuck out his hand. "Welcome to the

family, Pad."

"Thank you, sir."

Cari pulled the couple deeper into the house. "This calls for champagne." She pulled open the cabinet door and Ray picked up a tray with four glasses.

Ellie looked between her parents. "How did you know?"

"Ellie, they've had a heads-up. I asked your mother if I could marry you."

"Oh, Pad," she cried. "This moment is even more romantic."

She pecked his lips and paused. "Does anyone else know?"

Pad chuckled. "I told Paul. But I'm sure before the night is over, most of the town will know. After this toast, we need to drive out to Aunt Winnie's."

Ray passed out the glasses and Cari raised a crystal flute.

"I'd like to propose a toast," Cari said.

"Padraic, when I met you, it was one of the worst nights of my life. Ellie was lying in the emergency room with a gash in her head and her gallery in shambles. I'm positive you saved her life that night. Afterward, you moved in and watched over her, and I could see love blossom. But like some people, you both were stubborn. You let the fear of losing the person you love most overrule your heart." She smiled at Ellie. "But we couldn't be happier than to welcome you, as an official member, into our family."

Cari raised her glass higher. "May you cherish the love you found, embrace the life you are about to start, and always remember you're at home in each other's arms."

Tears streamed down Ellie's face, and Pad choked back a few too. The glasses tinged, and the young couple intertwined arms. Savoring the bubbles on their tongues, Pad said, "Thanks, Cari. Your words resonate."

Ray slung his arms around Ellie's slender shoulders. "Kiddo, when's the big day?"

"Ray, we've been engaged for less than thirty minutes, and I want to revel in our engagement. As soon as we set the date, you two will be the first to know." She winked. "I promise."

"Give us at least a month's notice," Ray teased.

"Ha, if you recall, you and Mom gave us eight days."

"Did I ever tell you Ray popped the question on Christmas Eve and they got married on New Year's Day? It didn't leave time for planning."

Ellie pointed out the kitchen window. "But in the midst of a snowstorm, they tied the knot under the arbor. It was the most romantic wedding I've ever been to." Ellie sighed. "I would love something simple, small, and very romantic."

Pad wrapped his arms around her and rested his chin on the top of her head. "You can have whatever you want, but I'll plan the honeymoon."

Ellie hugged him tightly. "Deal."

"Why don't you give Winnie a call before

driving out there? It's getting late, and I wouldn't want to alarm her by showing up."

"Yeah, you're right." Pad pulled out his phone and walked into the other room.

Ellie twirled in a circle. "Want to see the ring again, Mom?" Cari took her hand to admire the rock on Ellie's slender fingers.

"It was Pad's grandmother's. Isn't it incredible?"

Cari kissed Ellie's cheeks. "It's breathtaking, sweetheart, and it suits you perfectly."

Ray admired it. "It's feminine and sophisticated. Pad knows your style."

Pad entered the room and said, "El, Auntie's waiting for us. I think she has some idea of what's coming since we haven't made it a common practice to see her this late."

"Then let's put a wiggle on it." Ellie kissed Ray and then Cari. "Call you tomorrow, Mom."

Cari blinked back a tear. "I can't believe my baby girl is getting married."

Ellie gave her mom one last hug, "Oh,

Mom, we'll talk tomorrow."

A short rap on the door stopped Dani and Paul's conversation on the merits of cooking hot dogs on the grill or an open fire. Dani peeked out the small side window.

"It's Ellie and Pad."

"We didn't expect to see you again tonight."

"I hope it's not too late." Ellie grinned. "Can we come in?"

Dani ushered the couple inside.

"Hey, Paul. Sorry to barge in on your date." Pad looked like a cat who swallowed the canary.

"Would you like…"

Ellie interrupted her. "After you left, Pad asked me to marry him," Ellie squealed.

Dani grabbed her left hand and held it up. "Oh, my gosh, that ring is ah-mazing."

Ellie giggled at how Dani enunciated the word. "It was Pad's grandmother's."

"Have you told your mom and Ray?" Dani asked.

"We went there first, and then we stopped at Winnie's. The rest of the family knows. I called Kate, and Abby and Shane, and of course Jake and Sara. And we just had to stop and tell you two."

Paul clapped Pad on the back. "Congratulations, you're a lucky guy."

"I couldn't agree with you more." Pad shook Paul's hand.

"Have you set a date?" Dani looked at Ellie. "Will it be a fast wedding or long engagement?"

"We're not in any rush."

Pad said, "Whenever Ellie wants to get married, we will. But hopefully, it won't take years." He chuckled. "I want us to have kids while I'm still young enough to pick them up."

"Pad," Ellie scoffed. "It's not like you're Groucho Marx."

Dani pulled Ellie into the tiny kitchen. "Let's open a bottle of wine to celebrate."

"No, I think I'm all wine and champagne'd out. We had some at Mom's and Winnie's." Ellie saw the quick flash of hurt slide across Dani's face.

"But I'd love a cup of tea or decaf coffee."

Dani brightened. "I'll put on a pot of decaf."

"Count me in, Dani," Pad called.

Paul said, "Me too."

Dani took mismatched mugs from the cupboard and grabbed a small pitcher for cream and sugar. She laid everything on the table.

"I'm happy for you, Ellie. You guys make a great couple."

"Thank you. We had kind of a rough start with the problems at my gallery, and then he left and I thought I'd never see him again." Ellie sighed. "I'll never forget when he knocked on my door. It was right before Christmas. Wow, almost two years ago, and when our eyes met, I knew a life without Pad was empty. I never looked back."

"Time sure has flown by. It will be two years already?" Dani's eyes grew misty.

"Dani, what's wrong?"

"Nothing. It gives me hope. Maybe I'll find someone to share my life with, and Derek won't be looming over my future."

Ellie wrapped her arms around Dani. "Derek is your past and who knows? Maybe your future is talking to my fiancé?"

Dani giggled. "Paul is a nice guy, but I'm sure he only asked me out because he felt bad for me."

Ellie snorted. "Don't be so sure."

"Look at me. I'm short, covered in freckles" —she paused to push up her glasses—"and I wear glasses."

"Half the population wears glasses. What does that have to do with anything?"

"Have you looked at me? I'm not exactly beautiful. Not like you or Kate." Dani's gaze dropped to the floor.

Ellie pulled Dani's chin up and looked her in the eye. "Take another look in the mirror."

"Derek always said I should wear more makeup to cover my freckles."

"He was a jerk. Derek wanted you to feel bad about yourself. It made him feel powerful."

Ellie prodded Dani to look in the small bathroom mirror. "Dani," she said. "Look."

Dani studied her reflection.

"You have thick hair and those waves, women pay a lot of money to get those put into their hair. Your freckles dust your nose and cheeks, and a guy could get lost in counting them. You are hiding your eyes behind the oversized frames, but they sparkle when you talk." Ellie laid her cheek on Dani's. "You're beautiful and don't ever forget it."

"Do you really think Derek just said those things to be mean?"

"I do."

Pad came to the door. "Is everything okay in here?"

Dani smiled. "We were just talking about freckles."

Pad searched Ellie's eyes, and she winked.

"Well then, let's have coffee and make some plans for a hike or something."

"You heard our hostess, coffee is ready." Ellie pulled Pad back into the living room.

Dani passed Paul a cup, and with her eyes twinkling, she said, "Are you up for an adventure?"

Paul did a double take. "I'm not sure what you girls were cooking up, but count me in."

Dani and Ellie laughed.

10

Dani stirred a large pot of soup, humming a song from the radio. Time to open was looming, and she had finished filling the front case.

Cari and Luke arrived, each moving like a well-oiled machine. Opening the café was easy; it was at closing time that they did all the hard work.

A knock on the front door caught Luke's attention. He flipped the lock.

"Not one but two officers as your escort this morning, Ellie?" he teased.

Ellie entered the shop arm in arm with Pad. "We have news and didn't want you to hear it from someone else."

"Do tell."

"We're engaged!"

Luke hugged Ellie and then shook Pad's hand. "This is awesome news. I'm happy for you."

"And before you ask"—Ellie laughed—"we don't have a date."

Paul broke in, "Yet." Before Ellie could make contact, he stepped through the swinging doors. "Morning, Dani."

"Good morning, Paul." Dani's heart skipped a beat. "I didn't expect to see you today."

"Pad and Ellie are making the rounds, so I thought I'd sneak in and see what you're whipping up." He peeked into the large mixing bowl. "I've developed an affinity for cupcakes recently."

Dani wasn't sure if he was flirting or serious. "Repeat customers are good for business."

Dani felt the heat rise on her cheeks. "I'm making a simple chocolate cake with marshmallow filling."

"Like those cakes we had as kids? Devil dogs?" Paul's eyes lit up. "I loved those."

"You did? I thought they were dry. The cake was like sawdust in my mouth. The only thing saving it was the cream filling." Using an ice cream scoop, Dani filled the paper liners on the baking tray. "This cake won't be dry, and the filling will enhance the chocolate, topped with a light swirl of buttercream frosting. You'll forget all about those mass-produced cakes."

"You know you're defaming a national treasure, right?"

Dani arched an eyebrow. "Really?"

"Well, one of my sacred childhood memories." Paul grinned. "What time do you think they'll be ready? I don't want to miss the chance to sample one."

"I'll put a couple aside, and you can swing by after your shift."

"The shop's closed then. Can I stop at your place?"

"Sure. If you have time, we could have coffee." Dani's voice dropped. "I'm sure you have better things to do than hang around with me again. I'll have the box ready."

"Wait, I'd love to have, spend, see—" After each word, Paul sputtered. "I'd like to hang out for a while."

Pad poked his head in the kitchen. "Paul, we gotta roll. Dani, he'll see you after work."

Paul shrugged his shoulders. "You heard the man. I'll see you later."

Dani was leaning against the counter when Ellie walked in.

"Earth to Dani." Ellie waved a hand in front of her face.

Dani blinked. "Huh?"

"Were you daydreaming about a handsome blond officer?"

"I don't know what you're talking about." Dani slid the cupcake tray into the oven. "We were just talking about cupcakes."

"And?"

"Well, if you must know, Paul's stopping by after work for coffee and a cupcake."

"He is? Nice."

"Ellie, do you think he's interested in me? I have nothing to offer a guy like him, except trouble with my ex."

"Obviously, Paul disagrees."

"What if I'm not ready for a relationship?"

"Dani, who says you have to jump into a relationship? Right now, you're getting to know a nice guy who understands an ex-boyfriend is harassing you. You've done a great job of being a country mouse with your oversized glasses and shapeless clothes to make sure no one would notice you."

Dani looked at the floor. "It's easier to be invisible."

"For heaven's sake, why?" Ellie sat down on the stool. "You're funny, sassy, smart, nice, and very pretty."

"If I was invisible, I was safe."

"Oh."

"I used to dress differently when I lived in Chester. I wore makeup and shopped for clothes, but what happened changed me."

"Because you felt isolated. Derek chiseled you away from everyone in your life. You had to rely on him. Your mom bought into his line of bull. Slowly, he cut you off from friends. But he under estimated your courage and strength."

"How do you know all that about me?"

"We all have our own issues. I tried to keep Pad at arm's length and he with me. We were afraid. Instead, we closed the door on love, our future. For months, we didn't even talk. It's not exactly the same, but it amounts to holding ourselves away from emotional attachments."

"I want to move on, but I feel like I'm carrying a two-hundred-pound monkey on my back."

Ellie smiled. "You've already started. Self-defense class, a date with a hot cop, you're talking to your mom, and look at us. We're friends."

"It's been a long time since I've had a close friend." Dani hesitated. "Maybe we're kindred spirits."

Ellie hugged Dani. "I know we are. Other than Kate and Mom, I've never had close friends."

Dani squeezed Ellie tighter.

"Dani." Ellie looked her square in the eyes. "Promise me, despite what Derek says or does, you'll remember the truth. Soon, he'll be a distant memory."

"You haven't seen him in action. Would you take another class with Judy?"

"Sure, any night except Saturday. The gallery is pretty busy on the weekends."

"All right, I'll let you know." Dani's timer went off.

"Hey, save me two of those little gems. I'll pick them up after my run."

Ellie breezed out the back door and ran into a human wall. Hands clenched her arms at her sides.

"Let me go!" Ellie tried to wrench her arms

out of a viselike grip.

"You're gonna march in there and tell Danielle to come out here. Now."

"I will do no such thing. Get out of here and never look back before you're arrested for trespassing." Ellie's heart pounded. She tried to push him away. "*Let me go*!" She stamped on his foot, but he still didn't release her.

He shook Ellie, making her head snap back. "I told you…"

At the sound of sirens growing closer, he shoved Ellie to the ground. She put her hand out to break her fall. Pain radiated up her arm as pavement and palm connected.

Dani pushed open the back door, wielding a granite rolling pin. "Ellie!"

Ellie blinked tears from her eyes, struggling to her feet. Dani reached out to steady her. "Where is that SOB?"

She was wobbling on her heels when Pad thundered through the back door, Paul a close second.

With blood dripping down her hand to a

widening puddle, Pad scooped her into his arms. "Ellie, honey, are you okay?"

"I'm okay. You can put me down. My hand hurts, not my feet."

Pad kept his arm around her. The trembling started to subside. Ellie asked, "Did you see him?"

"No. Dani called Paul as soon you screamed, and we got here as fast as we could, but he took off. Although"—he scanned the area—"Paul went to double-check and call in the attack."

Dani went inside. She came back with a wet kitchen towel. "Ellie, wrap this around your hand." Dani choked back a sob. "I can't believe he hurt you. It should have been me."

"Danielle, stop it right now." Ellie stamped her foot. "If he had gotten to you, heaven only knows what he would have done."

"You're bleeding." Dani tried to wipe away the pebbles on Ellie's hand and forearm.

"Ouch, it hurts." Ellie winced as she leaned against Pad. "Where's Mom?"

"She went to the bank, but I'll send Luke to get her."

They went inside and Ellie stuck her hand under the running water and watched as the river of red became pink. She bent closer, and upon examination, saw a good-sized shard of glass sticking out. Her knees buckled.

Pad wrapped his arms around her waist. "We're going to the hospital."

"Can't you pull it out for me?" Ellie looked up. Her big blue eyes filled with tears. "It looks really gross and it hurts worse."

"I might not get it all, and it could lead to infection." Pad smoothed back her hair. "Don't worry, I won't leave you."

Dani handed Pad a white towel. "Take care not to catch the glass."

Paul came through the door. "He isn't any-where in the vicinity."

Pad gave a curt nod. "We're headed to the hospital. Ellie has glass in her hand, and she might need an X-ray on her arm."

Paul leaned toward Dani. "She's going to be fine, maybe a few stitches."

"It's my fault she's hurt."

"No. You didn't do this. Derek attacked her. When we find him, he'll be charged with assault and battery. Ellie going to the ER strengthens the charge."

Paul put his fingers on Dani's lips. "I called for another squad car. I'm too close to this situation, given our personal relationship. Having someone else handle it is best for prosecution." Paul walked out of the room, leaving Dani staring after him.

Slowly, she shook her head. What did Paul mean, given their relationship? Did he mean their friendship or something more?

Luke popped his head in. "Cari's on the phone. Do you want to talk to her?"

Dani picked up the receiver. "Hi, Cari. Pad

took her to the hospital to have a laceration looked at, but she'll be fine." She paused. "Okay, I'll see you shortly."

A sharp rap on the door broke her train of thought as she hung up the phone. Judy walked into the room. "Dani, how are you doing? Paul said they believe it was Derek Ryan who attacked Ellie. Can you answer a few questions?"

Dani wrung the towel in her hands. "Of course."

Judy ran through the standard questions: Had she heard from Derek recently? What made her call the station, and did she see which way Derek ran?

Dani carefully answered each question as she replayed the event in slow motion in her brain.

Judy said, "My partner is taking some photos. Are you sure it was Derek and what was he wearing?"

"I caught a glimpse of him as he was running away. He had on black jeans and a black

T-shirt, sneakers, and a ball cap. Oh, and dark sunglasses."

"And you're sure it was Ryan? Was there anything distinctive about him?"

"The cap had a Chester Fire Department logo. It was turned around backward, and it's the kind I've seen him wear."

Judy made a note and snapped her notebook closed. "Dani, you don't need to worry. He's going to get cocky, and if he keeps up on this path, we'll have a slew of charges against him."

"I know. Paul has said the same thing. But what if next time…"

"Don't even go there."

"Before Ellie left, we had decided to ask you for another lesson." Dani pushed her glasses up to the bridge of her nose. "Do you have some time?"

"For you two, absolutely." Judy pulled out her cell and scrolled through a few apps. "Here we go. My calendar is wide open tomorrow night."

"Ah, we might want to let Ellie's hand heal up. What about next week?"

"Sorry, I wasn't thinking. Next Thursday?"

Dani smiled. "I'll ask Ellie later. Can I give you a call?"

"Sure. You've got my number, and you can always have the guys give me a message."

An officer poked his head in the door. "I'm ready to roll, Judy."

"Wait, before we go, I'd like to introduce you to Dani Michaels."

Dani was struck by the officer's jet-black, almost blue hair and black eyes. He wasn't tall but he was powerfully built; his features looked chiseled.

"Dani, this is Hoyt Walker."

He grasped her outstretched hand. "Walker. Pleased to meet you. I wish it was under different circumstances. Judy has told me you've been studying self-defense. In light of recent events, it seems to be a good idea."

"It's nice to meet you." Dani glanced out

the window. "Did you find anything out there?"

"No. I'm afraid not." Walker caught Judy's eye. She nodded.

"We need to get going. Paul should be back in. He was finishing up."

"Oh, okay." Dani's head started to spin. She grabbed the counter and Walker put out a hand.

"You should sit down."

Paul rushed through the door and to her side. "What's going on here?" His eyes were glued to Dani's pale face.

Judy handed Dani a glass of water, and she brought it to her lips, taking a tiny sip.

"I got a little light-headed. Walker had me sit down before I hit the floor."

"Paul." Judy tapped him on the shoulder. "If you've got this, we're going to head to the station."

"Dani?" Paul rubbed her small hand in his. "Are you feeling a little better?"

Dani looked at the cops. "I'm not some hot-house flower."

Judy knelt down. "Dani, your friend was just threatened by your ex, and adrenaline flooded your system. It's only natural to be a little knock-kneed."

Dani forced a smile. "I'm sorry for being rude. I didn't expect to see him today."

"I think you and Ellie both need to be prepared, which is why we're going to have advanced self-defense classes."

"Thanks, Judy." Her smile grew. "You guys should get out of here and stop coddling me." She grabbed Paul's hand. "I want you to check on Ellie."

Dani stood, wobbled a little, and announced, "I have customers to feed. Derek isn't going to stop me from doing my job."

"I'm going outside with Judy and Walker. If anyone knocks, call Luke before opening it."

Dani's eyes widened. "Do you think he's coming back today?"

"I doubt it, but we're going to take more precautions moving forward."

He flipped the lock on the back door before closing it.

Cari saw Walker talking to Luke when she stormed through the door.

"Did you get him?" she demanded.

Walker rested his large hands on his belt. "Mrs. Davis?"

"Yes. And you are?"

"Officer Walker, ma'am. I'm Officer Bell's partner."

Cari pushed past him. "What's going on here?"

"Ma'am, Pad took her to the ER. She has glass in her hand, and it needed to be cleaned and dressed."

Cari eyed the newcomer.

"Ellie requested you call her cell."

Luke handed Cari her handbag. Cari paced

the room, waiting for someone to pick up the phone.

Walker waited.

Cari slipped the phone into her bag. "Ellie asked me to stay here until they're back. At least this time she wasn't hit over the head and locked up." Cari's hand flew to her mouth. "Is Dani alright? I didn't even think to ask about her." She rushed into the kitchen.

"Dani, oh my stars. Are you okay?" Cari wrapped her arms around the girl.

"Cari, I'm fine. I'm sorry Ellie was hurt."

"I just talked to Ellie, and she said it was a small cut. Pad wouldn't pull the glass out in case something broke off. And she's not sure when she had a booster for tetanus."

Paul walked in. "Dani, I'll be back soon."

"You don't need to hang around here. You've got work to do, tickets to write and all." She smiled. "Really, go. Do your thing."

"I'm going to see Luke before I go." Paul left the kitchen in search of him.

Paul saw Luke wiping off the counter and

staring out the front windows. "Luke. I was hoping you could do me a favor?"

"Sure, what do you need?"

"Will you keep an eye on things until I get back?"

"Yeah. If I see anything, I'll call, and it goes without saying Dani won't go anywhere alone." He swallowed hard. "I don't want this to come out wrong, but…"

"I know. How long before we arrest Ryan?"

"Well, yeah, it's been a while now. Can't the cops in Chester help or something?" He held up his hands. "The guy is huge, and I don't care how many self-defense classes Dani has, she's tiny."

"Luke, we're doing everything we can. But it's not easy to lock him up," Judy said.

Luke gave Paul a hard look. "What's it going to take, for him to really hurt her before he's arrested?"

"Look, I know you are friends and you're frustrated. Be our eyes. I'm sure Cari won't mind keeping the back door locked at all times."

"Cari would do anything for Dani. She looks at her like another daughter."

Walker said, "Luke, we will get this guy. You have my word."

"You'd better before he does anything else. Dani's the closest thing I have to a sister, and I don't want anything to happen to her or Ellie."

Paul said, "We don't either. But right now, we need to get going. Will you call me before you close up? I want to be here when Dani goes up to her apartment."

"Yeah, I'll call."

The police officers walked outside and slid shades into place.

Paul spoke first. "Walker, did you find anything useful?"

He held up a small evidence bag. Inside, there was a handwritten note. He handed it to Paul, who passed it to Judy.

"With this, we can issue a warrant for his

arrest." Paul's voice was low. "You know he isn't going to stop unless we stop him first."

Judy handed the bag to Walker. "I know Dani asked me to wait until next week, but I'm going to line up the community room for tomorrow night. If you don't have any plans, feel free to drop in around five. I'm sure Pad and Paul will both be there. I know you taught self-defense too; maybe you can use me to show some new things to the girls."

"Happy to help if you don't think they'd mind a newcomer?"

"The more the merrier, and another set of trained eyes won't hurt. We're certain he's watching her."

"That's a given," Walker said. "Paul, are you okay with me jumping in?"

Paul studied Judy's right-hand man. "Yeah, we need to get Dani ready for anything. I've got a bad feeling. He's coming unhinged, and I'll do anything to protect her."

Walker gave an abrupt nod. "Judy, are you ready?"

"I'll check in with you later, Paul." Judy followed Walker to the patrol car.

Paul scanned Main Street. How could Ryan move around without being noticed? Paul slid behind the wheel. He needed to talk to Ellie.

Pad and Ellie walked out of the emergency room doors as Paul parked. They waited for him on the sidewalk.

"How's your hand, El?"

She shrugged. "No big deal. I didn't need an X-ray. They picked out the glass, cleaned it, gave me a shot, and used some kind of super glue to pull the edges together. Bottom line, it's not as bad as someone"—she jerked her head in Pad's direction—"had thought."

"In my defense, you had glass sticking out of your hand. It needed a professional's intervention."

Ellie stood on her tiptoes and kissed his cheek. "My hero."

She redirected her gaze at Paul. "Why are you here?" Ellie's eyes widened. "Did he come back? Were you able to cart him off to jail?"

"I wanted to ask you a few questions, away from Dani. I was hoping you'd remember something more."

"Everything happened so fast." She rubbed her arms where Derek pinned them. "I remember he grabbed me, demanding I get Dani, and I refused. Then he shoved me to the ground and took off."

"Why did you go out the back door?" Paul asked.

"I wanted to take the shortcut to the gallery."

"You're using the front door until this mess is behind us all, right, Ellie?" Pad pulled her chin up and looked her in the eye.

"I already said I will. But what about Dani? She lives out the back door."

"For starters, your mom has agreed to keep the back door locked, and we're all meeting Judy and Walker, her new partner, tomorrow night for another lesson."

"What Judy taught us isn't going to help. His hands were like a viselike grip. I tried to pull loose, but the way he held me, I couldn't connect to any body part that would cause him any pain."

Paul rubbed his chin. "Do you think he was on drugs?"

Ellie thought carefully. "I couldn't say. I didn't look at his face. I was too busy trying to get away." She straightened up. "Wait, I stomped on his foot, and it didn't faze him. It felt like I had stepped on a brick or stone."

Pad's eyes narrowed. "Steel toes?"

"Yeah, we know he pretends to be a fireman; maybe he's wearing safety boots like cops and firemen."

"One more thing. Pad, this time, he left a note." Paul shook a finger at Ellie. "For now, don't say a word to her."

"She has to know."

"And she will," Paul agreed.

"What did it say?"

Paul winced. "Soon, they'd be together, and for all time."

11

"What the hell?" Dani stamped her feet. "I can't go home until I have a police escort?"

"Dani, listen," Luke shouted. "Paul asked me to wait with you until he got here. For now, you wait, and then bring it up to him."

Dani flung the towel she had twisted into a knot. A sharp rap on the back door sent her heart racing.

"I'll go." Luke looked out. "It's Paul."

Dani scowled at Paul. "Would you mind

telling me why I need a police escort across the back parking lot?"

Paul hesitated. He pulled a cell phone from his shirt pocket, hit a couple of buttons, and handed it to her.

"See for yourself."

Dani's hand flew to her mouth. "What does this mean?"

Paul took his phone and handed it to Luke. "You should see this since you spend a lot of time with Dani."

Luke's color paled. "Does this mean he intends to hurt her?"

"We don't know for sure. He was here today, and we have no idea where he went. We're not taking any chances. Everyone on the force is taking this very seriously, and we've issued a warrant for his arrest for the attack on Ellie. If anyone sees him, anywhere in town, he'll be picked up."

"What do I need to do in the meantime?" Dani grabbed Paul's arm. "I spent the last couple of years living in fear." She whipped a cookbook down onto the stainless-steel counter. "I won't live like this, not again. If I have to, I'll disappear where he won't find me."

Paul steered Dani to a stool. "Dani, the man is unbalanced, and he'll keep searching for you. We have to stop him. If you run, there won't be anyone who has your back. You'll be alone, defenseless."

Dani dropped her head in her hands. A lone tear hovered on her lashes. "I don't care if he does. He won't hurt anyone else."

"I care." Luke knelt down and looked into her eyes. "And you know the entire McKenna family cares. You've made good friends and a life here. Let us help you."

"Dani, I promise. Pad, the department, and I will do our best to keep everyone safe and arrest this guy before he can carry out his threat."

"Do you think he'll be arrested?" Dani said.

"I do. In fact, Pad has a call into the Chester

Police Department. He's hoping they can help us since Derek left a note. We have proof of something brewing."

"But he's a fireman. Don't they all stick together?"

"He's not a fireman. Remember, we found out he's a photographer. Besides, the police wouldn't care if he was in the department. If there is proof he's breaking the law, with the oath they took to protect and serve, they'll do what they need to do."

Dani's wheels were spinning. "What do I need to do?"

"That's my girl." Paul grabbed her hand.

Dani felt a tiny smile creep across her face. "Your girl?"

Paul flushed crimson. "Do you need to go to the store or anything before we go to your place?"

Dani grinned. "Oh, we're going to my place?"

Paul sputtered. "We can do anything you want, but at some point, you have to go home, and I'd prefer you didn't run out for milk."

"Paul, you're awfully cute when you're nervous."

Luke chuckled. "It seems you're in good hands, Dani. I'll see you in the morning."

"Luke, hold up."

"What do you need?"

"Would it be asking too much for you to come in early tomorrow and wait for her at the bottom of the stairs? I'm going to run over to Chester and poke around a bit."

"Yeah, sure." Luke clapped a hand on Paul's shoulder. "Don't worry. I'll look after her."

"Guys, you know I'm standing right here and can hear you."

"And I'll be over at quarter till six. Wait for me."

Dani threw up her hands. She may be stubborn, but she was sensible. Walking into the shop with Luke was better than running into Derek.

"See you tomorrow," Dani said.

Luke left out the front.

Paul said, "I'm sorry if I came off heavy-handed. But I care about you. I couldn't stand it if something happened to you."

Dani laid a hand aside Paul's firm jawline. "I care about you too. You've become a good friend."

"Maybe, when this is over, we could become more than friends?" Paul's gaze intensified.

"I'm not ready for anything more than friendship. I'll understand if you don't want to hang out or share an occasional meal."

Dani looked at the floor. She hated lying to him. In her heart, she knew he was the kind of guy she could fall for, and hard.

Paul tilted her chin up. "Then we'll be best buds." He gave her a big smile. "Friends?"

Dani grinned. "Friends."

Dani gave him a quick hug, the brief contact causing her blood to tingle. "If the offer stands, I've love to go to the market and cook dinner with you."

"How about at my place?"

Dani batted her eyelashes. "Sure. But you're the cleanup crew."

"Do I get to keep the leftovers?" Paul teased.

"Depends on how hungry I am," Dani said. She grabbed her bag and said, "Let's go, Officer Greene."

Paul and Dani went out front to where his car was parked. Paul held the door for her. When she glanced up, he said, "Years of my mom hammering into my head good manners."

"Sounds like a smart woman." Dani slid into the passenger seat, and Paul jogged around the car.

"Do you want to go to Blake's Farmer's Market or the super center?"

"Do you have any requests for dinner?"

"How about spaghetti and meatballs? It's my favorite." Paul pulled into traffic.

"The super center then. Have you made sauce before?"

"You mean like open the jar and heat it up?" He looked out of the corner of his eye and smirked.

"You just answered my question. We'll make a quick simmer sauce and then bake some meatballs in the oven. It won't take long, and you can freeze the leftover sauce for another night."

Dani noticed Paul glancing in his rearview mirror a few times. The car sped up.

"Hey, can't you get in trouble for running a red light?" Dani asked.

"I can get a ticket. No one is above the law. I just misjudged the timing."

Satisfied, Dani pulled out a notepad and jotted down a few ingredients.

Paul parked close to the entrance of the market; all the while, Dani was talking about the merits of homemade sauce.

"It sounds good." Paul pushed the cart and followed her inside.

"Are you sure you want to have dinner tonight? You seem distracted."

"No, I'm just thinking about dessert."

"We could have gotten something at the café."

"Let's pick up a pint of ice cream."

Dani dropped items in the cart. Coming down the last aisle, she said, "How long do you think before it's over?"

Paul looked at her sideways. "A few days if we're lucky, at most a couple of weeks."

"Why doesn't he just get the hint and chase some other girl?"

"No idea."

"I wouldn't wish this on anyone, but I never dreamed he'd come after me after such a long time. I guess it was wishful thinking." She laid her hand on Paul's arm. "Can we get a restraining order?"

"We can if you're ready to take the next step."

"What do I need to do?"

Paul looked around. "Let's talk about this when we get back to my place. It's not really a conversation we should have in the dairy aisle."

Dani smiled. "Once again, you're right."

As the pair pulled into Paul's driveway, Dani's eyes grew wide.

"Wow, I had no idea you owned a house." Dani's gaze took in the sweeping wraparound porch on the large rambling farmhouse and carefully maintained but haphazard flower beds.

"It was my grandparents' home. When they moved to the retirement complex, I bought the house. Primarily to keep it in the family, but really it made my gram really happy to know I was setting down roots."

"It's beautiful. There are many wonderful homes in Loudon." Dani got out of the car and turned around. "It's so peaceful."

"But technically we're still in town." Paul grabbed the bags of groceries.

"Come on. I'll give you the nickel tour."

Dani followed Paul up the wooden steps. Her fingers trailed over the back of a rocking chair.

"Do you sit and watch the world go by?"

Paul chuckled. "You sound like you've never been on an old-fashioned front porch before."

"My parents always had a modern house. You know, clean lines, lots of glass, and open spaces. Our home was beautiful, but it didn't invite one to linger in a chair and do nothing."

Paul pushed open the front door. "I haven't had much time for renovation. It's pretty much the same as when I was a kid."

Dani stepped into the soaring entrance. Her mouth fell open.

"You might catch a fly with your mouth hanging open. Let me give you the tour." Paul dropped the bags on a table.

"Straight ahead is a three-season porch that

extends across most of the back of the house. To the right the kitchen, and it opens into the family room, which connects to the porch. Of course, the stairs go up to three bedrooms and a full bath, and tucked behind the stairs to the left is the master bedroom and bath, which adjoins the screened-in porch."

Paul proudly showed off each room, flipping on lights which highlighted the crown moldings and wood details.

Dani ran her hand across the chair rail in the entrance and peeked into the screened porch. "May I?"

Paul held open the door, and Dani sucked in a deep breath.

"If this was my house, I'd spend most of the time right here. I'll bet a lot of wildlife strolls through your backyard."

"It does, and I do. This is my favorite room too." He pulled open the bedroom door. "As you can see, there are windows looking out over the entire property. Gram loved lots of windows."

"When you see her, tell her I agree, lots of windows are essential." Dani wandered back into the main entrance and picked up the bags.

"We should start the sauce and then"—she grinned—"we can have wine on that fabulous porch, and you can tell me how to get the restraining order against Derek."

"It's too bad we have to mix unpleasantness with good company." Paul handed Dani a big pot.

Dani placed it on the stove. "We'll need a cutting board, sharp knives, and olive oil."

Paul retrieved all the items and grabbed two wineglasses. "White or red?"

"Red, of course. We're having spaghetti." She shook her head and teased. "Peasants."

The pair soon had a pot of sauce gently simmering. With glasses in hand and an open bottle, Paul ushered Dani into the spacious sunroom.

"Have a seat."

Dani sank into a floral chaise lounge and

propped up her feet. "You don't need to ask me twice." She took a glass from Paul.

Bringing it up to her nose, she inhaled the light floral, fruity fragrance. She studied the glass as she swirled the liquid. "I love the rich crimson color. It reminds me of old velvet cushions."

"I never thought of it like velvet, but since you mention it, I have to agree." Paul leaned back in the chair. "How long should the sauce simmer?"

"About an hour. It needs time to thicken and the flavors blend. It'll be even better the next time you eat it."

With a crooked smile, Paul said, "You'll come over and share it with me?"

"We'll see, but you might want to have a different dinner guest." Dani shifted in her seat.

"Let's talk about Derek," Paul said.

"I know we have to, but that topic puts a damper on everything." Dani gazed out the window. "You know, I never thought I'd end up like this, with a stalker."

"No one ever thinks about this in the first stages of dating. It goes both ways, you know."

"Do you speak from personal experience?" Dani's eyes widened. "Oh, wow, you had a crazy ex-girlfriend."

Paul held his palms up. "We all have a past, some more, shall we say, colorful than others."

"Tell me about her."

"There's not much to tell. It didn't last long. I figured out pretty quickly she had issues."

"And…"

"We went out on a few dates, you know movies, dinner, hiking, and each date she asked to meet my family. I wasn't in any hurry, and it was way too early for those kinds of introductions."

"Why do I think you're going to say she ended up meeting them?"

Paul let out a belly laugh. "You guessed what's coming." He took a sip of wine.

"I had plans with the family for my gram's birthday, and we were having the party here. She had asked me to hang out, and I said I couldn't. I didn't want to tell her and make it awkward. I kind of knew this relationship wasn't long term."

Dani leaned forward. "Go on."

"Well, the night came and my entire family was here—grandparents, cousins, the whole gang. Just as we're sitting down to eat, I hear a knock on the door and without waiting for me to answer, guess who waltzes in?"

Dani's hand flew to her mouth, smothering a laugh. "No. She walked in?"

"Wait, there's more." Paul hopped up and stood in the doorway.

"She stood in this very spot and said, before we all got too far into the birthday celebration, she knew we couldn't keep our news a secret any longer."

"You're kidding, right?"

"She announced we were engaged." Paul flopped onto the couch.

"She told your family she was engaged to you?" Dani asked.

"She did. At first, everyone was stunned into silence, and then my mom hugged her and welcomed her to the family."

"What did you do?"

"I blew up and escorted her to the door and locked it, with her banging on the glass on the other side. Then I went back into the house and explained to my entire family we had gone on a few dates and apparently, she was a whack job."

Dani dissolved into giggles. "I can just see you now, the tips of your ears bright red and clenching and unclenching your hands. Like you do when you're really mad."

"How do you know what I do when I'm angry?"

"I've seen you in action. Dealing with my problem the last few weeks has piqued your temper."

"Well, anyway, after I got my parents to be-lieve that I wasn't hiding some deep dark secret, we enjoyed what was left of the birthday party. The highlight came the next day. I had to see her and find out what the heck she was thinking."

"Was she devastated you rejected her?" Dani asked.

"When I finally caught up to her, she was miffed I denied our relationship in front of my family. I reminded her we had gone on a handful of dates, and after her little stunt, there wouldn't be another one."

"Did she get the hint?"

"It took about a month of her calling, dropping by the house, and so-called bumping into me in town. But eventually, she knew it was over between us."

"Where is she now?"

"Last I heard, she had hooked up with some guy near the city and is married. She got what she wanted, and I'm happy she moved out of town. For a while, it was a bit awkward, never knowing when she would pop up."

"Jeez, I wish Derek would have gotten the

hint after all this time. But he's like a punching bag toy, you know where you hit the clown face, and it keeps popping back up?"

"Eventually, he's going to get the hint and leave town for good." He reached out and touched her hand. "I promise."

Dani squeezed his hand. "For the first time in a long time, I feel like this really will be in the past, where it belongs."

Dani didn't want to let go of his hand. She liked how the warmth of his touch flowed straight to her heart, melting the hard, icy shell Derek's mean, hurtful words had created layer after layer.

Dani pulled her hand away and brushed back her bangs. "I have to stir the sauce."

She could feel Paul's eyes follow her. The butterflies flitting in her stomach slowed to an intermittent flutter. Taking the wooden spoon, she stirred the deep-red sauce, drinking in the pungent, sweet smell. She used the moment to drift away.

"Dani?" Paul's deep voice pulled her back to him.

"I just didn't want the sauce to burn." Dani rapped the wooden spoon on the side of the pan and set it on the counter.

She wasn't ready to talk about anything on a deeper level.

"Paul, I'll make the salad if you can start the pasta water."

Paul moved with quiet confidence.

"You seem at home in the kitchen?" Dani spoke softly.

"It comes natural, I guess. My mom and gram are great cooks, and they shared with me the love of cooking."

Dani washed the lettuce and was surprised to find Paul handing her a salad spinner. "Most men don't have the niceties in their kitchens."

"You'll discover I'm not most men." Paul handed her a vegetable peeler and a wooden cutting board. "Can I help?" Dani moved to make room at the butcher-block island.

Working like they'd been cooking together for years, they had dinner ready in no time.

Paul held out a chair for Dani. He sat next to her, at the head of the farmhouse style table. He topped off her wineglass and did the same for his.

"I know we still need to talk about why you agreed to have dinner with me, but let's table it until after dinner. This looks too good to have us distracted by anything other than two friends enjoying a meal together."

Dani held her fork and tablespoon in midair. "Do you twirl or cut spaghetti?"

Paul let out a belly-busting laugh. "I'm a twirler from way back."

"Me too!"

Pleasant conversation filled the room as the plates were wiped clean with the last of the bread.

Dani pushed herself back from the table and patted her belly. "I don't remember when I've eaten this much at night. If we keep having dinner, I'm going to have to take up running."

"We can do it together."

Dani's mind slipped to a different activity, and her face grew hot. "I'm going to clear the table." She dropped a fork on the floor. As she bent down to retrieve it, she bumped Paul's head.

"Ouch." She rubbed her forehead.

"Here, let me take a look." Paul studied her face and leaned in, gently brushing his lips against the small bump.

"Mom always said there's nothing a kiss can't fix."

Dani pulled back. "Um, thanks."

She carried the stack of plates into the kitchen. Bracing her hands on the edge of the sink, she swallowed hard and turned.

"Paul?"

His gaze never left her. "Yes?"

"Am I crazy, or— Oh, never mind." She turned back to the sink and started rinsing the plates off. Paul turned off the faucet.

"Dani, look at me." He gently turned her to face him.

Her gaze matched his. "We can't do this."

"Why not? We both feel it, don't we?"

Dani hoped her thundering heart didn't betray her. "Paul, I will not get involved with anyone until Derek is out of my life. If you want to be my friend, fine, that's all I can handle for now."

Paul slipped his arms around Dani and held her tight against his chest.

"Please, just be my friend."

"Relax, we'll be the best of friends."

Dani held him close, reveling in the feel of his warm, hard body against hers. "Thank you for understanding."

Paul continued to hold her tightly.

"Let's talk about the restraining order. I don't want you to be alarmed, but really, it's to create layers to eventually wrap Derek up in legal mumbo jumbo. We don't want him to wiggle away."

Dani stiffened. "You mean it's not going to stop him from coming after me?"

"Unfortunately, I've seen other men like Ryan and it doesn't stop them when they think they're above the law. But it will show the courts, when we do arrest him, you followed the letter of the law, and it will help convict him of stalking."

Dani pulled back. "Let's do it. I'm done being afraid."

12

Over the next few days, Dani went to the courthouse and filled out paper-work for the restraining order and had a date and time to appear before the judge.

Dani held up a simple floral print dress. "What does a person wear to request a re-straining order?"

Ellie flipped hangers. "You should wear this."

She handed Dani a short-sleeved pale-green top and a simple floral skirt. "You can add a cardigan in case it's cool inside."

Dani threw the dress on the bed and held up the new outfit. "I think this will work. Give me five minutes to change."

Ellie hung up the dress and straightened out the closet.

Dani peeked her head out of the bathroom. "Do you think Derek will be there?"

"From what Pad said, he was served. If he doesn't show up, it won't look good for him."

Dani stepped into low-heeled sandals. "What if he tries to talk to me?"

"I don't think he'll dare start trouble, especially in the courthouse. There are cops everywhere, and if he does something stupid, I'm pretty sure Paul would love to arrest him."

Dani frowned. "He'll try to have the judge eating out of his hand before it's done."

"Stop worrying. It's all about the facts. You have strong evidence, and if needed, you have me as a witness."

Dani draped the sweater over her shoulders. "Will you drive? I'm too nervous."

Ellie squeezed her hand. "You're going to be fine, you'll see."

Ellie parked in a space. The brick and stone structure rose three stories, large white columns supporting the immense overhang.

Ellie pointed to the stone stairs. "We've got company."

"Oh, no." Dani shrank into the car cushions. "It's Paul."

Dani peered through the windshield. She exhaled. "And Pad's with him."

Paul jogged down the steps and approached her side of the car. He was dressed in full uniform, complete with handcuffs, nightstick, and his sidearm in its holster. He pulled open the door and offered his hand.

She absorbed the warmth of his touch. "I'm surprised to see you here." Her eyes looked deep into Paul's.

"Did you think I wouldn't be here to support you? Walking into a courthouse can be intimidating."

"I really appreciate it." Dani smiled at Pad. "And thank you too."

"I wouldn't miss the opportunity to see Ellie in the middle of the day." Pad grew serious. "And besides, my partner couldn't stay away."

Flanked by her three closest friends, Dani squared her shoulders, took a deep breath, and said, "Let's go inside."

She marched up the stairs, pulled open the thick wooden door, and stepped into the vestibule. Before her, an officer stood next to the metal detector and another officer was focused on a monitor, examining contents of a briefcase. Dani grasped Paul's hand. "What do I do?"

Paul steered her forward. He nodded at the officers. "Joe, Nick."

"Hey, Paul. We didn't think you and Pad had a case today?"

"This one's personal."

Joe nodded.

Paul said, "Put your handbag on the belt and wait for Joe to tell you to walk through."

Dani waited.

"Step through, please."

Cautiously, she walked through, taking care to not touch the metal sides.

Once Dani was on the other side, he said, "Hold out your arms, parallel to the floor please, Miss."

Dani became a statue as Officer Joe used a wand to scan her arms and legs. Nick picked up her bag and handed it to her.

"You're all set."

Ellie went through the same procedure. Pad and Paul secured their guns in the small lockers on the left of the security station.

"Good luck in there," Nick said.

"Who's the judge today?" Paul asked.

"Judge Stanton."

Paul said, "Good." He turned to Dani. "You've got nothing to worry about. She's tough but fair."

"Easy for you to say. You don't have a

crazy ex-boyfriend as big as an oak tree harassing you."

"After today, you won't either."

Dani flicked her thumbnail with her forefinger.

"Dani, I'll be right by your side." Paul took her hand. "Remember, we have backup. Super Cop's got our six."

Dani couldn't hold back her laughter. "Who's that and what the heck is our six?"

"Pad's got our back." Paul laughed. "And believe me, there isn't anyone better, well, except me, of course."

"Hey, Paul, I can hear you." Pad jabbed him in the back. "Watch who you're saying is the better cop."

Dani stopped mid-stride and sucked in a breath. "Look."

Derek sat in the front of the room, right behind the half wall that kept the onlookers from the defendant and plaintiff tables.

"Look at how respectable he is, wearing the perfect suit and tie." Dani froze in place.

"Dani, let's sit down." Ellie gently pushed Dani toward the opposite side of the room.

Dani's eyes were riveted on Derek Ryan. Her mouth had gone dry. Her heart pounded in her chest. "I can't do this," she croaked.

Ellie stood in front of Dani, blocking her line of sight. "Look at me. Just me."

Dani focused on Ellie's eyes.

"Close your eyes and take a couple of deep breaths, in through your nose and out through your mouth, and listen. Shut out everything else except the sound of my voice."

She listened to Ellie's melodic voice.

"Derek can't hurt you. We're here today to show him you're not afraid, not anymore. We're sending him a strong signal. If he tries to mess with you, he messes with all of us."

Dani's head slowly moved up and down.

"Are you ready to open your eyes?"

Dani's eyes fluttered open. "I'm okay now. Thanks, Ellie." Without looking at Derek, she slipped into a row and slid down, putting Paul between her and Derek.

Ellie and Pad sat behind them.

Charlie Bell, an excellent lawyer and an old friend of the McKenna family, walked in and sat next to Dani. "Are you ready to talk to the judge?"

Dani blinked rapidly. "I'll be glad when today is over."

"Don't worry; I'll be with you every minute, and this particular judge takes a dim view on stalkers."

The waiting was excruciating. A door behind the judge's podium opened, and a tall woman in a police uniform came through and announced, "All rise for the Honorable Louise Stanton."

Chairs scraped across the wooden floor. Everyone got to their feet. The judge glanced around the room as she took her seat.

"You may be seated."

Judge Stanton leafed through the stack of papers in front of her. She peered over her glasses and passed a folder to the bailiff.

"Michaels versus Ryan. Are both parties present?"

Dani felt a shiver race down her spine.

Charlie rose. "Charles Bell, Your Honor. My client, Danielle Michaels, is here."

The judge gestured for them to take their place up front.

Derek shuffled to his feet. "Derek Ryan, Your Honor." He flashed a tooth-filled grin.

"Mr. Ryan, do you have representation?"

"I do not."

"You'd like to proceed without a lawyer?"

"I would, ma'am. I feel this is just a misunderstanding between two old friends."

"Very well. Take a seat up front."

Derek approached the vacant table and sat.

Judge Stanton turned to Charlie. "Attorney Bell, I'd like to hear from your client, please."

Dani glanced at Paul.

Judge Stanton's voice boomed. "Ms. Michaels, you may begin, from the beginning."

"Judge Stanton." Dani wiped her hands down the sides of her skirt. "Six years ago, I lived in Chester and worked in a bakery. Derek used to come in every day with his firemen buddies, but I've recently learned he is not a fireman. We started talking, and he asked me out on a date. Right from the beginning, we dated exclusively and life was wonderful. Eventually, Derek asked me to move in with him, and I did. Afterward, I started to see a change in Derek. He started to criticize my cooking, what I wore, and even accused me of having a relationship with someone else."

"Were you having a relationship with someone else?"

Dani's hand flew to her heart. "Of course not. I was in love with Derek and wanted to marry him."

"Go on." Judge Stanton jotted down a note.

"We started to have terrible arguments. Over time, I stopped seeing my friends, I went to work and home. It was easier. He went everywhere with me, except work. The only time I was alone was when he was working his shift at the firehouse."

Dani clasped her hands in front of her. "I started to feel like I was walking on eggshells. I suggested we take a break and re-evaluate our relationship. We had a huge fight. All the while, his fists were in a ball, you know, like when someone is going to punch something or someone."

Derek jumped up. "Hold on. She's lying."

The judge gave Derek a withering stare. "Mr. Ryan, sit down. You'll have your turn." She turned back to Dani. "Ms. Michaels, continue."

"I thought it was only a matter of time until he'd use his fist on me. There was no discussion; he said we weren't going to break up. I packed up and left."

"Had he ever hit you?"

"He grabbed me once and left a bruise on my arm, but he apologized and said he was sorry."

"When was that?"

"About a month before I left."

"Did you tell him where you were going?"

"No. I took what fit in my car and drove away. My boss was in the process of closing the bakery. They were retiring and the timing was right."

"Ms. Michaels, have you been in contact with Mr. Ryan since leaving Chester?"

"No, ma'am. I wanted a fresh start. About two years ago, I found my way to Loudon and saw a help wanted ad for What's Perkin'. I applied and Mrs. Davis hired me on the spot."

"How did Mr. Ryan come to find you?"

"He had been calling my parents. I had asked my parents not to tell him where I was, but I never said I was afraid for my safety."

Derek jumped to his feet, the chair flying back into the wood partition. "She's a liar!"

Judge Stanton banged her gavel down. "Mr. Ryan, I won't tell you again. Sit down. You'll have your turn." The judge's eyebrow arched. "Ms. Michaels, why didn't you confide in your mother?"

"She thought Derek was a great catch, good job, nice home, handsome, and very charming.

I didn't want her to know. I was embarrassed and felt like a jerk. A few weeks ago, I had to tell her the truth. It was after the phone calls started, flowers began arriving, and Derek was lurking outside my apartment. Then he assaulted Ellie McKenna when she refused to get me from the café."

"You're asking the court today for a restraining order against the defendant?"

Charlie said, "Yes, Judge Stanton. We want the defendant to cease contacting Ms. Michaels, and he can't come within one thousand feet of her."

The judge made some notes and turned to Derek.

"You may speak now."

Derek's face flushed crimson. He stared at Dani, hands clenched at his sides. "Everything Dani said is a lie. I never restricted her comings and goings. She had friends. I didn't check up on her, and she could do whatever she wanted. We had a great relationship, and when I found out she was just a couple of towns away, I felt compelled to reach out and try and win her back. She's the only girl I've ever loved."

"Mr. Ryan, do you know a person has the right to break off a relationship at any given time?"

His nostrils flared. "But I love her."

"I wouldn't term what you have been doing in recent months love, Mr. Ryan."

"Your Honor, we belong together." Derek's voice was laced with smarmy sincerity.

"Not if Ms. Michaels doesn't agree. No means no, Mr. Ryan."

The judge picked up her pen and wrote something down.

"I don't have to think about this. I find for the plaintiff. Mr. Ryan, you're to stay away from Ms. Michaels. Zero contact. Which means no phone calls, no flowers, no stopping into her place of employment, and if you so much as see her walking down the street, turn around and go in a different direction. Do I make myself perfectly clear?"

Derek glared at the judge and then turned his venomous glare on Dani. "Yes."

"The case is adjourned."

Dani threw her arms around Charlie. "We did it!"

"You did it, Dani. You were strong and told the truth."

Dani watched Derek storm from the room. She danced across the short aisle. She threw her arms around Paul's neck. "Can you believe it? He's gone!"

She hugged Pad and then Ellie. "I just can't believe it. I don't have to look over my shoulder anymore."

"It's great, Dani, but I still want to take the rest of the self-defense classes, if for no other reason than to throw our guys on a mat."

Dani giggled. "Sounds like a fun time."

Dani stopped doing her impromptu jig and said, "Paul, I couldn't have done this without you here for moral support."

"You could do it all along, but I'm glad I helped."

"I'm buying lunch. Any takers?"

The foursome left the court, stopping to get Paul and Pad's handguns before stepping into the bright sunlight. Dani squinted and changed her glasses to sunglasses. She gasped and stumbled.

Derek was leaning against the stone wall at the bottom of the stairs, waiting.

She grabbed Paul's hand. "I'm not afraid of him."

She strutted down the stairs and refused to acknowledge Derek.

His icy voice stopped her. "Danielle, you had better think about what you just did."

"Derek, I would strongly suggest you get out and stay out of Loudon," Paul growled.

"Or what, you'll sic your cop buddies on me? I have friends too, you know."

He took two slow, menacing steps toward Dani. "This isn't over. Not by a long shot."

Dani flinched at his tone and watched Derek stalk away.

Paul held her close. Speaking low, he said,

"He won't hurt you. I promise I'll keep you safe."

Tears dampened his shirt. Dani mumbled, "You can't protect me. He's smart and he has friends."

"But what you need to understand is, anyone who vows to protect and serve, and means it, won't break the law, and that includes firemen."

Dani stepped out of the security of Paul's arms, her pale-blue eyes filled with tears.

"Paul," she pleaded. "You never saw Derek with his buddies. They're tight." She pointed to Pad. "Like the two of you, it's like you saying Pad's got your six."

"Pad would never break the law for me. If Derek thinks his buddies in the department will, then I'll bet my last dollar he's in for a surprise."

Derek's tires squealed as he roared past Dani. She tore her eyes from Paul's.

"I'm telling Cari I quit. I'll change my name and he'll never find me."

Ellie snapped, "And let the jerk win? Force you to leave your home, job, friends, and a good life? I didn't take you as a quitter."

"Ellie? You've already been caught in the crossfire of Derek's rage."

Dani dropped next to Ellie on a stone bench. She dropped her head in her hands. "Ellie, I don't know what to do. My instincts are screaming for me to run, fast and far. But my heart is another story. I don't want to leave what I've built. For the first time since my parents moved away, I belong. My journey led me to Loudon."

Softly, Ellie said, "Then don't leave. Stay and let us help you. You're strong, but we're stronger together."

Dani looked from Pad to Ellie, and finally, her eyes rested on Paul. "I don't want to run anymore."

Paul did a pretend wipe of his brow. "Whew, the best news I've heard today."

"Ellie, can we have dinner at your place tonight? We need to make a plan. I want to be prepared for whatever Derek has up his sleeve."

"Absolutely, but only if we can take a dip at the lake first, and you're bringing dessert. Pad can grill and I'll make a salad."

Dani's smile slowly reached her eyes. "It was my lucky day when I stumbled into Loudon. Dessert's on me."

13

Paul gripped the steering wheel, his knuckles white. "Pad, you know he'll be back."

"Yeah, he's fixated on Dani, and he's not going to stop unless we stop him."

"What's our next step?"

"We investigate. Tear his life apart, find out what's really going on with the fire department. Something still doesn't fit for me."

Paul looked at Pad. "What do you mean?"

"How you feel about Dani is clouding your investigative skills. If he's obsessed with her, is she the first girl he's done this to? And how in the heck does he pass himself off as a member of the CFD, and do they know?"

Paul slammed his hand on the steering wheel. "Of course. There must be other women he stalked."

"Duh, you're in love with Dani, and it's clouding your judgment. But don't worry. Remember, you've got Super Cop in your corner." Pad burst out in laughter.

"Sorry, man, I thought it would help Dani feel more comfortable."

"No big deal." Pad took a sip of cold coffee. "Does Dani know how you feel about her?"

"She's not ready for a declaration of love."

"Maybe it would help if she knew."

"Nah, once this is over and we spend more time together, without this cloud hanging over her, I'll see if she has feelings for me, other than a cop protecting her."

"Paul, you've sold her short. I see how she looks at you. She's crazy about you. It's not gratitude."

The radio squawked of an accident outside of town. Pad answered the dispatcher, then they were en route to the scene.

With lights flashing and sirens wailing, Paul negotiated the gawkers with skill. Before the car had come to a full stop, Pad leaped from the car.

Up ahead, Ellie's SUV was crushed against an ancient maple tree, and the passenger door was open. Paul's eyes scanned the scene. He could see Ellie slumped over the steering wheel but no Dani.

With years of practice with auto accidents, Paul clicked the mic attached to his shirt and called for an ambulance and the fire department. He watched as Pad pried open the crumpled driver's door. He was calling for Ellie to open her eyes. Paul ran to the other side of the vehicle. He scooped up Dani's handbag from the grass. He looked inside; her cell phone was missing. Frantic, he called out for her, turning in a full circle, scanning the tree line.

"Dani!"

Silence. "Danielle, answer me!"

Birds chirped in response.

Sirens grew louder as the seconds ticked. Paul ran to the car. Pad pleaded with Ellie to open her eyes. Paul prayed she would be able to tell him what had happened to Dani.

Pad rubbed Ellie's hand in his.

"Has she said anything?"

"No. I can't risk moving her before the paramedics arrive. Her head's bleeding and she's unresponsive. At least she's breathing okay."

"Pad, she's tough."

Pad looked at the vacant passenger seat. "Where's Dani?"

Paul's gaze roamed the surrounding area. "I don't know. I found her purse, but there isn't any sign of her anywhere."

"The paramedics are here. I've got Ellie. Canvas the scene and see if there was a witness."

Paul didn't need to be told twice. He strode over to the small group of onlookers. It consisted of a couple of teens on bikes, a woman with a large shaggy dog, and a young couple pushing a baby stroller.

"Excuse me, did anyone see what happened?"

A lady with a dog said, "Sorry, I didn't see the accident; I heard the crash. I was already down the street when I came back to see if I could help."

"Did anyone see what happened to the other girl in the SUV?"

A scrawny, pimple-faced boy spoke up. "Well, there was a pickup truck speeding down the street, and the SUV swerved to miss it and hit the tree. Then the guy stopped, backed up, and got out. He went over to the lady who had just gotten out, you know the passenger, 'cause the other lady driving couldn't open her door."

"And?" Paul's blood pounded in his ears. "Then what happened?"

"The guy talked to the lady. It looked like she started to fall down or something. He picked her up, put her in the truck, and took off."

Paul felt the air had been sucked from his lungs. "Can you describe the guy or the truck?"

"Dark pickup, kinda new. It was all shiny. The guy was tall and jacked with short hair."

"Which direction did they go?"

The boy pointed down the street. "When they left, he wasn't driving fast anymore. You know, just regular."

Paul jotted down his information and called for another officer who had arrived to finish taking the other statements.

He hastened back to Pad and Ellie. "Has she woken up?"

Pad stood back, watching the professionals assess her injuries and prepare to extract her from the SUV.

"She did. All she said was *Derek*."

"Son of a... He walked right through the restraining order before the ink was dry." He ran his hand over his head.

"He deliberately drove them into the tree and he kidnapped Dani."

"Paul, how do you know it was Ryan?" Pad spoke in slow, measured tones.

"A kid watched it happen. The only good thing, Dani got out of the SUV on her own. She must not be hurt. But, Pad, he took her."

"Paul, focus. You need to call for reinforcements, now."

"You're right." Paul stepped away, leaving Pad to focus on Ellie.

Ellie was being loaded into the ambulance when Paul asked, "Did they say how she was doing?"

"She's regained consciousness, and of course, her first concern was for Dani."

"Was she able to tell you anything else?"

"Not yet. But drive me to the hospital, and tell Sarge I'm off the clock for the rest of the day."

"I'll drop your car at the hospital later."

Fellow officers cordoned off the scene with yellow tape. It was a crime scene. Ellie had confirmed his worst fear. Cold sweat ran down Paul's spine as he watched the police photographer take pictures of every minor detail.

"Paul. Ready?"

Paul walked away from the scene with slow, plodding steps. He turned and took one last look. "I'm coming for you, Dani. Just hang in there."

Paul parked in front of the emergency room entrance. "I'll check in later. I need to do something."

"Stay in touch." Pad leaned on the car door. "Once Ellie's stable, I'll help you track him down."

"Later." Paul watched Pad jog through the sliding doors. He backed up and swung away from the entrance. Time to head to the station and see what evidence was found at the scene.

Paul stopped at the sergeant's desk to let him know Pad was at the hospital with Ellie. He walked into the squad room, surprised to see Judy, in off-duty clothes, sitting at his desk.

"Judy, what are you doing here?"

"I heard about the accident. How's Ellie?"

"She got a nasty laceration on the head, I'm sure whiplash, and she's going to hurt all over, but thank heavens she was wearing her seat belt and the airbags deployed."

"Is Pad at the hospital?"

"I just dropped him off. I'm sure the rest of the McKenna clan is on their way too."

"I'm guessing you could use some help with research?"

Words lodged in Paul's throat. "He took her."

"I know. I heard it come over the radio."

"It was a dark-colored pickup truck but no one got the plate number. From the description of the guy, it's definitely Ryan."

"What do you need me to do first?"

"I'm going to Chester and ask some questions. Find out where he really works, lives, and track down the truck. He was driving a sports car the last time we saw him."

"You're not going anywhere in the state you're in. I've called Walker. We're both off-duty tonight, and he's meeting us here," Judy stated. "We're going to Chester. You're staying here and doing some research on the internet."

"I'm going with you." Paul's eyes narrowed. "When I find him, I'm going to beat the truth out of him."

"Exactly my point. You're staying here. If your emotions run away with you, it could jeopardize the court case. If we find something, it can be used to convict him for kidnapping as well as violating the restraining order. You screw up, well, we don't want anything getting thrown out of court."

Paul dropped to a vacant chair. "I told Dani she didn't need to worry, I'd protect her. And now, what she feared the most happened."

"Paul, you can't blame yourself. Nobody thought Ryan would do this today."

Walker hovered in the doorway, listening to Judy. Silently, he entered the squad room. "Paul, when someone is totally focused, like a stalker, it's hard to anticipate their next move. But from my experience, he acted impulsively, fueled by emotions. Mistake one, he should have waited until she was alone. He'll make others, and when he does, we'll use them against him."

"Walker, thanks for coming. I appreciate you wanting to help out."

"We're brothers in blue. When someone tangles with one, they best be prepared to mess with us all."

"You know, I've been thinking." Paul got up and fired up his computer. "Dani said Ryan was tight with his department buddies. But when Pad and I started investigating, we found he was never an active firefighter."

Judy said, "Paul, we'll check every angle, and I'll call you. See what you can find about a family home someplace where he could take Dani."

Paul nodded. "You're right. I'll text you if I find something."

He looked at the clock; the hours had dragged since Judy and Walker left. He wondered how long it would take them to get to

Chester and back. Patience was never his strong suit. He shot a quick text to Pad, checking on Ellie. Before settling in, he poured himself an oversized mug of strong black coffee, hoping the caffeine would kick him into overdrive.

One thought churned: how did he miss that Ryan was a loose cannon? Dani was kidnapped. The single word caused his blood to pound in his ears. He wouldn't rest until Dani was safe.

Paul's cell phone buzzed with an incoming text. It was from Pad. Other than some bumps and bruises, Ellie was going to be fine. Pad was going to take her home and stay until Cari could get there. Then he'd be at the station for an update.

Paul shot back a quick response.

Don't bother coming in. I'll come to Ellie's later.

Then he texted Judy. Are you in Chester?

No, was her response.

Paul pulled up the internet and typed

Derek's name into the search bar. It didn't take long for the results. Basic information such as address in Chester, social media accounts, and a few restaurant reviews popped up—nothing to send up flares. Next, Paul did an image search on his home address, and it was just as Dani described—a basic apartment building.

Shift change came and went before Paul finally logged off the computer. He'd run by Ellie's. Maybe Pad had an idea. For all of Paul's years on the force, his clear thinking and judgment were clouded.

Pad opened the door, still in uniform.

"Come on in. We can talk out back. Ellie's resting."

Paul followed Pad through the house to the back deck.

"Something to drink?"

"Anything wet."

Pad went inside and returned with a bag of pretzels and two sodas. "Keeping a clear head is wise."

"Yeah." Paul twisted the cap off and foam bubbled over onto his hand. Swearing softly, he wiped it off on his pants.

"Where do we stand?" Pad asked.

"Judy and Walker went to Chester, and I've been trolling the internet. So far, I haven't found anything remotely hinky."

Paul leaned back in the chair and rubbed his hand over his eyes. "The usual, address and stuff."

"Does Judy have the address of his apartment?"

"I sent it over, and they'll swing by to check it out."

"Do you think he'll have her at his place?" Pad asked.

"No, he's a crafty SOB. They won't be there, but maybe Judy will find something helpful."

"She's a good cop. She'll turn over some rocks."

Paul's hands played with the bottle cap. "What if he hurts her, or worse?"

"He won't do anything stupid. Ryan wants her in his life. My guess, he's taken her someplace with the intent to convince her this was in her best interest and he loves her."

"Would he really think it would work?"

"For a rational person, no. But Ryan's not thinking clearly."

"He's jeopardized his career. All because he can't let Dani go?"

Before Pad could respond, Paul's phone rang.

Paul looked down. "It's Judy."

"Hey, Jude, I'm with Pad. I'm going to put you on speakerphone."

Pad said, "What have you found out?"

"We swung by his apartment. His neighbors haven't seen him for a couple of days. But as we were getting ready to leave, his cleaning lady was going into his apartment. We asked her a few questions." Judy's voice was steady as she relayed the facts.

"Well, what did she say?" Paul demanded.

"It seems like she started cleaning after Dani left. He was always respectful, paid on time, and very tidy. When we asked if there had been any women staying with him, she said no. He mentioned his heart had been broken and he hoped someday to win back the love of his life."

"Did he happen to mention Dani specifically?" Pad questioned.

"No, he didn't," Walker interjected. "We showed our badges and asked if we could walk through the apartment, and she happily let us in, but then asked if we would promise not to tell Mr. Ryan."

Paul snorted in response. "She didn't realize you didn't have jurisdiction and she shouldn't let you in?"

"Nope and we weren't going to say anything more. We just looked around, thanked her, and left," Walker stated.

Judy said, "And before you ask, there was nothing to indicate Dani had been there recently. But there was a picture of them on his nightstand."

"After all this time, he's kept a picture by the bed?"

Paul began to pace the deck. "What's next?"

"Paul." Judy's voice cracked over the phone. "Sit down and listen."

Paul stopped mid-stride.

Pad said, "How did you know he was pacing?"

"It's his tell. Is he sitting?"

Paul dropped back into his chair, and Pad said, "Yup."

"Now, Paul, you need to listen very carefully."

"I'm all ears."

Judy plowed ahead. "We talked to a few of the men on duty and they all know him well. They confirmed he's a photographer. He takes pictures for the local newspaper."

Paul jumped up.

"Paul, it's been confirmed he flunked out of the academy. My guess, based on recent events, he didn't pass the psych evaluation."

Paul's body had gone rigid. He opened his mouth to speak and then closed it.

Pad said, "Bottom line, he hasn't been seen in Chester, and he's not a fireman, he's a freelance photographer? Do I understand the basics?"

"Perfectly," Judy said.

"Are you two coming back tonight?" Paul asked.

"We should be home in a couple of hours."

Pad pointed to the chair. "Guys, if you think of anything you've left out, give us a call; otherwise, we're going to start laying out the next steps."

"Will do. Talk to you both later." Judy disconnected.

"How are we going to figure out where he took her?"

"I'm going to check on Ellie and see if she's

up to eating something. You'll stay. If, and only if she wants to talk about the accident, we can see if there is something I missed."

"I'm sorry Ellie got hurt."

"I know you are, but remember, it's not your fault or mine."

"I should have realized he was desperate."

"Pad, I'm going to go pick up a whiteboard. Maybe we can set it up and review what we know. It might help me think more clearly."

"While you're out, do you want to grab some dinner? I'll let Cari know she can head out."

"I'll be back in about an hour. I'm going to swing by the house and change."

"Take your time. We'll be here."

Paul trudged to his car. Suddenly, it hit him. The longer he felt like a failure for not protecting his girl, the longer it would take to find her.

Paul shouted through his car window to Pad. "I'll be back in thirty!"

Pad held up his hand, acknowledging he had heard.

Paul tore off down the street. He was a damn good cop, and it was his job to protect the innocent and solve crimes.

14

Paul dropped the takeout bags from Panda Express on the kitchen counter. He returned to the car for the large whiteboard jutting out from the trunk of his car. The edge scraped the paint off the back door. Oblivious, Paul hurried inside and discovered Ellie sitting in a recliner with her eyes closed.

"Hey there, you're looking better than the last time I saw you."

Ellie's steady gaze caught Paul's eyes. "You're not."

"Leave it to you to cut right to the chase." Paul leaned the whiteboard against the sofa and flopped down. He hated to think about Dani's condition after the accident and prayed her injuries were minor like Ellie's.

"Tell me what you know. Pad's holding out on me."

"We've confirmed he hasn't been home in a few days and no one seems to know where he is."

"What about the truck? Has anyone been able to find it?" Ellie demanded.

Despite Paul's mood, he chuckled. "Have you ever thought of being a cop?"

"I'm going to marry one. It comes with the territory." Ellie smiled.

"I was going to wait for Pad."

On cue, Pad entered, carrying a tray of glasses and soda. "Did I hear my name?"

Ellie took the newspaper off the coffee table.

"I was just about to tell Ellie about the truck."

"Good, I didn't want to miss the details." Pad settled on the arm of Ellie's chair.

Paul let out a heavy sigh. "We found a truck matching its description at the mall in Rockdale. It was unlocked with keys in the ignition. No sign of Ryan or Dani. Oh, and it was stolen late yesterday in Morrisville."

"We can assume Ryan stole the truck, left his car at the mall, grabbed Dani, and made the switch. I presume we have a BOLO out on his car?"

"We do." Paul drummed his fingers on the side table. "But we're not doing enough. It's been eight hours. He could be a third of the way across the country by now." He wiped clammy hands on his pants.

"Paul," Ellie said. "Sit down. You don't know that, and you're not doing Dani any good by flipping out."

She patted Pad's leg. "Sweetie, would you get us some plates and forks? We can eat and start to build the board."

Pad cocked his eyebrow. "Have you taken up detective work?"

"No, smarty-pants. Well, maybe, but you two are so busy beating yourselves up over what happened, and one of us needs to put emotions aside and think logically."

Ellie turned to Paul. "Now that we're going to be fed, did you bring markers?"

Paul grabbed an unopened box. "I got the rainbow assortment." He grimaced. "I'm scared. I've never felt this way about a case before."

"Dani's not just some case, to any of us. She's my best friend, and well, I guess the two of you are sorting out what you are to each other."

Ellie grimaced and slowly rose from the chair. She held up her hand to stop Paul from helping. "I'm fine. A few muscles want to protest, but my headache is down to a dull ache."

She held out her hand for a marker.

Ellie started by writing down a timeline,

adding details as she went from the morning right up until she was forced from the road.

Pad walked into the room and frowned. He opened his mouth and then closed it. He looked at the board and raised his eyebrows.

"Here's what I know, and if I miss something, you can fill it in."

"At eight we were in court and left by eight forty-five. We stopped at What's Perkin' for coffee and Mom told Dani to take the day off. Then we got here around nine thirty-ish."

Paul watched Ellie lay out the details. He was impressed with the way her mind worked.

Ellie paused and took a sip of water. "Dani had grabbed her bathing suit and we drove straight here to change, since we were going to Shane's to hang out on the dock, and we left here around ten-ish."

Paul jumped in. "Around ten twenty, the accident came over the radio. We arrived on the scene at ten twenty-seven and Dani was gone." Paul's heart constricted, and the blood roared in his ears.

Pad picked up a different color and added more information to the timeline.

"Judy and Walker went to Chester and discovered Derek hasn't been seen in a couple of days. It's confirmed he doesn't own a truck and seems to have been pining for Dani."

"Next step, we follow up with his family."

"Hold on. What about social media? Has anyone looked up his profile to see if he's been posting?"

Paul grinned. "You two are just like those in *The Thin Man* movie series, with Nick and Nora."

Pad said, "I'll get your laptop."

He quickly returned, and Ellie flipped open the top.

She hit a few keys. "Found him." She handed the laptop to Paul.

"I'm going to eat something while you scroll."

Paul studied the small screen. "It doesn't

say much. He seems to like the outdoors, including water sports. Some of these pictures are at a lake and he's driving a motorboat." Paul turned the screen around.

Pad peered at the image. "There's a cottage in the background but not much else."

"Can you see any cars in the picture? Maybe you can find out if it's in the state," Ellie said.

Paul shook his head. "Nope, nothing. This is a good start. People are creatures of habit."

Pad wrote down the information. "El, did Dani mention anything about going to a cottage with Derek?"

"She didn't talk about her life before moving to Loudon. But it would make sense; she loves the water and boating."

A knock on the back door made Ellie cringe. "Jeez, that makes my head throb."

Pad said, "I'll be right back."

Paul peered out the window. Shadows crept across the yard. Dani, where are you? He filled a plate and shoveled forkfuls of noodles into his mouth. As with other investigations, Paul ate for nourishment, not for enjoyment.

Pad returned with Judy and Walker. "Look who's back in town."

With a curt nod, Paul said, "Did you learn anything more?"

Judy looked at Ellie and then Pad and said, "Paul. We don't have anything new. We knew you'd be setting up a board and thought two more heads might be helpful."

"Sorry I barked. Thanks for coming."

"Paul, take it easy, buddy." Judy laid a hand on his arm. "You know we're making progress."

"Can you imagine how scared Dani has to be, alone with a crazy man? One minute she's with Ellie and the next speeding down the road with him."

"Judy, do you guys want some Chinese? There's plenty," Ellie said.

"I could use a bite. Walker?" Judy sat down on the couch and grabbed a plate.

"How are you feeling?"

"Other than muscles weeping and my head banging, I'm fine."

"Do you mind if I ask a couple of questions?" Judy looked sideways. "I'm sure you've been questioned to death, but sometimes you can remember something later, or if asked in a different way."

"Fire away. I'll do anything to help Dani."

Walker filled himself a plate and took a seat across the room.

"When did you first notice the truck?"

Paul leaned forward and Pad stopped what he was doing.

"Um, let me think." Ellie closed her eyes. "When we came out of What's Perkin', I saw an unfamiliar truck parked down and on the other side of the street." Ellie's eyes popped open. "You know, by midmorning, most pickups aren't hanging around town. We're a working truck community except for weekends."

Judy nodded. "Go on."

"We left there and stopped at my place. We

weren't inside long, and the truck cruised by, you know, kind of slow. Most locals drive slow down this street because of the park and all."

"Did the truck turn around?" Walker asked.

"No. We went that way when we left here. After going about a mile, the truck pulled over, and we drove by. We were talking a mile a minute, and I didn't think anything about it at the time, but now..." Ellie's hand flew to her mouth. "He was waiting to follow us."

"It's okay, Ellie." Judy patted her hand. "Then what happened?"

"He blew past us, and I remember telling Dani I must be driving slow for a change. We laughed because everyone who knows me says I've got lead in my shoes. It was just a couple of minutes later that I saw the truck in my lane. I swerved to avoid hitting him head-on and lost control, crashing into the tree instead."

Tears filled her eyes. "I don't remember

anything else until I heard Pad urging me to open my eyes."

Ellie's eyes narrowed. "Wait. There was a voice. He was speaking very quietly. He told Dani not to worry and everything was going to be fine. She reached for my hand, but her fingers slipped away." Tears fell unchecked down Ellie's cheeks. "She didn't want to go with him."

Pad tenderly kissed the top of Ellie's head.

"You did great, sweetheart. You gave us a couple of good details. One, Dani didn't want to go with him, which we knew, but it's confirmed. And two, he was stalking you."

"But you knew she'd never want to go with him. She's terrified of him."

Paul paced and said, "Our next step is to figure out where he took her, and I think the clue is the picture of the lake and cabin."

Walker left the room. Judy watched him go and followed.

"Where are they off to?" Paul's voice was strained.

Pad called after Judy. A few minutes later, everyone returned, and Walker unfolded a large map.

He taped it to one side of the whiteboard.

"Ellie, do you have any Post-it Notes?"

"Yes, there are some in my desk. I think they're in the top, left-hand drawer."

Judy asked, "Do you mind if I grab them?"

"Not at all." Ellie glanced at Walker. "What else do you need?"

He shrugged. "I'm not sure."

Judy returned with various sizes and passed them to Walker. He took a bright pink one. "This is the scene of the accident."

He took an orange Post-it and placed it on the map, indicating Chester. Placing a blue one, he said, "Here is where the truck was abandoned."

"You can see between here and Chester, there are a few lakes, but none all allow motorboats. These are pretty small. The lake we're looking for has to be larger. We need to look to the north, south, and west of Chester. The map shows some large bodies of water."

Paul watched as the map took on a new look, nodding. "Once we narrow down where he might have taken her, we'll have a better chance of finding them."

"Guys, take a look." Ellie pointed to the screen. "You need to interview some of these people in the pictures. Derek didn't tag everyone, but I'll bet a few are firemen."

Judy went into the gallery and came back with pads of paper and pens. She handed one to Pad and sat down with the other one.

"Ellie, can you give me the list of names of people tagged? I'll run the list against the roster of firemen, and Pad you can work with Walker and Paul on the lakes."

The stranglehold on Paul's chest loosened just a bit. This was something he could control, research.

The group worked for several hours, compiling data. Pad saw Ellie rubbing her temples.

"Team, we're going to need to call this a

night. Ellie's had a horrible day and needs to rest."

Judy rolled her shoulders. "You're right. We could all use some rest and start fresh tomorrow."

Paul protested, "Wait, we can't quit now. We're making progress."

Pad placed a firm hand on Paul's shoulder. "I know you want to find her. We all do, but we need rest, and we'll start again first thing tomorrow."

"Would you rest if it were Ellie?" Paul demanded.

"I wouldn't want to, but hopefully, I'd have good friends to talk some sense into me." Pad's voice diffused the thick tension. "We need clear heads to find her."

"Come on, Paul. Walker will drive your car, and you can ride with me. We're working second shift tomorrow, but if Ellie doesn't mind this being our makeshift headquarters, we'll start working in the morning."

Ellie piped up. "I want to help too."

"You are helping. Despite knocking your noggin today, you've been clearheaded and have come up with some good ideas."

Ellie put her arms around Paul. "I'm sorry I couldn't stop him."

He held her tightly. "There was nothing you could have done. I'm just thankful you're okay."

Ellie's tears flowed. Pad wrapped his arms around her, murmuring softly in her ear.

Paul closed Ellie's back door, silently admonishing himself for not remembering Ellie was a victim of Ryan's insanity too. He'd text Pad later to check on her.

Walker was waiting next to Paul's car, and Judy was in her driver's seat.

"No need to drive me home. I'm fine."

"Judy wants to talk to you. I'll be right behind her."

"But really."

"Paul. We all have a stake in what happened today. Dani's one of our own. Humor Judy and let her drive."

Paul's shoulders slumped and his steps slowed. "Walker, I know you just met Dani, but thanks."

"You'd do the same for me." Walker jumped into his car and started the engine.

"I'm all yours, Jude." Paul buckled up, staring into the passing darkness.

Judy drove in silence and was headed out of town when Paul said, "Do you really think she's safe?"

"Paul, I don't think Ryan wants to hurt her. He had opportunity for days before we knew he was in town. In his warped mind, he's rescued her. He wants to convince Dani this was all a big mistake."

"What you're really saying is Derek Ryan is delusional, and he's going to convince Dani they belong together and will live happily ever after?"

"In his mind, yes." Judy glanced away from the road. "Dani knows you'll come after her, and hopefully, she can play the crazy game long enough to give us time to find her."

"She's a smart girl," Paul spoke softly. "She'll find some way to get a message to me."

"I have no doubt. Keep your phone fully charged and the ringer at high volume at all times." Judy pulled up to the house. Walker parked in front of the garage.

"You gonna be all right?"

"Yeah."

He got out of the car and waited until Walker got in. "See ya in the morning."

Paul lingered on the front porch, remembering when Dani was here with him. "How could a freckle-faced imp dominate every waking thought?"

Crickets chirped in response. Shaking off the fear clenching his heart, he went inside.

15

———————

A cool breeze wafted across Dani's arm. She blinked at the bright sun streaming in the window. She sat up straight, shaking the fog swirling in her head. *Where am I?*

Her bare feet touched the smooth wood floor, and she tiptoed to peek out the window. Her gaze took in a view of a large lake which seemed to have no beginning or end. Clarity took hold. Derek. He brought her here.

She dashed to the door, smashing her shin on the bed frame. The smooth brass doorknob didn't yield under the pressure of her hand. Dani jerked on it, praying the door would swing open, beating on the hard wood, calling out for someone to answer her.

Leaning against the door, she studied the room. There were two other doors. One might lead to the outside. She scurried to the first closed door, and the knob turned. Dani pushed it open, revealing a large luxurious bathroom complete with a skylight, oversized tub, huge walk-in shower, and a deep-pink bathrobe hanging on a hook. Walking in, she did a three-hundred-and-sixty-degree circle. Dani pulled open each drawer and door. Every space was stocked with all her favorite hair products, toothpaste, and makeup.

She walked back to the bedroom. Pulling on the final door, she discovered a closet. She examined the clothes. They were her size and preferred style. The truth hit her like a ton of bricks. Derek had planned every last detail.

Dani clutched her heart and sank to the floor. Silent tears coursed down her cheeks.

She was afraid to make a sound. Tears had always made Derek angry.

She willed the fogginess from the corners of her mind. She had to be clearheaded if she was going to find a way out. She grabbed some clothes and secured the bathroom door with a chair under the knob. She rushed through the shower. Feeling a measure of self-control, Dani dressed and sat on the bed to wait.

Unable to sit still, Dani crossed the spacious room. The lake was calm. Was anyone out there? As far as she could see in all directions, nothing stirred except the leaves on the maple tree just outside her window.

Heavy footsteps were running up the stairs and stopped outside her door. Dani heard a click. Her legs felt weak. She didn't want to turn and see who was watching her.

Her heart raced. Slowly, she turned.

"Good morning, Danielle. Did you sleep well?" Derek's smile didn't reach his eyes. His bulk filled the doorway.

"Derek, what are we doing here?"

"Breakfast is ready. I've made your favorites—waffles, extra crispy bacon, strawberries, and of course, plenty of dark roast coffee just the way you like."

"Then will you take me back to Loudon?"

"We'll talk about what comes next later. But I do want to show you the cottage. It really is lovely." Derek stepped back. "Please join me."

Dani hesitated.

"I won't hurt you. We're former lovers reconnecting."

Dani waited. Derek shrugged and retreated down the stairs. "It's getting cold, Danielle."

Torn, Dani longed to see where she was, but she didn't want to give Derek the satisfaction of her company.

Dani's stomach rumbled. She was running on empty. The smell of coffee lured her to the balcony. Glancing down, she saw Derek was right; the cottage was lovely with an open floor plan with gleaming wood and lots of oversized windows, sun streaming in from all angles.

Dani crept down the stairs, keeping an eye on Derek moving around the kitchen area. The cottage seemed to be somehow familiar.

Derek smiled. "Have a seat, and I'll fix you a plate."

Dani struggled to keep her voice calm. "You don't need to wait on me."

"I should have done this when we lived together. Please, have a seat."

Dani pulled out a chair facing the kitchen and closely watched Derek move with ease in the space.

"Since when did you learn to cook for two people and not vats of pasta?"

"After you moved out, I found you had spoiled me. So I devoted some time to learning the art of making simple and tasty meals for two." He chuckled. "But nothing up to your standards."

Derek set an overfilled plate in front of

Dani, picked up a glass filled with juice, and proclaimed, "Fresh squeezed."

As soon as Derek turned his back, Dani switched plates.

He picked up two mugs and a carafe of what Dani assumed was coffee.

"This looks like enough calories to cover me for the day," Dani said.

"Eat what you like." Derek smiled again.

Dani's stomach turned over. This is creepy.

Derek drowned his waffle in syrup and dug in. Between bites, he said, "You'll love the syrup; it's from a local farm as is the bacon."

Dani picked up a slice and sniffed, it smelled like regular bacon. She eyed Derek.

With one eyebrow raised, he said, "It's not poisoned, Danielle. Our little getaway is designed for you to fall in love with me again. I don't want to hurt you." He sipped his coffee. "Mmm, rich and hot. An acquired taste but I think it's your favorite brand. You can check out the pantry later and let me know if I've forgotten anything."

Since he didn't seem to feel any ill effects of the food, Dani bit off a tiny corner of the bacon. It was good. Dani cut the waffle in half, placing the extra on a napkin. She added a splash of syrup.

Derek flashed a warm smile, but his eyes were still cold. "I told you they're pretty good."

Dani ate slowly, waiting for signs of internal distress or an overwhelming urge to sleep. Nothing happened. She finished her breakfast and leaned back in the chair, sipping coffee and studying Derek.

"What did you think? Not bad, right?"

"It was very good. Thank you." Dani peered into her coffee cup and then looked up. "Derek, what happened yesterday?"

Shrugging his shoulders, he said, "I kind of lost it when the judge said I had to stay away from you. I'm not proud of my actions, causing the accident with your friend, but I had to get you away from those people. They were turning you against me. I love you. I've always loved you, and we're supposed to be together. After the girl drove into the tree, you fainted. I brought you here."

Dani suppressed a shudder. "Where exactly are we?"

"This is the cottage I bought for you." Derek walked around the room. "Remember, you cut out pictures of your dream house?"

Dani didn't want to hear what he was about to say.

"I was going to throw away your house folders, you know, after you moved out. But something told me to wait, so I did. I decided to find you the perfect house and decorate it just the way you would."

Dani stared out the window. "You. Did. This. For. Me?" she stuttered.

Derek's head bounced up and down. "Yup. I've been working on this place for over a year."

Dani's eyes bulged. "You've been planning this for a year?"

"Well, not the way it happened, but I've

been planning on winning you back ever since you left." He tilted his head to one side. "Did I surprise you?"

"Yes, you did." Dani's voice cracked.

Derek smacked his forehead with his hand. "I really didn't do right by you when we were together."

Dani pushed her chair back. She picked up the plates and silverware and placed them on the counter. She looked around, noticing this was the exact kitchen layout she dreamed about. Instinctively, she knew each cabinet's contents right down to the kind of peanut butter on the shelf.

"Danielle, I'm sorry. Did I miss something about the kitchen? You seem, well, unhappy."

Through clenched teeth, Dani said, "Derek, you don't just take someone from the scene of an accident and whisk them off to a cabin, God knows where, and expect them to be overjoyed."

Derek's smile turned into a thin, hard line.

He took several deep breaths. "I'm going out for some air. When I come back, we can talk."

Dani watched out of the corner of her eye as he unlocked the door with a key and heard the lock turn again once he was on the other side. She quickly dried her hands and ran to the window. Derek headed down toward the lake. Dani ran from door to door to the windows. Every form of exit was secured. Dani sank to the floor and tears pricked her eyes.

How long she sat there, Dani wasn't sure, but feeling sorry for herself was not going to get her back to Loudon. She needed to be ready for Derek's return. Maybe she could reason with him and convince him to let her go. Outsmarting him was something Dani could work on, as physically overpowering him was out of the question.

Dani heard the click of the lock. She flipped open a cooking magazine to the middle, trying to appear engrossed in an article.

"I'm sorry I took off, Danielle, but you've always been able to push my buttons."

Dani looked up, hoping to appear casual. "I'm sorry too, Derek. I don't want to fight with you. I'm trying hard to understand what's going on here. If you were in my shoes, you'd feel out of sorts too."

"Yeah, I can see where you're coming from." He dropped into an overstuffed chair and propped his feet up. "Did you explore the cottage?"

"Not yet. I'm a little sore from the accident. My back and neck are stiff and I have a horrid headache. I will when I'm feeling better." She batted her eyelashes. "I'm sure you understand."

Concern flooded his face. "Can I get you something? There's aspirin in the medicine cabinet."

"I'm going to lie down for a bit. I'll get some when I go upstairs."

"Feel free to do as you'd like. This is your home now."

Dani bit back a frosty retort. She needed to clear her head.

"What are you going to do?"

"I'll go outside and fish. The lake is stocked with trout and bass. If lady luck is on my side, we'll have fresh fish for dinner."

Dani forced a smile. "Sounds delicious." Before heading up the stairs, she grabbed a bottle of water from the fridge and took stock of the contents, noticing there was enough food for roughly a week.

"Have a good nap," Derek called out as she climbed the stairs.

Unable to force another civil word, she lifted her hand as her response. Closing her bedroom door, she sagged against the door-jamb. The tears she held back all morning coursed down her cheeks. When her tears were spent, she pushed a chair under the door-knob and sank into the upholstered chair and ottoman, pulling up a soft knitted throw, then she fell asleep.

Dani woke with a start and remembered where she was. Shadows had crept across the room. Out of habit, she looked at her wrist but remembered she'd taken her watch off before she and Ellie started out to the lake. Yesterday was a lifetime ago. She listened to the silence and wondered where Derek was hiding. Debating if she should stay in the safety of these walls or go downstairs, she dropped the blanket on the ottoman. In the bathroom, Dani peered at her reflection. Her ice-blue eyes were rimmed red as she splashed cool water over her face. She straightened her shoulders, determined to find out what Derek's plan was. Did he intend to keep her here indefinitely or would she be free to go home? Too many unanswered questions.

Dani softly walked down the wide staircase, wishing they had carpet on the treads to hide the sound. She scanned the lower floor with no sign of Derek. She reminded herself to slow down her breathing. Taking the chance, Dani began to examine the room, inch by square inch, looking for a key to unlock a door or find a phone. She longed to call Paul, to hear his deep soothing voice which had become a balm to her jagged nerves. And Ellie, who had become Dani's most trusted friend, how badly was she hurt in the accident? Somehow, she'd have to convince Derek to make a phone call, but first, she had to earn his trust.

Glancing at the mantle clock, she noticed it was almost four. Dani needed to stay busy, and it would help clear her head. She'd do what she did best: bake.

Footsteps clomped on the side porch, the one which led into the kitchen. Dani heard the lock click, and Derek walked in with two largemouth bass, cleaned and ready for the frying pan.

"Look who's awake." He ran a finger through the almost empty bowl and licked it clean. "You're baking cupcakes?"

"I am. It's a new recipe I've been working on. I hope you don't mind being a guinea pig."

Derek's grin warmed his dark eyes. "Just like old times."

He pulled a shallow baking pan out of the cabinet and slid the fish onto it. Wrapping it with plastic wrap, he said, "I'm going to put this in the outside fridge. Be right back."

He stepped out through a different door. When he came back in, she asked, "What's out there?"

"It's the garage. But also, a cabinet with canned goods, a freezer, and an extra refrigerator too. I've stocked them all so we don't have any reason to leave for a few weeks. It'll give us plenty of time to get reacquainted, uninterrupted."

"Seems you've thought of everything." Deep in Dani's heart, she could feel it fracture, slivers of hope breaking off. Derek was planning on staying here without an end in sight.

"Wine?"

"Um, no, thanks. My head. You know, it is still bothering me."

Derek's eyebrow arched. "You can't use your head hurting as an excuse forever, Danielle." The undercurrent in his voice caused a shiver to run down her spine.

"Derek, it has literally been just a day since the vehicle I was in hit a tree head-on."

He shrugged. "You're right. I apologize. I'm looking forward to doing things with you when you're feeling better."

He walked around the bar and sat on a stool on the other side, watching Dani cream butter and sugar.

"Frosting?"

She nodded. "Derek, do you know if Ellie was okay? I mean, from the accident."

"How would I know? We left before anyone got there."

"Do you think I could call her, just to check on her?" Dani bit her lip. "She's my best friend."

Derek remained silent for a few moments before shoving the stool. It hit the floor and it skidded a couple of feet. He strode across the room and went out the sliding glass door.

Dani kept her hands busy as her brain whirled. Underneath her breath, she said, "He didn't say no."

It was growing dark when Derek finally returned. The door slid open, and Dani was horrified; she had missed her chance. It hadn't been locked. She silently vowed to pay closer attention when Derek dropped a cell phone in her lap.

"You have two minutes. You can ask if she's alright and tell her you're safe. But tell her not to call you. When you have time, you'll call her again."

Dani's eyes were like saucers. "You're giving my phone back?"

Derek snorted. "Not permanently. For this one phone call."

Dani dialed Ellie's number at the gallery and prayed she would answer.

"Hello, The Looking Glass."

"Ellie?"

"Dani, are you okay? I've been out of my mind with worry. Where are you? I'll come get you."

"Ellie, I only have a couple of minutes. Things are a little crazy here. But I wanted to make sure you were okay after the accident." Dani fought to keep her throat from constricting.

"I've got a wicked headache and whiplash but nothing serious. Did you get hurt?"

Dani could hear the questions but knew there was so much more Ellie wanted to ask. "I've got some sore muscles and a headache like you, but otherwise, I'm okay."

Derek was tapping his watch.

"I need to go, but I'm glad you're not hurt."

"Dani, wait," Ellie pleaded.

"I'll call again, Ellie. Please, I have to go now." Tears pricked Dani's eyes.

"Where…" Ellie began.

"Bye, Ellie." Dani hit the disconnect button and placed the phone in Derek's outstretched hand.

"You did good. There might be a short call to your mother in your future." Derek slipped the phone into his shirt pocket. "I'm famished. I'll make dinner, and you just relax."

Dani stayed on the couch. Her inner monologue was in high gear, grateful she had talked to Ellie but wishing there had been some kind of message she could have gotten through to her. She'd be better prepared next time.

One day slid into the next for Dani, with Derek seeming to become more relaxed each day. Every morning he made her breakfast and then left for hours at a time. When Dani had asked where he spent time, he was vague. She thought he must be working since there was a pattern to his comings and goings.

Every chance she had, Dani searched the cabin, looking for her cell or a way out. She had to admit, Derek was being nice, but she knew his moods changed on a dime. She could sense something was lurking under the surface. Derek continued their conversations at every opportunity. He wanted their relationship back on track, to get married and have kids. Rescuing Dani from the people in Loudon gave them this special time in their lives.

Dani was revolted by the thought of

staying with Derek. She knew the only way out was to gain his trust, showing Derek she wouldn't take off at the first chance a door was left unlocked. He left the door to the garage unlocked, but the exterior doors were still barred. Although there was access to the garage, it did her no good. There weren't any tools in sight. It was time to see if Derek would let her go outside. By her count, she had been in this cottage for six days without the sun gracing her skin.

Over dinner, Derek's conversation revolved around the lake and the warm temperatures.

Dani took the plunge. "Maybe tomorrow we could sit outside."

Derek's fork stopped in midair.

Dani avoided his eyes and concentrated on cutting a piece of chicken on her plate. "You know how much I love the outdoors."

Dani knew Derek's mind would race with the potential scenarios.

She chewed the tasteless chicken, effectively ignoring the topic.

The balance of the meal was finished in silence. After the kitchen was tidied, Dani picked up a book from the side table. "I'm going upstairs to read."

"Danielle, wait."

Dani raised an eyebrow. "Why do you persist on calling me Danielle?"

"Would you like to sit outside? We can have a fire and toast marshmallows unless you'd prefer to read."

"Let me change. I'm not dressed for the cool air." Dani suppressed her joy, lest Derek change his mind.

"Don't take too long."

Dani took the stairs two at a time and flung open the door, careful so it didn't bang. She pulled on sweatpants and a sweatshirt over her T-shirt and shorts. Figuring it might be chilly, she grabbed a small quilt off the bed. All in all, it didn't take five minutes before she returned to the living room.

"Danielle, let me be very clear. No funny stuff. If you try to take off, you won't smell fresh air for a very long time." Derek looked at her through slits in his eyes. "Understand?"

Dani looked at the floor. "Absolutely."

Dani stepped onto the deck. The cool, fresh air caressed her cheeks. She tipped her head back, drinking in the woodsy scent deep into her lungs. She would never take the ability to walk outside whenever she wanted to for granted again.

Derek pointed to an Adirondack chair next to the fire pit. "Have a seat."

Dani all but skipped to where he pointed and slid onto the wooden chair. For now, she was going to enjoy just being outside. Later, she would assess her surroundings.

16

"Calm down? What do you mean, calm down? It's been eight days since Dani called Ellie. Other than knowing she wasn't hurt in the accident, we've come up with zip on her location."

"Paul. You're going to wear a path in the squad room. Sit down." Pad's voice was low and demanding. "Dani said she'd call again, and she'll find a way. She's smart and by this time, she knows what Derek expects from her. If you don't keep your wits about you, when the opportunity comes, you'll be a loose cannon."

Paul perched on the corner of Judy's desk. "I'm losing it, Jude."

"You're worried. There's a difference."

Walker entered. Reading a paper, he said, "I got a report on any real estate transactions for the last twenty-four months on any lake property in a two-hour radius from Chester. Nothing under the name of Derek Ryan."

"Another dead end," Paul muttered.

"Maybe not," Pad said. "What if he didn't buy the property? It could have been in his family."

"I checked. No one by the name of Ryan owns lake house property in the vicinity we've been checking."

"Let's expand the search to three hours," Pad suggested.

Judy was already clicking keys and doing a search. "There are two more large lakes which fit our criteria."

Paul sat up. "Another thread to tug." He looked at Walker. "Will you check into it?"

"Right after our shift is over."

Judy rested a hand on Paul's shoulder. "We'll work together and hopefully have something by tomorrow morning."

"You look exhausted. Why don't you head home and get some rest?"

"I'm going for a run. It'll clear my head, and maybe I'll think of something." He looked at his friends. "I know this is a case for the feds, but you understand, it's personal for me."

"You'd do the same for us, Paul," Walker said.

Pad said, "If I remember correctly, you and Judy had my back from the first day we met. You didn't much like it when I horned in on your investigation when Ellie was attacked in her gallery, but without your help, we wouldn't have solved it as fast."

Judy's head bobbed. "We've got this. Take off. If we find out anything, I'll text you."

"Come on, bro. We can walk out together."

Paul and Pad signed the duty log and left the building. "Care to go for a run?"

"Yeah, if you want company. It sounded like you might like some solitude."

"All I can think about is what I want to do to Ryan when we find him."

Pad chuckled. "Finally, a nice, normal reaction."

"Wouldn't you feel the same way if it were Ellie?"

"Hell, each time something happened at The Looking Glass, I saw red. Especially when we found the crushed replica of the shop on her porch. I wanted to hurt whoever was scaring her."

"Man, I always took you as cool and detached."

"In the beginning, it was easy to keep my distance, but as feelings for Ellie took over, it was harder for me to be detached."

"I never thought how it must have been for

you." Paul grew quiet. "I was a territorial jerk. Worried about who got the collar."

"No harm. We got the perp, and she's locked up for a long time." They stood next to their vehicles. "In the end, I got the girl, and everything worked out just fine."

"You really think we're going to find her, right?" Paul's voice cracked.

"You forget, I'm Super Cop. Remember?"

Paul's smile was weak. "I'm gonna hold you to it."

"Paul." Pad's voice commanded Paul's attention.

"We're good cops, and Dani didn't choose to leave. Ryan took her. We'll lock him up and bring her home."

Paul cleared his throat.

"And when we do, you'd better not waste one moment with her. Trust me, I know. When I left Ellie and took off for Scotland, I thought I was doing the right thing for both of us. All I did was break Ellie's heart and make myself miserable."

"How did you know to come back?"

Pad raised his eyebrow. "I don't know if you'll believe me or not, but I was taking pictures on this tiny island. I'm looking through the lens, lining up the shot. The sun was just sinking below the ruins of a castle when I hear a man's voice say, 'Ye a damn fool. Leaving a fine woman like Eleanor McKenna. Git ye head on straight and git back to her before ye lose her forever.'"

"What? Who was with you?"

"That's the weird part. When I looked around, I didn't see a soul. I took a few pictures, and all I could see was her smile and those big blue eyes. I was lost without her."

"And then?"

"It took about a week to wrap up the shoot, book a flight, and get back to the States." Pad grinned. "And I've not had one moment of regret. I'm a lucky guy. I'm marrying the girl of my dreams, and professionally, I'm a cop and a photographer. Life can't get any better."

"Did you ever figure out who you heard on the moor?"

Pad shook his head. "You know, Scotland is supposed to be full of fairies, and if you look at their flag, it sports two unicorns. How could something like hearing voices not happen?"

"Did you tell Ellie?"

"I was telling Aunt Winnie about it when Ellie casually mentioned it was more than likely her father's ghost."

"What?" Paul's eyes popped. "Ellie believes in ghosts?"

"One better, her mother, sister, and even Ellie have talked to her long-dead father, Ben McKenna."

Paul's whistle said it all. "It sounds like it all worked out for the best."

Pad clapped a hand on Paul's shoulder. "And it will for you and Dani."

ani glanced at Derek as she clenched her hands. He was leaning back in the chair with his eyes closed. But Dani knew he was aware of everything around him.

"Derek?"

He slowly opened his eyes.

"Um, do you think I could call my mom?"

Dani plucked at her pant leg. "I haven't talked to her in over a week, and I don't want her to be worried. I'm not sure if you remember, but we usually talked a couple of times during the week."

Derek looked out over the water. He looked toward the house and then at her. "Wait here."

Derek disappeared into the house. Dani's mind raced. Her fist slammed against the arm of the chair. If only she knew where they were.

The back door banged, and Derek lumbered across the grass. He dropped her cell phone into her lap.

"Call your mother, but remember I can hear

every word. If I think your conversation is straying, I'll cut it short."

"Thank you." Dani turned the phone on, noting it was fully charged. She quickly dialed her mom's cell number.

Dani's mother answered on the second ring. "Hello."

"Hi, Mom. It's me, Dani."

"Sweetheart. How are you? Where are you? I've been worried sick. Ellie's called me every day to see if I've heard from you. She told me what happened with Derek."

Forcing a smile in her voice, Dani said, "I'm fine, Mom. Derek and I are lakeside just taking a break from our hectic day-to-day schedules."

"Are you alone?"

"No, the weather is perfect."

"He can hear you?"

"We could use a little rain, but the water seems to be at the right level."

"Sweetheart, how can I help you?"

"I'd love to visit, but I'm not really sure how long we'll be here. We're just hanging out, eating some fresh caught largemouth bass, and soaking up the warm sun."

Derek leaned back in his chair and closed his eyes. But Dani knew he was listening closely.

"Is he holding you against your will?"

"Yes, the temperature has been very pleasant and it's sunny."

"And you have no idea where you are?"

"No, we grilled the fish."

Dani heard her mother start to cry.

"Well, I should get going. Tell Dad I said hi, and I'll try to call again in a few days."

"Dani? Be careful."

"I love you too, Mom." Dani brushed away the lone tear trickling down her cheek. "Bye, Mommy."

The phone dropped in her lap, and Dani let the tears flow. She didn't care if they'd anger Derek. She longed to see her parents, her friends, and her little apartment above the café.

Squaring her shoulders, Dani announced,

"I'm going inside." She didn't wait for permission. She desperately hoped the subtle clues of type of fish, weather, and the absence of road noise would be things her mom would pass along to Ellie.

⁂

The guys had just started the return trip when Paul's cell vibrated in his armband. He stopped and pulled it out. Glancing at the text, he shouted, "Pad. Hold up. Ellie sent me a text."

Pad peered over his shoulder. "What did she say?"

Paul punched a series of numbers. "To call her immediately."

"Ellie, Paul. What's wrong?"

"I just got a call from Olivia Michaels. She talked to Dani."

"Where are you?" Paul demanded.

"I'm at the gallery."

"We're on our way." Paul took off at a dead

run with Pad keeping a steady pace beside him. The two didn't speak until they approached Ellie's back door.

"Whatever Ellie tells us, you have to keep a level head."

Between deep gulps of air, Paul said, "I will."

Paul went inside first. Ellie was waiting in the kitchen with two glasses of water.

"Let's go out back."

"Ellie." Paul's tone was terse. "Just tell me."

She pointed to a bench. "Sit."

Paul knew it would do no good to argue.

"Dani called her mother this afternoon." She held up a hand as Paul's mouth formed the beginning of what would be a barrage of questions.

"From what she said, Dani is lakeside, as we suspected, but doesn't know exactly where she is. They've eaten largemouth bass, it's been sunny, and the temperature is moderate. Derek is with her, but for the moment she's safe."

"And?" Paul demanded.

"She didn't answer any questions, so I'm going to assume she's okay."

Paul let out a deep breath. "Thank God."

Pad said, "Did she give any other clues about their location?"

"Dani said it was very quiet there, and Olivia said there wasn't any background noise of any kind."

Paul paced the long deck. "We're back at square one."

"No, we're not."

Ellie's head snapped at the tone in Pad's voice. "Pad, there's no reason to bark at Paul. He's worried."

"I know he is, but Dani did a great job giving us information. First, she knew her mother would call you. Second, she's being held against her will, but she's playing the role thrust upon her. And, finally, we know the weather of her location, they're lakeside, it hasn't rained, and there must not be a lot of people nearby if he has allowed her to go outside. Lest we forget, she also told us the type of fish they're eating. We can use this to narrow our search."

Paul turned in the threshold. "Are you coming? We need to add this to the board."

"Can you give us a minute?"

Paul left Ellie and Pad alone, giving them privacy, as Ellie sought comfort in Pad's arms.

❧

*P*ad murmured into her hair, "I'm sorry I'm sweaty."

Ellie slipped her arms around his waist and held him tightly. "I don't care."

Pad waited for Ellie's breathing to slow before asking, "Did you tell us everything?"

He felt her nodding against his chest. "I'm scared, Pad. I thought we'd find Dani by now. Do you think we will before his patience runs dry?"

"We'll find her. Walker has been searching real estate transactions, and something will pop." He planted a kiss on the top of Ellie's head.

"Let's go check on Paul."

"He's fallen hard for Dani. Has he figured it out yet?"

"I have a sneaking suspicion that when she gets back, he's going to kick things up a notch or two."

"She likes him. She was scared about making another mistake. She misjudged Derek and didn't want that to happen again."

"Paul would never hurt her. He's a tough cop, but she couldn't find a better man."

"Present company excluded." Ellie stood on her tiptoes and kissed Pad's lips. "I figured we'd be calling the team of J and W. I called out for takeout."

Pad's brow wrinkled. "J and W?"

"Judy and Walker. I called them after I talked to Paul. They're going to drop in on their dinner break."

"You think of everything, don't you?"

"I do try. It's one of the many reasons I

agreed to marry you. You need someone who can keep up with your runaway brain."

Pad let out a belly laugh. "I guess."

He draped his arm over her shoulders. "I hope you ordered enough. Paul had us beating feet, and I haven't run so fast since I was in pursuit on the streets of Chicago."

Ellie grinned. "Two large pizzas, double order of wings, and salad."

Pad went into the living room. The whiteboard was propped against the wall.

"Hey, Judy and Walker are swinging by. Let's add the new intel to the board before they get here."

Paul was like a caged animal. "I'm so angry I can't think straight. When I think about him holding her, my blood boils. I've never felt this out of control. I'm a damn good cop. Where's my professional edge?"

"Bro, this isn't just a case. You have feelings for this woman. Believe me, I get it. It's how I felt when Ellie was in danger. Hell, I felt that when I took her to the ER after the accident."

Ellie called from the kitchen, "Pad, can you open the front door? Pizza's here."

"Coming."

Paul flopped onto the couch and bounced his knee rapidly. Ellie carried in a tray, and he hopped up.

"You should have said something. I could've grabbed the tray."

"It's not a big deal." Ellie cleared off a stack of books from the coffee table. "You can set it here."

Pad came in carrying a tower of containers on top of two very large pizza boxes.

"You weren't kidding when you said you'd bought food. You have enough for a small army."

Voices drifted in from the back. "Anyone home?"

Pad yelled, "Back here."

"I heard a rumor of pizza and new information," Judy said.

She read the board. "Walker, we've got a

few more details on the location. Do you think you can do something with it?"

He took a picture of the board with his cell phone. "Yeah. I'm waiting to hear back on a promising lead. When I have something concrete, I'll fill you in."

Paul's hand stopped midway with pizza hanging in the air. "What is it?"

"Nothing I'm ready to talk about yet." Walker looked at the eight eyes staring him down. "All right, I came across a transaction which looks odd. A lake house was purchased about eighteen months ago, by D.D. Michaelson."

Paul felt the heat rise as blood pounded in his veins. "What are we waiting for? Let's go."

Pad cleared his throat. "Paul, we need to check it out before we go charging down the highway."

Walker said, "I'm doing the research, and as soon as I know something more, I'll tell you immediately."

Ellie announced, "I'm going to try Dani's cell."

The room fell silent. "We know Dani called her mother today, which means she was able to use the phone. Don't you think it's worth a try?"

Pad draped his arm over her shoulders. "You have to love a logical woman."

Ellie put the phone on speaker. After the fifth ring, a deep voice said, "Hello."

"Hi, is this Dani's phone?"

"Who wants to know?"

"This is her friend, Ellie McKenna. I was hoping to speak with her."

Silence.

"Is she available?"

Again, silence.

Her patience was rewarded.

"Hold on."

They heard rustling, and then a familiar voice said, "This is Dani."

Ellie choked back the tears. "Dani, it's Ellie."

"Ellie, how nice to hear from you. This is an unexpected surprise."

Paul opened his mouth, and Pad jerked his arm and mouthed, No.

"So, how are things going?"

"Everything here is fine." Dani's voice betrayed her ability to talk freely.

"You owe me some beach time, girlfriend." Ellie blinked away a tear.

"Hopefully, we can get together at some point. Right now, Derek and I are spending quality time together. I think tonight we're going to cook some homemade spaghetti sauce together and share a nice bottle of wine."

Paul dropped to the sofa. His head fell into his hands. The plans were a dagger to his heart.

Ellie continued. "Sounds like a nice evening."

Silence answered her. "Well, I just wanted to check in and see how things were going."

"Thanks for calling, Ellie."

"I miss you, Dani."

"I do too. Bye."

The line went silent and Ellie clutched the phone. "Pad, how do you think she sounded?"

Pad had a ten-second internal debate.

"How could she go on about making sauce and sharing wine with a monster?" Paul demanded.

Judy's temper flashed. "Paul. As your former partner and friend, listen to yourself. You're walking around like she chose to leave with him. Think. What do you think she was really trying to say?"

"What?" Paul slapped his forehead. "Oh, shoot. She was trying to remind me about the dinner we shared. Reassuring me, when it's Dani who needs comforting."

Walker said, "I hate to break up this self-revelation, but Judy, we need to get back on patrol."

With a quick hug for Ellie, Judy said, "We can touch base tomorrow. If Walker's information pans out, we'll make and execute a plan to get her."

"I'm making a promise to each of you." Paul studied these four people. "Each one of you is like family to me. You've carried me the last eight days. As of now, I'm focused and putting my personal feelings aside. I'll document everything about tonight's phone call and everything we've found out so we can share the intel. Tomorrow, we'll do what needs to be done."

17

---

aul tossed and turned all night. In his dreams, he was sharing a plate of pasta with Dani. At first light, he jumped out of bed, anxious to get the day started. Today was the first real step to bringing her home.

His cell rang, and he grabbed it off the counter. "Hello?"

"Hey," Pad was on the other end. "Have you heard anything yet?"

"Not yet. I expect Walker will stop in at the station this morning if he connected the dots."

"Okay, see you in a while."

Paul got ready for his shift. He leaned against the counter, picturing Dani laughing and smiling.

He pulled himself out of the sweet memory; time for work.

*P*aul and Pad reviewed the previous night's lack of activity. It made for an easy morning. Sometimes, small-town living had its perks.

"Ready to head out on patrol?" Pad studied his partner, only imagining what was going through his head.

Paul glanced at the doorway. "I was hoping we'd run into Walker before we left." He shoved his chair back, metal legs scraping the black-and-white linoleum. "Let's hit the road."

Paul tossed the keys to Pad. "You drive. I'm too keyed up to pay attention to the road."

Pad caught the keys in midair. "Probably a wise decision."

Paul adjusted his sunglasses. He was waiting for Pad to unlock the car when Walker pulled in.

Paul leaned into the driver's door window. "Any news?"

"I'm pretty sure I know where Derek is holding Dani."

"And?"

"I've called the local PD and apprised them of the situation. They're going to do a drive-by and get the lay of the land."

"Okay." Paul looked over the top of the car.

"Pad, we've found her." Paul glanced at Walker. "Well, we're pretty sure. The house is in…"

"It's in a small town on the south end of Lake Champlain on the New York side, Chazey Way."

"When are we going?" Pad asked.

"Today," Paul said.

"Tomorrow," Walker said. "We need to let

the local police check things out. They won't
spook Ryan, and it will give us time to get coverage for our shifts."

"You guys don't need to go. I can go in and
get her out."

Pad chuckled. "You're going in as the lone
ranger? Not contacting the feds or locals? I
think not. We go as a team."

"Judy plans on going too," Walker stated.

Paul shifted from one foot to the other. "I
won't tell you again; you don't need to come.
I'll work with the locals."

"Walker, will you let them know?" Pad
asked.

"I already have. They're expecting us at
nine."

"Why so late?" Paul's face flushed red.

"We need time to drive up there, and Judy
and I have to work tonight."

"I forgot."

"Speaking of which, Paul, we need to get
on patrol."

"Okay, Walker, we'll catch up at shift change and firm up the details."

"Sounds good. Catch you later."

Paul slammed the car door and waited for Pad to ease the car onto the street.

"Patience has never been my strongest asset."

Pad laughed. "Like I have any? Over the last couple of years, you've seen me in stressful situations, and by comparison, you have a lot."

"How the heck am I going to wait for twenty-four hours before I get to throw cuffs on this guy?" Paul drummed his fingers on his leg.

"Let's stop at What's Perkin' and fill Cari in on the news."

"Yeah, at least it will make me feel like I'm doing something positive. You should give Ellie a call."

Pad had his phone out. "One step ahead of you."

Paul overheard the easy banter between his partner and Ellie. He longed to pick up the phone and call Dani. He was surprised how much this girl had come to mean to him in such a short time.

"Ellie's coming down in a few minutes."

Paul locked the doors with a push of the key fob.

"Why don't you go in? I'll wait for Ellie."

Paul entered the brightly lit café.

"Hi, Luke. Is Cari around?"

"Sure. You look like hell, if you don't mind me saying so," Luke said.

Paul snorted. "Nah, just like a man with a lot on his mind."

Luke stuck his head into the kitchen. "Cari, Paul's out front."

She wiped her hands on a towel as she walked through the swinging door.

"Morning, Paul. Any news?"

"Yes, ma'am. As a matter of fact, we're pretty sure we know where she is, and hopefully, later this morning, we'll have confirmation. If all goes well, we're going after her tomorrow."

The bell on the door jingled and Ellie, with Pad right behind her, entered.

"Hey, Mom, Paul, Luke." Ellie glowed. "Did you hear, we're going after Dani tomorrow?"

"El, Paul and I are going after Dani. You're going to be right here in Loudon." Pad spoke in a firm tone. "I don't want you anywhere near this crazy man."

"You said Walker and Jude were going too."

"They're trained professionals and you're not."

A glint shone in Ellie's eyes. "All the more reason I need to be there. Dani's going to need me."

Oblivious to anyone else, Ellie focused on Paul. "You agree with me, right?"

"Ellie, it's not for me to say one way or the other, but it could be dangerous. We don't know what we're going to find. Pad would kill me if you got caught in the crossfire."

"Mom, help me out here."

"Ellie, I've seen you in enough danger to last me a lifetime. But I understand why you want to be there. I think we'd all like to be there for moral support."

Pad's eyes narrowed. "I'll make a deal with you since you're not going to let this go."

Ellie squealed and threw her arms around Pad's neck. "Thank you. I promise I won't get in the way."

"After our shift, we'll have dinner, the three of us, and come up with a compromise. You'll need to promise to do as we say and not argue with me once we get there."

"Absolutely. As long as I can be there for Dani."

Pad kissed her forehead and looked at Paul. "It's easier to give in now and come up with a plan. If I said she couldn't go, she'd probably follow us."

Paul gave him a sideways glance. "I'm a little surprised you caved so fast."

Ellie looked between the two cops. "Pad knows me. I would have followed you. It's better you know where I am and where I'll be. It'll free everyone up to do their jobs."

Paul's radio crackled. "Gotta run, Ellie. See you later."

He grabbed the keys. "Kiss your woman goodbye and let's hit it, partner."

"Hey, Luke." Ellie smiled. "How's business been?"

"Brisk as usual. Your mom is amazing, you know?"

"Lucas, I'm standing right next to you and can hear what you're saying. Are you trying to butter me up?"

Luke laughed. "Nope. I speak the truth."

Ellie looped her arm with Cari's. "Can't blame the guy, Mom. You've been holding down the kitchen since all this craziness started."

"Keeping busy has kept me from worrying

about what might have happened to you and what did happen to Dani."

"I know; I keep thinking about what I could have done differently to avoid the accident. But it could have been much worse. My car took the brunt of the impact. I'm fine now, and when I talked to Dani, she said it was just muscle soreness."

"I'm not thrilled you're walking into heaven knows what."

"I'll have four cops with me, including my dear Pad. The locals and a few feds will be there too. Mom, I really feel like I need to be there. She's friendly with Judy, but we've become really close. I can help."

"Promise me you'll be extra careful."

Ellie couldn't help but laugh. "Pad won't let anything happen to me."

"Once this is behind us, do you think we can plan a wedding?"

"Is this your way of trying to get me to think of something happy?"

Luke interjected, "You might as well agree

to set a date. I think your mom is looking for something to think about today. Otherwise, she's going to worry about all the things she can't control tomorrow."

"Then you can start planning, but remember, I want small and simple, but elegant."

Luke went into the kitchen. He called back over his shoulder, "I don't think small or simple is in any mother's vocabulary when it comes to her baby girl's wedding."

Cari said, "Keep your head together tomorrow, and after this is over, you and Padraic will set a date."

Ellie threw her hands up in the air. "You win. Once Dani is home safe and sound, we'll set a date. It'll make Aunt Winnie happy too."

*E*llie had laid out a cold supper. She moved the plates and silverware again and then put them back. She had plenty in case Judy and Walker swung by. She glanced at the clock and then out the window. "What could be keeping them?"

Hearing a car door slam, Ellie hurried out to the driveway.

Pad allowed his lips to meld with Ellie's. "Hello, darlin'."

"I was starting to worry about you both." Ellie pulled Paul by the arm.

"Jeez, for a petite girl, you're plenty strong." Paul rubbed his arm in mock pain.

"Never underestimate any girl, no matter her size," Ellie admonished with a glint in her eye.

"I won't make that mistake again." Paul munched on a slice of roast beef. "J and W will be here soon."

"Don't hold me in suspense." Ellie looked between the men. "Did Walker get confirmation? Is it them?"

Pad nodded. "He did and it is."

"What time are we hitting the road?"

"Walker will have the details. He talked with the local PD."

Two voices drifted through the open windows. Judy paused on the step.

Ellie called out, "No need to knock; come on in."

She waved toward the table. "Let's fill our plates, and then we can talk."

The group filed out to the back deck, and before Walker could even sit down, Paul demanded, "Can you fill us in on the plan?"

Ellie said, "Paul, it's a good thing Walker understands your impatience. But you should let him take a bite before you jump down his throat."

Walker got comfortable in his chair and speared a pickle. "We need to leave at five thirty. It should take us about three hours to get there, and we head right to the station. They'll have a small team ready. The cop I talked to confirmed he caught a glimpse of Dani in the yard, but she avoided all eye contact with him. He got the impression Ryan wanted to keep her out of hearing range." He paused and took a bite of salad.

Paul sputtered, "Was she okay?"

"Per the report, she looked fine."

Paul nodded.

"The house is pretty remote and about twenty minutes outside of town. The four of us will hike in from a designated location."

Ellie interrupted, "Five."

Walker raised an eyebrow and continued. "Two officers will approach the house and ask to speak to the woman inside."

"If he refuses?" Ellie asked.

"They'll say they have reason to question her in an open investigation. Hopefully, Derek will agree."

"He won't want to," Ellie spoke.

"Derek thinks he's above the law, and he'll probably never guess we've been able to find the house. He underestimates many people. After all, it took him several years to find Dani."

Walker finished his dinner before continuing. "We're going to be in place as backup only, in case Derek tries to take Dani and run. We are not to engage Ryan unless absolutely necessary." His gaze strayed to Paul, who seemed to wither under the intensity.

Walker pushed the dishes aside and unrolled the paper he'd carried in. "These were filled out with the town clerk's office when he did a major renovation. We have no reason to think they're not completely accurate." His finger trailed over the blueprints.

"Here's the layout. All exterior doors, except one, lead into the woods on either side. There is a sliding glass door that faces the lake."

He pointed to the tree line on each side.

"We'll be here."

"If he takes her, we'll get him. If he goes alone, we'll get him. No matter which way you look at it, Derek Ryan is done." Walker turned to Paul.

"Since I've been in contact with the locals, I'm going to run point for our team. Are you good?"

Paul's lips formed a thin, hard line. "Yeah,

I'm good. I don't care who leads what as long as we get Dani out of there."

Judy said, "I'll be with Ellie. Walker, Pad, and Paul will all have separate vantage points."

"No disrespect, Judy, but Ellie's with me."

"Sure, I just thought if you need to get into the thick of it…"

"I'll take care of Ellie, and I'll have your back too."

"Understood."

Judy glanced at her watch. "Walker, we need to roll. Dinner break is over."

He pushed back his chair. "I'm going to leave this map with you. You guys look it over and get familiar with the lay of the land."

Paul extended his hand. "Walker, this is above and beyond, man."

"Brothers in blue. You know the code." Walker clasped his hand.

"I owe you."

Ellie hoped this plan would go smoothly, and in a few days, they'd be sitting on the deck under the summer sky, throwing back a couple of beers until the stars lit up the night sky. "We'll see you back here bright and early."

"Pad, let's go over the prints until we know it as well as our own houses in the dark."

Ellie leaned in. "Count me in."

The trio huddled over the photos and map until their eyes blurred.

Paul straightened up, easing the crick from his back. "I think I'm gonna call it a night. Want a lift?"

Pad said, "I'm gonna crash in the spare room tonight."

Pad walked Paul to his car. "Just an FYI, we're waiting until the wedding night."

Paul clapped him on the back. "You're one of a kind, Stone."

"Whatever my girl wants. This is really important to Ellie, so it's important to me."

"I wondered why you still had your apartment."

"We're still trying to decide where we'll

live after the honeymoon, here or look for a house."

"I respect you even more."

"Thanks. Try to get a decent night's sleep. Tomorrow is gonna be wild and wooly."

"Yeah, but for Dani, this is the last night she has to sleep under that maniac's roof." Paul's fist balled at his side. "If he laid one finger on her." Fury rolled off him like heat from a bad sunburn.

"Hey, I think he was trying to wheedle his way back into her heart by isolating her. Making Dani dependent on him was the way he was going to do it. Not with physical intimidation."

"I'm just saying…"

"Paul, I know, buddy. I know how you feel, and I'd think the same thing in your shoes. Derek will pay for what he's done. We'll make sure of it."

18

The first rays of sun were creeping over the horizon when Paul pulled into Ellie's driveway. He had a restless night, but his energy level was in overdrive, and his thoughts were clear. Pad loaded a cooler in the back of his SUV along with a duffel bag. Ellie finished locking the door and approached Paul's window.

"Hey, guys. Are you ready to hit the road?"

Pad nodded. "Change of plans. We're meeting Judy and Walker at What's Perkin'. Cari called last night and asked us to stop in."

"Mom's sending us off with food. I'll give you guys a minute to talk."

"She's pretty intuitive."

Pad snorted. "You have no idea."

"You'll have to tell me sometime." Paul looked down the street. "I've checked the route to the local police, and we should be there before nine."

"And we're letting them take the lead, right? We follow orders. This isn't our jurisdiction, and they know the area. They're giving us professional courtesy."

Paul bit back a sharp retort. "I'll follow orders. I promised her parents and Dani knows, in her heart, I'm coming for her."

"We won't let her down."

Paul waited for Pad to climb behind the wheel before easing down the driveway. He was glad Pad understood why he needed to be alone, but he was rethinking the decision. Maybe Dani would want to be with Ellie on the drive home. Having her best friend around her could be comforting after her ordeal.

The group gathered in the cozy coffee shop, and on the counter were several to-go bags. Cari hugged her daughter and reminded Pad to keep an eye on Ellie since she tended to listen to the voice in her head and go against the grain.

Paul asked, "Is she psychic or something?"

Ellie looked Paul directly in the eyes. Her blue eyes shimmered. "Sometimes I know things. Most times it helps me in tough situations. I know Dani is safe, angry, and confused, but the most important thing to remember, she's unharmed."

Paul was stunned. "Um, Ellie."

Ellie touched his arm. "It's fine. There are many people who don't believe people can be in tune with more than what they can see and touch." She jerked her thumb toward Pad. "Take your partner. It totally freaked him out when I told him."

Pad put his arm around Ellie. "If El says Dani's okay, you can trust her."

Paul looked around at his ever-expanding

group of friends. "Would you mind if I rode with you and Ellie? I'm sure when the day is over, Dani's going to want to be with Ellie."

Judy said, "A great idea. Fewer cars to hide when we get to the lake."

Cari handed Ellie a bag. "I went up to Dani's apartment and grabbed a couple of out-fits. She's going to want to change into her own clothes."

Cari handed out another bag. "Sandwiches, cookies, and anything else I could think of to keep you well-fed."

The town clock chimed six. Paul said, "Ready?"

With promises to call, the group of four cops and one civilian left What's Perkin'.

*P*aul watched the road signs. "Take the next left. The station should be on the left."

Pad followed directions and Walker

pulled in next to them. The tension was pal-
pable as they walked toward the main
entrance.

Paul pulled the heavy metal door, and Pad
held it open for the group as they waited in the
large barren vestibule. Paul hit the intercom
button.

The speaker crackled. "Please hold your
photo ID up to the camera."

Paul held up his credentials.

Moments later, on the buzz, the lock re-
leased, and the door opened.

"Officers Greene, Stone, Bell, and Walker,
and Eleanor McKenna. We're here to work
with Officers Stewart and Booker on the
missing person case of Danielle Michaels."

"We've been expecting you. If you'll wait a
minute, someone will be out."

Paul and the group moved away from the
desk. Paul's irritation grew.

"You'd think they'd be waiting for us."

"Easy, partner. Put your cop hat on," Pad
murmured.

"I wouldn't keep people waiting this long," Paul snapped.

Pad made a low rumble in his throat. Paul glanced at him. "I know it's only been a couple of minutes. But it feels like forever."

A door opened at the far end of the room. "Are you the team from Loudon?"

Paul stepped forward. "Paul Greene."

"Officer Stewart. Come with me."

Paul wasn't surprised at the stature of the officer. His voice was deep and commanding. A cop who is used to being on the job.

The group followed the officer down a long, well-lit hallway, their hiking boots clomping over the beige linoleum floor. At the end, Stewart walked through an open door into a large window-free conference room. There were whiteboards on every available wall space and a large table with chairs on one side. Several were occupied with men and women in outdoor type clothes, but with the telltale sign of body armor underneath, much like Paul's team.

Stewart made quick introductions of each team member. Paul and his group took open seats.

Stewart stood in front of one whiteboard with a detailed map posted. "Here's what we're dealing with," he began. "We've had a patrol car drive out there to see if the woman you reported as abducted was in fact with Derek Ryan."

Paul opened his mouth and closed it.

"The officers went there on the guise there had been break-ins on several vacant cottages. Mr. Ryan came to the door, and we did get visual confirmation that Ms. Michaels is there. When the officers tried to speak with her, Mr. Ryan stated his wife wasn't feeling well and needed to rest."

Paul leaned forward, hands clenched, knuckles white, as Stewart gave his report.

"They asked to look around the perimeter, just to check for any evidence their cottage might be next and Ryan quickly volunteered to escort them."

My officers did a thorough inspection and noted all the exits from the building. It helped us determine how to approach the house and how many we need to be stationed in the woods."

Paul examined the board. "To be clear"—he pointed to several areas—"this is where teams will be posted?"

Stewart nodded. "And our plan will be to send two different officers in, as a follow-up to the break-ins."

"How do you plan to get Dani out of the house?" Paul demanded.

"I'm Booker." A tall, lean woman stood. "I'm going to be one of the uniforms today. I'll ask to speak with Ms. Michaels, and if Ryan refuses, I'm going to insist."

"This sounds like a disastrous plan," Paul said. "Ryan's radar will be up."

"We're going to have the cottage surrounded, and we'll have to go to the main entrance. We can't just bust in."

"And what do you expect my team to do?"

"Each member of your team will be paired up with one of mine. Everyone will be mic'd. We'll keep in constant contact. If you need to move in and breach the house, you will, and being with a local will keep it legal."

"Stewart," Pad said, "Ellie stays with me."

Stewart nodded. "I understand she's not a cop, and, frankly, I think it might be better if she stays at the station."

Ellie jumped up. "I'm going!" She looked from Pad to Paul.

Paul's gaze was steady as if weighing the pros and cons. "If Pad says she's safe with him, Ellie goes."

"Are you armed?"

Ellie shook her head. "Just pepper spray."

Stewart surveyed the room. "We leave in five. We're going to take different routes to the lake." He pointed to Judy and Walker. "You're with Hal and Aaron, Paul you're with me. Pad and Ellie, go with Keith."

The groups paired up and got into various types of plain cop SUVs with the exception of

Booker and another uniform. They walked toward a black-and-white patrol car.

"I'll radio in when I'm close. Once everyone's in position, we'll get this show on the road."

Paul got into the passenger side of Stewart's SUV. "I appreciate you allowing us to help out."

Stewart studied Paul. "I get it. It's hard to be a cop and sit on the sidelines."

The landscape changed from moderate-sized town to lush forest. "How far is the lake?"

"About fifteen more minutes. Once we get there, we'll have a short hike to the cottage."

"And the others?"

"All about the same timing, except for the patrol car."

"Are they there?"

"Nah, they're taking the scenic route. On the off chance Ryan is outside when she pulls up, her story will hold water."

Paul frowned. "This still sounds, oh, hell, I

don't know. I'm having trouble staying objective."

"That's why you're in a support role and not taking the lead. If I were in your shoes, I'd want to beat the guy to a pulp, grab your girl's hand, and run. This way, he's arrested and charged, clean as a whistle to make the conviction stick."

Paul had nothing more to contribute to the conversation. Stewart pulled off the road and turned off the vehicle.

Paul leaned on the hood. "Should we start?"

"Not yet, we need to get the reports from the rest."

"Have you ever had someone you care about taken?"

"Nope. I've never been in your shoes. I've worked cases where people have disappeared."

Stewart's unspoken words chilled the blood in Paul's veins. All too often, the victim didn't come home alive.

The radio squawked. "Boss, this is Hal, we're in position."

"Ten-four."

A few minutes later, Aaron and Keith announced they were in place too. Stewart radioed Booker.

"Everyone is ready to get in position. Give us eight minutes and then make the final turn."

"Ten-four, boss."

"Ready?"

"I thought you'd never ask." Paul checked his ankle harness and pulled his ball cap low over his eyes.

The two men stalked cautiously through the woods, alert for any movements.

Paul caught sight of the cottage and noticed most of this side had no windows, just one side door.

Paul pointed to the door. "Does that lead into the garage?"

"Yeah." He pointed to their left. "There's a small ground floor window on the side and larger windows on the second floor, which we assume is a bedroom. The lake side has a full wall of sliding glass doors, and then, of course, the main entrance is near the driveway."

"So, where is everyone?"

"Hal will be to our right, Aaron will be down below, and Keith, who is with Pad and Ellie, will be facing the house from the lake. There's good cover in all locations."

The crunch of tires on the gravel driveway caught Paul's attention. "Booker?"

Stewart gave a curt nod. "Her mic will be open. We can hear what's going on."

Paul held his breath. A sharp rap on the solid door rang out.

Nothing.

Another sharp rap. "Hello, police department."

Paul heard Booker whisper, "I hear footsteps."

The clarity of the microphone was excellent.

"Officer? Is everything okay?" Derek's

smooth voice made Paul's skin crawl. He longed to take off at a dead run. It took all his will to stay put.

"Officer Booker. I was on patrol. I know you were made aware of the issues of the past week or two we've had with cottages being broken into."

"Yeah, someone stopped by a few days ago."

"I was wondering if I could talk to you and your wife for a few moments, just to see if maybe you've seen something new which could help us."

Paul's gut flipped at the word wife.

"Well," Paul could hear the hesitation in Derek's voice. "We're on the back deck. If you'd care to come in…"

Booker turned and gestured to the car. "My partner wants to ask a few questions; he's an expert in these types of situations."

"We don't need an expert in B & E," Paul hissed.

Stewart's voice was low. "He's an expert in

hostage negotiation."

"You could have told me before?"

"Greene, get ahold of yourself. You're not thinking like a cop."

Paul ran his hand over his head and looked for the rest of the team.

Stewart spoke into his mic. "Everyone, be ready on my orders."

Voices came over the radio.

⁂

"Sweetheart, this is Officer Booker, and I'm sorry I didn't catch your name," Derek said.

"Ma'am, Officer Goodwin."

Dani's heart raced. It couldn't be a coincidence. The police stopping twice in less than a week. She stood up and said, "Danielle Michaels…"

Derek interjected, "Ryan. We're recently married. She's still adjusting to her last name."

Dani's mouth went dry. "How can I help?"

Dani noticed the subtle movement of the female officer putting herself between Dani and Derek.

"How long have you been living in the cottage?"

"I've been here maybe a little over a week?" Dani's eyes darted from Goodwin to Booker.

"I see you have a bruise on your forehead. Did you fall?" Booker asked.

"Um, no, I was in an auto accident." Dani's voice cracked. "I'm fine now."

Goodwin looked at Derek. "Mr. Ryan, were you injured?"

"No, just Danielle, but as you heard, she's fine now."

Dani watched Derek lick his lips. "I'm sorry but I don't know what her bruise has to do with vandalism."

Dani took a step back. The tone in Derek's voice was all too familiar. She caught a flash of movement from the side of the deck, and she froze. More cops.

"Mr. Ryan," Goodwin said. "We have reason to believe this young woman was taken from a motor vehicle accident against her consent."

"Danielle, tell these cops you're my wife."

Dani bolted to the screen door. She fumbled with the handle as she tried to slide it. She heard pounding footsteps getting closer. Pain seared her shoulder. Her fingers lost their grip on the handle. Derek's arm was a vise around the base of her throat.

"Come on." He picked her up from her feet. Dani's legs dangled in the air. "We're getting out of here."

"Ryan, stay where you are." Booker's voice penetrated the roaring in Dani's ears. "Nobody needs to get hurt."

Dani felt a cold sharp prick at the base of her throat as Derek held her in a fierce hold. Dani tried to get her feet on the floor. He was backing them toward the deck.

"I don't know what you think is going on here, but Danielle and I are enjoying some

much-needed alone time to rekindle our relationship. I'm gonna sue the police for harass-
ment. Now, get off my property."

Dani could feel the cold steel bite deeper
into her skin. She sucked in a breath and
whimpered, "Please, let me go."

"Derek, if this has been a misunderstanding, let's sit down and talk about it. You don't
want to hurt Danielle." Goodwin's voice was
smooth and soothing.

Dani was still being partially dragged backward when they stumbled. Derek held tight.

"Derek, there's no place for you to go,"
Goodwin said. "Let Danielle go."

Paul watched the events unfolding on the
deck. Without thinking, he took off. Pad intercepted him, and together, they drew their
handguns, training them on Derek.

Paul's eyes were locked on the knife at
Dani's throat. He could see a few drops of
blood.

"Derek, you have nowhere to go. Drop the
knife and we can talk about this."

Derek watched the police presence grow around him. His eyes blinked rapidly, scanning the area.

A sob escaped Dani's lips, and Derek's grip tightened.

"She's mine. I love her, and we belong together."

Dani's lower lip quivered. She cried, "Derek, please. Let me go. This isn't how you want me with you, by force."

Derek whispered in her ear. "I can't lose you. You're all I have."

Paul's eyes were locked on Dani's. They were filled with terror.

"Ryan," Paul's voice rang out. "You're surrounded, and the only way out is to release Dani. Now."

Derek pushed Dani away with astonishing force. She cried out as she fell to the deck. Derek raced down the steps and grabbed Ellie. Using her as a shield, he dragged her toward the boat dock.

Booker stepped forward to help Dani, and Paul ran with Pad after Derek and Ellie.

In mid-stride, Paul heard a loud howl burst from Derek. He was on the ground, writhing.

Ellie was standing over him, feet planted wide, emptying a canister of pepper spray in his face.

Pad reached Ellie and pulled her into the safety of his arms. Paul turned and ran to Dani.

He dropped to the deck and held Dani as she sobbed.

"It's okay; it's over," Paul murmured in Dani's hair.

She looked at Paul, her blue eyes red, and asked, "Did he hurt Ellie?"

Paul snorted. "He didn't get the chance. She hit him with pepper spray."

Paul liked the feel of Dani's head on his chest.

"Dani." Ellie knelt down. "It's time to go, honey. Do you want to get anything from the house?"

Dani shook her head. "There's nothing except my cell phone."

Paul said, "I'll get it."

Dani shuddered. "No, don't leave me."

Paul wrapped his arms tighter. "Pad, would you look for her cell phone?"

Over Dani's head, he watched Pad and Ellie, hands clasped, walk toward the house. A buzz of activity was going on with police in and around the building, taking pictures and gathering items in evidence bags.

"Dani, you need to give your statement."

He felt her nod against his chest.

"Will you stay with me?"

"Nothing can pry me from your side." He kissed the top of her head and pulled her upright.

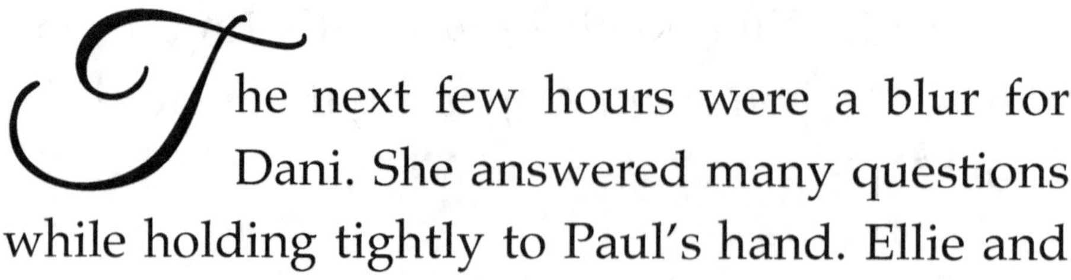

The next few hours were a blur for Dani. She answered many questions while holding tightly to Paul's hand. Ellie and

Pad were in the room the entire time, and she could never begin to express how much their support meant to her. For over a week, she'd been isolated and drew on a strength she hadn't known she possessed. Once the final questions were answered, Officers Booker and Stewart said she was free to go home.

Dani looked down. She pulled at the collar of her shirt.

Ellie crouched down.

"Dani, Mom packed you a few outfits. She thought you might be more comfortable for the trip home."

Dani's shoulders slumped and tears fell. "Cari thought of fresh clothes?"

"Would you like me to go into the restroom with you?"

"Yes, I don't want to be alone."

Dani squeezed Paul's hand. "I'm going to change, and then I need to call my mom."

"Dani, you can relax. She knows you're safe and said to call when you had a free minute."

"Who called her?"

"I did. Right after we pulled into the parking lot."

Dani wiped the tears from her eyes. "What else did you think of?"

Ellie's eyes twinkled. "Some of Cari's cooking for the ride home."

Dani hiccupped. "Can I change?"

"Sure."

Dani wrapped her arm around Ellie's and held tight. "As soon as I take these off, will you throw them out?"

Booker intercepted the girls and handed Ellie a large, clear plastic bag. "Dani, we'll need them for evidence."

Dani dropped her head. "Will this ever be over?"

"The worst of its behind you. Each day you move forward means you're healing. You're a lucky girl. You've got great friends."

Through her tears, Dani said, "I have the best friends in the world. They came after me."

"If it wasn't for them, we wouldn't have

found you as quickly. Your friends were determined."

Dani's heart beat a little faster. "Paul? He wanted to be here?"

Ellie squeezed Dani's arm. "I'll fill you in on all the details after the guys go to work tomorrow. Oh, and for the record, you're sleeping at my place for as long as you want. It'll be fun being roommates."

Dani didn't know if she should cry or laugh or be over the moon with happiness. Her throat was choked with tears. "I guess my life began to change the day I walked into your mom's café. It really was the beginning of the end to my nightmare. I just didn't know it at the time."

She took the large plastic bag. "Give me five minutes, and you can have the final bit of evidence from me. I'm calling Mom, and then I want to go home."

ani's eyes flew open. Her heart pounded deep in her chest. She squinted to look at her surroundings, taking in the pale-blue walls and curtains with tiny dark-blue checks. The duvet cover was a field of wildflowers, and the sheets were velvety soft and a pretty shade of blue. It was pure luxury. It took a few moments until she realized this was Ellie's guest room. She sat up in bed, hugging her arms around herself as she wept with joy. It wasn't a dream. She was home, free from the beautiful prison Derek

Ryan had kept her in for nine days. Every day an eternity.

A soft knock on the door caught Dani's attention.

"Are you awake?" Ellie cracked the door open.

"Yes, come in."

Ellie carried a tray with two mugs of what Dani hoped was coffee.

"I thought you might like a slow start today. I ran down to the café and picked up breakfast."

Dani smoothed out the blankets so Ellie could set the tray down.

"You didn't need to do this, El."

"Yes, I did. And later, if you're up for it, I think we should drive out to the lake and soak up some rays."

Dani froze and her heart began to pound. "Um, Ellie. I don't know if…"

"I have a surprise at the lake. Please say yes." Ellie's eyes shone. "You won't be disappointed."

Dani shook her head. "I don't think I'm up to an adventure today." Dani pulled the covers up. "I'm really tired."

Ellie handed her coffee. "Here, take a sip."

The mug touched Dani's lips.

"Careful, it's hot."

Dani let the smell waft and tease her senses. "I feel like I've been gone forever."

Ellie patted her leg. "You're home now and safe."

Dani's color paled.

"Is that why you want to stay here today? You feel safe?"

Dani swallowed hard. "I know it must seem silly since Derek was arrested and I know he's in jail. But we were just minding our own business and having a girls' day when, out of nowhere, a car accident happens, and you could have been killed." Tears welled up in Dani's eyes. "I couldn't have lived with myself if you had died."

"I had a few bumps and bruises. After the first day, I was fine. You had to deal with the abduction and isolation of the cabin."

The tears fell unchecked down Dani's bright-pink cheeks. "You know, every day I worried he might try to, well, you know, force a physical relationship. But he didn't. I wasn't free to go outside when I wanted to. I was a prisoner inside the cottage. When I was allowed to go out, Derek was never any farther away than one arm's length. I was scared but more from what I thought might happen than what actually did happen." Dani looked at Ellie. "Does that make any sense?"

"Of course, it does. I'm sure every waking moment you were trying to figure out a way to escape. You had to be on high alert."

Dani nodded. "It was weird. The cottage Derek bought and furnished? It was exactly like something I had mentioned in passing years ago when things were still good between us. I remember ripping out pages from a magazine about a lake house and the way it was decorated. He must have saved them and thought this would have swayed my opinion of him."

"Dani, Derek is very sick. He needs help."

"Well, I'll settle for him going to prison for a very long time."

Dani looked down and her mug was empty. "Would you mind if I made some breakfast?"

"I have a much better idea. Eat what I brought back from Mom's. Why don't you run through the shower and meet me downstairs? We'll have breakfast and maybe you'll feel up to going out to the lake."

"You're not going to give up, are you?"

Ellie grinned. "You know I'm not. You might as well slather on sunscreen when you get out of the shower and put on sun worshipping clothes."

Dani watched as Ellie left the room. She sighed and sank into the pillows. Picking up her cell phone from the bedside table, she hit the speed dial labeled, MOM. The phone went to voicemail. Dani frowned and left a short message for her mother to call when she had a minute.

She flipped back the covers, letting her feet touch the thick carpeting. She padded to the adjoining bath and then back into the bedroom. She crossed the room and flipped the lock and went back into the bathroom.

After a soothing shower, Dani walked down the back stairs toward the smell of cooked bacon. The lure of food and her friend caused her steps to quicken.

Ellie had the table on the back deck set for two. She looked up when Dani came out. "How was the shower?"

"Hot and you have the best soap. You'll have to tell me where you buy it."

"You got it." Ellie pointed to the carafe. "Will you grab the coffee? I'll bring out our plates."

The sound of car doors slamming stopped Dani in her tracks. "Are you expecting someone?"

"Oh, it's the guys."

Dani relaxed just a bit. She had wondered when she'd see Paul again.

Pad walked into the kitchen and kissed Ellie on the lips. "Good morning, sweetheart. I see we're just in time."

Paul's eyes caught Dani's. Her heart thudded in her chest, and she glanced at the floor and then back up, meeting his eyes.

"Good morning, Paul."

"Did you sleep okay?"

"I did, thank you." She held up the carafe. "Can I interest you gentlemen in coffee?"

Pad grabbed two mugs from the cabinet and pointed to the bag with a familiar logo. "Muffins."

Dani stammered, "Is Cari mad I didn't come in today?"

Ellie put the plates on the counter and took Dani by the shoulders. "Dani." She pushed Dani's chin up so they were eye to eye. "My mother doesn't expect you back at What's Perkin' until you feel you're ready. If it's next week or next month, she and Luke have everything under control."

"I'm letting everyone down." Dani's shoulders drooped. "How could I have let this happen? Why didn't I fight him off? I should have stopped him from taking me!"

Dani's voice grew louder with each word she spoke until she slumped into a chair.

The room fell silent. A chair scraped over the floor, and a large hand took both of hers. Holding gently, Paul's thumb caressed the top of her hand.

"Dani." His voice was quiet but firm. "There was nothing you could have done differently, and you have no way of knowing if you had fought back if Derek might have hurt you or worse. You survived."

"But." Dani fought back the tears. "I should have done something."

"What could you have done? He was determined. You had just suffered a car crash, and you weren't thinking clearly. I would guess you may have even passed out."

Dani's eyes narrowed. "I don't remember much about the drive to the lake." She pushed her glasses up her nose. "I vaguely remember Ellie driving, and then I was in Derek's car. We had just pulled into the garage. That's the last thing I remember—well, sort of remember—until I woke up the next day in my bedroom."

Dani looked at her concerned friends' faces. "Do you really think I couldn't have changed anything?"

Pad shook his head and said, "No. If anyone is to blame, I think Paul and I are. We underestimated him, and we shouldn't have allowed the two of you to drive out to the lake until we were very sure he was back in Chester."

Paul nodded as Pad talked. "I'm sorry, Dani. Once we knew what had happened, we did everything possible to find you."

Paul's voice dropped. "With each passing day, it was harder and harder for me to face the fact that I failed you. I promised to protect you."

It was Dani's turn to comfort Paul. "You had no way of knowing what he would do. I don't blame you or Pad. And the whole time I was gone, I knew you'd find me and bring me home."

"You did?"

Dani laid her hand on her heart. "I believed with all my heart. And look, I was right. You and Pad did the cop thing, and then here comes Ellie with her can of pepper spray and brings Derek to his knees."

A lump lodged in her throat. She croaked, "Besides my parents, you three are the most important people in my life."

Her gaze landed on the cold scrambled eggs. "I'm going to whisk up some eggs, and we can start putting this behind us."

Ellie squeezed Dani's shoulder. "You're going to take the coffee and Paul and go out to the deck. Pad and I can cook the eggs."

Pad glanced at Paul. "We don't really have time to eat. We're on duty. But coffee would be good."

"We'll need to take a rain check on hot food, but coffee and muffins, a perfect substitute."

Dani said, "Let's skip the eggs and just have a light meal. I'd rather we didn't waste another minute of the guys' break time."

Ellie was happy to agree, giving Pad's hand a tug as he leaned down to kiss her forehead.

He whispered. "You're a good friend, Ellie."

Ellie broached the idea of going out to the lake. "Do you think it'd be okay if we drove out to the lake today?"

Paul looked from Ellie to Dani. "Do you want to go?"

Dani's lower lip trembled. "It would be fun to do something today, but I'm not sure."

Paul said, "Would you feel better if we followed you out there? We could swing by after lunch, and once we get off work, Pad and I can meet you and then drive home together?"

Dani let out a huge breath. "You'd do that for me?"

"Sure, it's part of the job to protect and serve, ma'am," Paul teased her.

Dani smiled. "Ellie, looks like we'll be going to the lake after all, if you think Abby won't mind us crashing her beach."

"I'll just let her know what time we'll be there and see if she needs anything."

Pad tapped Ellie's head. "You know, if Dani's feeling up to it, we could have a cook-out, invite the family, and maybe Judy and Hoyt Walker."

"Who's he?" Dani asked.

Paul said, "Judy's new partner. Remember, you met him."

Dani nodded. "He looks like a nice guy."

"He did a lot to help us in the investigation." Paul hesitated. "When we were looking for you."

Dani didn't want a big party, but after what all her friends had been through trying to find her, and Cari and her family being understanding, she figured she could find a way to keep her nerves steady for a few hours. Besides, if Paul was around, she knew she'd be safe.

"Sounds like it might be fun. If Abby and Shane don't mind hosting. I could make some food to take out."

Ellie laughed. "Have you ever been to a McKenna-Davis event where there wasn't more than enough food for a small army?"

Dani couldn't help but laugh. "I'm sorry; I must have lost my head for a minute. Even so, I'll still make something."

As if on cue, Pad leaned over and lightly kissed Ellie's upturned lips. "I'll call you later to let you know what time we'll swing by, but it won't be until after one."

Ellie said, "We'll be ready."

Paul hesitated before dropping a friendly kiss on top of Dani's head. "I'm glad you're feeling a little better today."

Color flooded Dani's cheeks. "Thank you, Paul. For everything."

The tips of Paul's ears turned red. "Think nothing of it."

After the guys left, Ellie called Abby and then her mom about a cookout. After settling on a time, Dani and Ellie lingered over coffee.

"How are you really doing?" Ellie asked.

"It was good to see Paul," Dani said and quickly added, "and Pad, of course."

"I couldn't help but notice the sparks flying between the two of you. A blind man could have seen them."

"I'm sure it was just the adrenaline left over from yesterday."

"I spent a lot of time with Paul over the past week, and I can tell you, it's not what you think. This man has serious feelings for you."

Dani wished what Ellie said was true. "He'll change his mind once everything settles down."

"Why would you say such a thing? Dani, Paul is a really good guy. You should give it a chance with him."

"I'd love to see if we might have a chance, but I allowed myself to be verbally abused by a man who ended up kidnapping me. I've lived a secret life since moving to Loudon. How could Paul see me as anything but a woman who lies?"

"You're not giving him very much credit. He understands why you did what you did, to protect yourself. You loved Derek, and you trusted him. He lied. Everything Derek ever said to you was a lie. You did nothing wrong."

Dani frowned. "I don't understand. Why did he pretend to be a fireman?"

Ellie's head bobbed. "He failed the entrance exam to join the department. He couldn't face the truth, but he did the next best thing. He took pictures of fires. This way, it perpetuated his lie."

Dani grew quiet, sipping coffee, and Ellie didn't say anything more.

Dani pushed back her chair, and said, "Well, if we're going to party tonight, I need to whip up something delicious. You know what they say, the way to a man's heart is through his stomach."

"You are interested in Paul?" Ellie teased.

Dani winked. "Maybe."

"Do you want some help in the kitchen? It wouldn't hurt for me to work on my cooking skills."

Dani tapped her finger to her temple. "I have just the thing. Do you have any brown sugar?"

"Sure, why?"

"We're going to make homemade butterscotch sauce. We'll fill my go-to vanilla cupcake and then frost them with buttercream and drizzle with even more butterscotch sauce."

"I think I have some butterscotch sauce I bought at the store, from the last time we made sundaes."

Dani gasped. "If you're cooking with me, it's scratch baking, and trust me, it'll be worth the few extra minutes it will take."

Ellie laughed out loud. "I finally figured out who you sound like—my mom and sister."

Dani smiled. "Thanks for the compliment. Shall we get started?"

Dani led the way into the kitchen.

20

Cupcakes sat on cookie trays lining Ellie's kitchen counters. Dani was sure they had enough, and after making a large batch of butterscotch dreams, she whipped up some chocolate raspberry swirls. They were her mother's favorites.

Ellie strolled into the kitchen with a bag slung over her shoulder and went to stick a finger in the raspberry frosting when Dani appeared in the doorway.

"Do you really think you need to sample any more frosting, Ellie?"

"Darn it, if you had been just one minute slower, I would have gotten away with it." Ellie laughed.

Dani looked at the clock. "The guys should be here any minute. Can we load these into your SUV? But I think you should crank the AC."

"Sure."

The cruiser pulled up the driveway.

Dani waved to the guys. "We're just about ready to go. One more trip into the house."

Paul jumped out of the car and jogged over to the door. "Here, let me help."

"Thanks." Dani held the door as Paul carried out the last two trays. He smacked his lips.

"What did you make today?"

"Butterscotch and a chocolate cupcake with raspberry filling."

"Any chance you'd take pity on me and give me a preview?"

Dani giggled. "Well, maybe just one."

"Of each?" Paul's eyes twinkled.

"Are you going to share with Pad?"

"I wasn't planning on it." Paul glanced in Pad's direction. "If those are your terms of getting samples, I guess I can."

"Hey, Pad. Want a cupcake?"

"Of course, I do."

Ellie locked the back door and glanced at her watch. "Hey, enough talk of sweets, we need to hit the road."

Dani saw a look pass between Ellie and Pad and wondered what was going on.

"Is everything okay, Ellie? I didn't realize we might be late."

"Oh, I promised Abby we'd help her before we hit the beach chairs."

"Yeah, and this frosting shouldn't be in a hot car for too long, even with the AC. I don't want them to melt."

"Paul, I really appreciate you taking time out to follow us out to Abby's. You won't get in trouble, will you?"

Paul shook his head. "I cleared it with the chief. It's not a problem at all."

Dani gave Paul a fast hug and pecked his cheek. "I'm looking forward to tonight."

"Me too."

The girls drove down the road and Dani remarked, "This is a new vehicle?"

Ellie glanced over. "I didn't think you'd notice. It's the same make and model, just a year newer."

"Is it because of the accident?"

Ellie didn't take her eyes off the road. "Yeah, Pad thought the frame was sketchy. I did the deal and got new wheels."

"I'm sorry."

"For what?" Ellie did her best to lighten the mood. "I got new wheels, and I love that new car smell." Ellie took a deep breath in. "Come on, breathe in the newness."

"Girlfriend, do you always find a way to turn things into a positive?"

"I do what I can."

She put her blinker on and drove up the driveway. There was a small coupe parked alongside Abby's SUV.

Dani peered out the window. "Did we come at the wrong time? It looks like Abby has company."

Ellie dropped the keys in her bag. "I don't think so. Come on, let's go in."

Dani went to the back of the vehicle. "Are you going to pop the lock?"

"Let's go see where Abby wants us to put them. We don't need to move them twice."

Dani shrugged her shoulders. "If you want."

Ellie pushed open the door and then stepped to one side.

A river of tears broke loose. In a single breath, Dani said, "Mom," and walked into her mother's open arms.

There wasn't a dry eye in the room as Dani was reunited with her mother and father. They held Dani between them, crying and asking for forgiveness.

Ellie and Abby left the Michaels family to talk.

"I can't believe you came all the way out to the East Coast to surprise me." Dani sniffled.

"Once Paul called to say you were safe, we booked flights to get here as soon as we could. If we had known you'd be back in Loudon last night, we would have been waiting." Mom pushed back Dani's riot of curls and looked into her pale-blue eyes. "But we're here now."

Dani hugged her mom and dad tighter. "I'm glad you're here."

Amid lots of questions and time for Dani to fill her parents in on all the events leading up to the kidnapping, Mom held her hands and Dad kept his arm around her shoulders. She fed off their strength, and finally, she said, "I'm really sorry about everything."

"Dani, you have nothing to be sorry about. I feel just awful telling a monster where you were living. He was charming, and before I knew it, he had wheedled the information out of me."

"Mom, Dad, he had a lot of people fooled,

me included. Did you hear, he wasn't a fireman after all? He flunked the test."

"I wonder what else he lied about," Dad said.

"I think Derek's entire life was one big fat lie. But I'm glad you're here. You can meet all my friends at the same time." Dani looked around and noticed Ellie and Abby were missing.

"I guess you met Abby. She married into the McKenna clan, and Cari is her mother-in-law."

Mom said, "She's lovely. We came here from the airport, and she welcomed us like we were old friends."

"From Cari and Ray right down to the little kids, everyone is welcomed like family."

Mom kissed her cheeks. "I'm glad you made good friends."

"They are amazing."

"Your dad and I have been talking. If you don't think we're hovering, we would like to move here."

Dani blinked hard. "You want to move back to where, for about six months of the year, it's cold?"

"It's been too long since we've lived as a family," Dad said. "I can do my new job from anywhere. What do you think, Danielle?"

A frown flitted across her face.

"Well, if you don't like the idea, we don't have to." Mom spoke softly, attempting to mask her disappointment.

"No, Mom. I'd love for you guys to live nearby. It's just, can you never call me Danielle again?"

"For heaven's sake, why not?" Dad said.

"Derek called me Danielle. He never called me Dani. So, I'm going to officially change my name to Dani." She hung her head. "I'm sorry. I don't want any reminders of the past."

Mom and Dad wrapped their arms around Dani and held her tightly. "We'll support whatever changes you want to make." Mom smoothed her hair as she spoke.

"Thanks for understanding." Dani kissed

them both and gave them one last fierce hug. She glanced at the wall clock. "It won't be long before you're going to be elbow to elbow with my adopted family, and I want to help Abby and Ellie. Are you ready to come outside and meet the clan?"

Mom clasped Dad's hand. "This is going to be a fun night."

he cookout was in full swing, and the little ones were starting to droop.

Dani whirled around and fell into Paul's arms. He tightened his hold on her.

He had waited all night for an opportunity such as this, and he didn't intend to waste a second.

"It's nice your parents got here in time to celebrate with you."

Dani batted her dark-brown eyelashes, unaware of how it made Paul's heart race.

"I know I told you, but they're moving here." Dani tried to push away, but Paul wasn't ready to let go.

"I'm happy for you. Did they say how long it will take for them to make the move?"

"No. They'll have to sell their house and find something here. My place isn't big enough for them to stay with me while looking. I'll need to check a few places out for them."

"I'm happy to go with you, if you'd like."

Dani gave him a sweet smile, and his blood hummed.

"I couldn't possibly bother you."

"Dani, don't you know by now, I'd do any-thing for you?"

Paul caught the strains of a conversation growing closer. They were about to be discov-ered. Reluctantly, he let go.

"There you two are." Pad thumped his buddy on the back. "Are you almost ready to head back to Ellie's?"

Dani blushed and murmured she wanted to say goodbye to her parents.

"Your timing stinks, Pad." Paul watched Dani's hasty exit.

"Better me breaking you two apart than her Dad. He's still reeling with everything."

"I can't begin to imagine how her parents felt. I know how hard it was for me." Paul's gaze followed Dani as she hugged everyone with promises for more cupcakes at the next event. Little Devin was pulling her hand. Paul was curious, and he walked closer to listen.

"Dani. I missed you while you were gone, and I'm really glad you came home and made the little cakes." Devin threw his arms around Dani's neck and planted a sticky kiss on her cheek.

Pad nudged Paul's arm. "You might have some competition if you don't make your move, my friend."

Paul chuckled. "I think I can handle it."

Dani picked Devin up and held him tightly. She whispered in his ear, and he laughed and wiggled until she set him back on the floor.

Dani linked arms with Ellie, and the girls

waved to their guys as they walked out the back door. Paul and Pad made a hasty exit to follow them.

"I don't know about you, but I don't want to ride with you on the way back," Paul said as they caught up to Dani and Ellie.

Pad called out, "Ellie, I've got shotgun."

Dani turned and looked at Paul. "Shall I ride with you? If you don't mind driving me back to Ellie's place."

"I was headed there myself. Pad invited me to have coffee." Paul cringed. That sounded lame even to his ears. If Dani noticed, thankfully she didn't say anything.

Dani climbed into the passenger seat and buckled up. "This was a nice cookout."

"It was."

Dani giggled. "I think they're amazing how they just welcome an outsider in, and before you know it, it's like you've known them forever."

The couple rode in silence. Paul rehearsed

the words he wanted to say in his head over and over.

It was in the final mile that he worked up the nerve.

"Do you want to have dinner with me some night, or maybe catch a movie? Or if you want, we can do dinner and a movie." Paul peeked at Dani's profile. His heart hammered because she didn't answer right away.

"I'm not sure we should date, Paul."

"Why? We have fun together. At least we were—well, before."

"My life is really about before and now, after. I don't know how I feel about a lot of things." Dani turned in the seat to look at him. "Can you understand what I'm talking about?"

He did understand. Victims of crime often needed time to deal with the trauma. He berated himself for rushing her.

"Dani, of course. I'm sorry if you thought I was pushing too hard."

"Paul, it's very sweet of you, and if things

were different, I'd be thrilled to have dinner with you. But for now, can we just be good friends?"

Paul nodded, but inside he was screaming, I'm falling in love with you. "The best of friends."

Dani exhaled.

Paul parked and turned off the car. He rested his hand on the shifter. "Do you want me to keep my distance? I don't want you to feel uncomfortable in any way."

Dani patted his hand. "I want you to be exactly who you are. Don't change anything for me."

"We should go inside before we give the soon-to-be Mr. and Mrs. Stone something to talk about."

Dani pushed open the kitchen door and wondered why the heck she had done the exact opposite of what she wanted to do. After talking with Ellie earlier, she knew she wanted to go out with Paul again. Maybe she was screwed up in the head. Tomorrow, she was going to call her old counselor and make an appointment.

"Hey, Ellie. It's really nice of Abby and Shane to have my parents stay with them for a few days."

"Mom asked if they wanted to stay at her place, but I get the feeling your dad was partial to Shane's location." Ellie flipped on the burner under the teakettle.

"Tea?" Ellie asked.

"Sure. What about the guys?"

"They're having decaf."

Pad and Paul strolled into the kitchen. "Sweet cheeks, I'm going to make a small pot of coffee; are you sure you ladies want tea?"

"I'm having Sleepytime."

Dani said, "I'll have the same."

Ellie moved around the kitchen setting out mugs, spoons, honey, and creamer. "Does anyone want cookies?"

Paul patted his stomach. "I already have to run an extra mile due to someone's delicious cupcakes. I had three tonight."

Dani laughed. "I don't think anyone forced you to eat three of them in one sitting."

Paul groaned. "Oh, I forgot I had two earlier. I've eaten way too many sweets today. This means I have to run two extra miles in the morning."

Pad laughed. "Man, you are gonna need to learn to pace yourself when it comes to all the food around here."

Ellie piped up. "It took Pad almost a year to learn moderation."

"Well, maybe I'll learn to love running more. I'd hate to miss out on anything these people make. Every dish was better than the one before it tonight."

Dani sat next to Paul. She wanted to be close without making it seem like she was sending the wrong signals. If Paul thought it was odd she sat next to him, he didn't indicate it.

Dani's eyes were growing heavy. She had to say something before she fell asleep sitting on the couch.

"I hate to break this up, but I'm exhausted." She looked around at her best friends. "I don't want to get all mushy or anything, but you really are amazing individuals. and together, you're unstoppable."

Ellie kissed Dani's cheek. "Sleep well, Dani, and if you need anything, just let me know."

Dani's feet froze on the first step. Before she had the chance to say anything, Ellie dashed up the stairs, turning on lights, then pulled the shades in Pad's old room. On the way down, her hand grazed Dani's.

"You should be all set now."

In silence, Dani walked up the stairs at a quick, erratic pace. Once safely inside, Dani circled the room. She opened the closet door, moved on to the bathroom, and pulled the shower curtain aside. Satisfied, she changed into her pajamas and slipped beneath the covers.

*S*itting in the family room, Ellie waited until it was all quiet upstairs.

"Do you think this is normal? Her fear of the dark."

"Why do you think she's afraid?" Pad asked. "Ryan is locked up and can't hurt her, and we're here too."

"Didn't you hear the doors opening and closing up there and then finally growing quiet?"

Paul nodded. "How was she this morning?"

"After I woke her up and suggested she take a shower, I know she locked herself in. How long before she feels safe again?"

Ellie grasped Pad's hand. "When I was assaulted, I was furious. You were more worried than I was. But Dani, she's scared."

"It's a little different. When you were in the midst of your trauma, you had a support system. Dani was isolated. It was part of Ryan's plan to make her dependent on him for everything. It's a way of psychologically breaking her down," Paul said.

"It's going to take her time," Pad spoke softly. "But you're doing everything right. What she'll really need is to talk to a professional."

"I'll ask Judy to give you a few names. Maybe you can pass them along when she's receptive," Paul suggested.

Ellie chewed her bottom lip. "I guess I wasn't thinking about the differences between our situations. I've told Dani she can stay as long as she likes."

Paul said, "She told me she wants us to be friends for now, nothing more."

Ellie watched him. "How do you feel?"

"I wanted to shout at her and tell her not to let the bastard win. I care for her and want to have the chance to show her." Paul jumped up. "How do I show her if she won't go out with me?"

"Did she say she didn't want to spend any time with you at all?" Ellie asked.

"She didn't want to go out on a date with me."

Pad snorted. "Bro, you're about as obtuse as they come. I know how you feel about her, but she isn't even twenty-four hours away from the horror she went through, and you're asking her out. What were you thinking?"

Paul groaned. "Wow. You're right. How could I have been so stupid? I rushed her."

"Do ya think?" Ellie scolded him. "I know by the way she looks, she's running scared. I'm trying to get her to feel comfortable about riding in a car without a police escort, and you just want to pick up where you left off. Do you want to push her away?"

Paul hung his head. "No. Of course not." He looked up at Ellie. "What do I do?"

"You wait. And then you wait some more. Dani will know when she's ready to date you."

"How long do you think it will take?"

Pad said, "Paul, if you think this will be on your timetable, you don't know jack about women."

Ellie laughed. "Ask Pad, he's an expert on waiting for this woman."

Paul looked at them. "You're right. Dani is worth waiting for. If you get the chance, Ellie, will you tell her when she's ready, she needs to give me a neon sign?"

Ellie wanted to laugh. Paul looked almost comical. But in matters of the heart, Ellie knew to tread lightly to not hurt anyone's feelings.

"When Dani is ready, you'll know. But on the off chance you don't pick up on the signals, I'll make sure Pad clues you in."

Paul shook his head. "It's getting late. I'm gonna take off. Pad, do you need a lift home?"

Pad looked at Ellie. "I think I'm gonna bunk on the couch tonight. If Dani wakes up, maybe she'll feel better knowing there's a cop in the house."

"But she's already gone to bed?"

Ellie smiled and steered Paul toward the door. "You know I can tell her before I go to bed. Relax. We'll take care of Dani, and you get a good night's sleep. Tomorrow's a new day."

Paul gave Ellie a quick hug. "You're a really nice person. The first time I met you, I thought you were way too stubborn for your own good. But now, I'm glad you and Pad are, well, good friends."

At a loss for words, Ellie watched Paul.

"He's got the weight of the world on his heart." From behind, Pad wrapped his arms around Ellie.

"If he gets impatient, he'll blow it with Dani."

"Just like I almost blew it with you?" Pad nuzzled her neck.

Ellie sighed. "I'm glad you came back to Loudon."

"Me too." Pad turned her around to kiss her properly. "Now, what about setting our wedding date?"

Ellie murmured, "Later," and deepened the kiss.

21

----

or Dani, life was starting to get back into a routine. She had stopped in at What's Perkin' and brought a small pastry box back to Ellie's. Dani set it on the kitchen counter just as Ellie came in.

"What's this?" Ellie peeked inside. "Are you kidding! Cinnamon buns?"

Dani laughed. "Cari insisted I bring them. She said they're your favorite."

"I love everything with cinnamon. Let's split one over coffee before I open the gallery. You can fill me in on your chat with Mom."

"Mine or yours?"

"What do you mean? Your mom's at What's Perkin'?"

"Yup, she was handling the counter like a pro."

"I thought your parents were leaving tomorrow and were spending today house hunting?" Ellie cut an oversized bun in half and licked a dollop of icing from her thumb.

"Dad is on a conference call with his boss. Mom skipped out. She really likes the café and wanted to see your mom. From what she said, they got slammed by a tour bus, and she jumped in."

Ellie laughed. "Sounds like your mom is getting seduced by the family business."

"What is it about the McKennas? Do you put a spell on people to lure them into the fold, and then we don't want to leave?" Dani poured freshly brewed coffee into two mugs and set them on the kitchen table.

Ellie put a plate in front of Dani and joined her.

"We do. It's a top secret spell but un-breakable." Ellie laughed so hard, her hands flying, and she knocked into her mug, spilling a small amount on the table. Sopping it up with a napkin, she said, "I really think it's my mother. People seem to gravitate toward her. She has a big heart and has never met anyone she didn't consider a friend."

Dani speared a hunk of bun. "I've decided to go back to work tomorrow."

"That's wonderful news."

"I do have a favor to ask."

Ellie cocked her head to one side.

"Would you mind if I stayed here a little longer? I'm sure you want your privacy, but I was in the apartment this morning, and to be honest, I got spooked."

"The place is big enough for us both, and I'm enjoying your company too."

"I know it probably sounds dumb and"—she tapped her forehead—"Derek is safely behind bars. My therapist says it's residual stress, like PTSD. I need to give it time and deal with my feelings."

"Take all the time you need." Ellie's eyes twinkled over the rim of her mug. "Can you keep a secret?"

"You're asking me if I can keep a secret? Are you forgetting, I didn't tell anyone about my past for how long?"

"True."

Dani leaned in. "Tell all. Is it something to do with Pad?"

"We set the date, and you're the first person I've told."

Dani flopped back into the chair. "Oh, Ellie. That's wonderful. You haven't said anything to Cari or Kate?"

With a shake of her head, Ellie said, "Nope. We decided on an October wedding."

"This year?" Dani's hand flew to her lips. "What can I do to help?"

"Will you make the cake? Some unique flavor combination, just for us?"

"I would be honored to make your wedding cake. Do you think Kate will be disappointed you asked me?"

Ellie giggled. "No, she says your cakes are better than hers."

"Really? She said that?" Dani shook her head. "I promise the cake will be so amazing it will be the only thing you remember about your wedding day."

Ellie let out a belly laugh. "I hope I remember something more than the cake."

Dani looked sideways at Ellie. "Why haven't you told your family?"

"They're going to want us to have a big wedding, and I want something small and intimate. Maybe even outdoors with a tent."

"In October? It might be a little chilly."

"I've already looked at tents, and we can get heaters. The guests will be comfortable, and I'll book the White House just in case the weather is really bad."

"October can be a beautiful month with the foliage and all." Dani grabbed a pen and legal-sized pad. "You're going to need lots of lists.

October is right around the corner. Have you thought about a venue?"

"Dani, chill. Anyone would think you were the bride. And to answer your question, yes, I have chosen a venue. Pad and I are going to see Aunt Winnie tonight and ask if we can get married in her flower gardens."

"You know she'll say yes. She'd do anything for Pad, and Winnie absolutely adores you. And then your parents?"

"I'm going to see if Mom and Ray will meet us at Winnie's. I'd rather have one conversation and get all the questions answered at one time."

"You can count on me."

"Dani, I hope you understand, but since it's such a small affair, I'm only going to have Kate as an attendant."

Dani hugged Ellie. "Kate should be your matron of honor. I'm thrilled to help and, of course, be there when you say I do."

"You're my best friend. You'll be involved every step of the way."

The gallery doorbell chimed, and Ellie went to check on her customer, leaving Dani to start dreaming up new flavor combinations.

Dani wrote down Ellie's favorites: vanilla, chocolate, coconut, fruit filling, and buttercream frosting.

She studied the list. "What if I take a white chocolate cake, pair it with a raspberry filling, frost it with a vanilla buttercream, and then dust it with coconut flakes? I wonder if it would be too sweet?"

Then Dani jotted down a few menu ideas. Her gaze wandered to the window, and her thoughts drifted to Paul. He had stopped over every day for the last few weeks for a short visit. Dani looked forward to the end of the day. She was excited to tell him about going back to work. One more step in her recovery.

Her counselor had helped. She carried a heavy dose of guilt about Ellie being caught up in the mayhem of her abduction, and Derek's lack of remorse for her kidnapping was a lot to deal with. At the last meeting, she had asked

Deborah, her counselor, what she could have done differently. Deborah pointed out Dani had zero control over what Derek did or didn't do. Knowing Deborah was right didn't make it easier for Dani to forgive herself. Ellie's wedding would be just what she needed to force the darkness away and give her hope for the future.

Paul. Are my feelings for you based on gratitude? Dani stared out the window, not seeing the view. She longed to talk about these crazy repetitive thoughts looping in her brain. She grabbed her phone.

"Hi, Mom. What are you doing?"

Mom sounded out of breath. "Hi, honey."

"Did I catch you in the middle of something?" Dani asked.

"No, I was just going up the stairs to your apartment."

"My apartment? Why?"

"I wanted to give it a deep clean. When you're ready to move back in, it will be ready."

"Oh."

"Dani, you are planning on moving back into your apartment, aren't you?"

"Well, of course I am." Dani hesitated. "But Ellie said I can stay as long as I want with her. She likes the company."

Mom didn't say anything, and Dani couldn't stand the silence. "Do you think I'm wrong?"

"You need to do what is best for you in your own time."

"I gotta go, Mom. I'll call you later." Before Mom could answer, Dani disconnected and laid the phone on the table.

"Hey, did I hear you talking to someone?" Ellie plunked down.

"I was talking to Mom. She's at my apartment, cleaning."

"Why are you irritated?"

"Wouldn't you be? I mean, it's a little presumptuous for her to assume I'm going to be moving back soon. She should have asked me first."

Dani rapped her fingers on the tabletop. "I'm going over there."

"Okay, do you want company? I can close the gallery."

"No. Closing down at a moment's notice isn't necessary. Besides, I need to talk to Mom."

Dani tried to force a smile. "Don't worry. I'll call you later."

"Dani, you're strong. And remember, you were always safe in the apartment."

Dani's head bobbed. "It's not the apartment. It's the quiet when the shop is closed. I feel isolated."

Ellie hugged Dani. "I'll be here when you get back."

*D*ani's hand rested on the car door handle. Taking a deep breath, like her therapist suggested, she pushed open the door. Hearing the chirp of the door lock on the car, she dashed up the stairs where her apartment door was open wide.

She peeked inside. "Hey, Mom. Are you in here?"

A muffled "Yes" came from the back.

Dani went toward her bedroom. She found Mom on all fours. Grinning, she said, "No dust bunnies under the bed. I've finished dusting and vacuuming, and the last thing to do is clean the refrigerator and wash the windows."

"You didn't need to do all of this, but it's really nice to see the apartment have the Mom sparkle," she teased. "How about I make some tea and we can visit?"

"Sounds perfect. I'll run downstairs and see what we can have with it."

Panic strangled Dani's heart. "Mom?"

She was halfway down the stairs. "I'll be right back."

Dani closed the door and watched her mother slip through the café door.

She paced the small living room.

"You're safe. No one can hurt you here.

This is your apartment and you're safe." Dani continued to chant to herself over and over again. Slowly, her heart rate slowed, and her breathing returned to a semi-normal pattern. She glanced out the window and then at the clock. What was taking Mom so long?

Dani looked at her phone, tempted to dial the café. She was overreacting. Perched on the edge of the straight-backed chair, she waited, her feet tapping at a furious pace.

Footsteps were ascending the stairs, and Dani peered out the small glass in the door. She flung it open.

"Oh. You startled me," Mom said.

"What took you so long? I was starting to think you got lost."

Mom walked into the apartment and turned the burner off under the whistling teakettle.

Mom sat on the sofa and patted the cushion. "Dani, sit down."

Dani folded her hands in her lap, sitting ramrod straight.

Mom smoothed Dani's stray curl. "When you were a little girl, I had such a hard time keeping your curls under control."

Dani pushed up her glasses. "It's easier now. I wear these."

"I have to admit, I was surprised to see you wearing glasses. As soon as you were old enough, you convinced me to let you wear contacts. I didn't expect you to go back to glasses."

Dani shrugged. "Things change."

Mom lowered her voice. "I'm sorry Dad and I weren't here for you when you needed us."

"It's not your fault. How could you have known? I didn't tell you what was going on."

"I didn't exactly make it easy for you. Always touting Derek's wonderful qualities—well, what he wanted us to see. I blame myself."

"For what?"

"If I hadn't talked to him, he wouldn't have found you."

"Mom." Dani grasped her mother's hand. "He was determined. Eventually, he would have found me, and maybe the outcome would have been worse. There's no way to know."

"Paul's a good man."

"He's very sweet. I'm lucky; I've made some really good friends here."

"Is he more than a friend?" Mom asked.

"We went out a couple of times, and he's very handsome. It's confusing. I'm not sure if the feelings I have for Paul are simply because of what he did to find me, and nothing more."

"Dani, when he looks at you, he's not Officer Greene." Mom giggled.

"It's not the right time for me to get involved with anyone. I'm damaged goods."

"Did… did something happen you haven't told me?"

Dani's mouth flew open. "Derek didn't physically assault me. I was his verbal punching bag for a very long time. I don't exactly have a good barometer when it comes to relationships."

"What happened with Derek wasn't your fault. No one knows how to deal with an abusive situation until they're in it and they find the inner fortitude to make a change. Be proud of yourself. You left him. As far as the kidnapping, who would have dreamed he would go to such extremes?"

Dani's head rested in her hands. "I didn't."

"What are you going to do to prove to yourself the past won't dictate your future?"

Dani fell silent. Mom set two mugs and a plate with a small variety of mini cookies on the little round coffee table. Dani poured some tea into her mug. She nibbled on a butter cookie.

"Mom, when is Dad going home?"

"Tomorrow and I'm going to stay on and keep house hunting. Why?"

"Do you think you could stay here, with me?" Dani's voice broke. "I think if you were here, I could move back and find my rhythm again."

"I can move my stuff over today. Do you want to stay here tonight?"

"I'm not saying it'll be easy, but with you here it will be easier."

Mom smiled. "It'll be nice for us to have some time together. It's been a while since we've lived under the same roof."

Dani chuckled. "But you don't get to time my showers. I pay the bills around here."

"I wouldn't dream of it. Well, if we're moving in today, I should get the fridge cleaned and then restocked."

"We should finish the cookies first. It's going to be a busy afternoon." Dani exhaled. This is the first step to taking back my life, and I don't have to do it alone.

*E*llie's gallery phone rang, and she looked at the caller ID. "Hey, Dani. How's it going at the apartment?"

"I'm going to stay here tonight, with Mom."

"You don't need to rush if you're not ready."

"Ellie, you've been terrific, but Mom made me realize I need to face the fear and work through it. It works out so that while she's hunting for a house, she'll stay with me."

"Dani, time with your mom is just what you need."

"Thanks, and besides, I'm sure your handsome fiancé will enjoy some time alone with you. You have a wedding to plan."

"We do. I'll call you tomorrow and fill you in on the details since we're doing the parent announcement tonight. Wish us luck."

"You won't need luck, Ellie, you have love."

Ellie shot a text to Pad: Dani moved back to

her apartment. You might want to pass along the news to your partner.

Dani was waiting for her parents to arrive for dinner. She was serving pasta carbonara when she heard someone calling her. She whipped her head over her shoulder.

She cautiously opened the door. A genuine smile crept over her face and reached her eyes. "Paul, what are you doing?"

"Mind if I come in?"

"Sure." Dani held the door open as Paul entered carrying a huge bouquet of wildflowers and juggling a bottle of wine and a six-pack of beer.

He handed her the flowers and kissed her cheek. "I heard you've relocated. I hope you don't mind I've dropped by uninvited."

"You have an open invitation." Dani set the

vase in the middle of the coffee table. "The flowers are beautiful. Thank you."

Paul held up the wine and beer. "I'll put these in the fridge."

Dani's eyes followed him as he walked across the small room. "I didn't expect to see you tonight."

Paul said, "Hey, I'm sorry. I didn't know you were having company. I'll get out of your way."

"No, stay. It's Mom and Dad. I'm making pasta," Dani teased. "I happen to know how much you love pasta."

A car door slammed and Dani jumped. Fear flickered in her eyes. Paul said, "It's okay. I'm here."

Dani rushed to the windows. "They're here. I'll be right back. I'm going to help Mom with her luggage."

"I'm right behind you."

Paul greeted Mr. and Mrs. Michaels.

"It's nice to see you both. I dropped by and Dani's invited me to stay for dinner."

Dani noticed the quick look exchanged between her parents and wished she could say something to them. "You know me, I cook enough for the neighborhood."

Paul grabbed Mrs. Michaels' bags.

Mom spoke over her shoulder. "Paul, we're thrilled you could join us. Dani's told us all about you."

For her mother's ears alone, Dani said, "Stop pushing, Mom."

Mom smiled from ear to ear. "Moms always know what's best for their daughters."

22

Paul put the luggage in the bedroom. Dani handed him a bottle of beer when he returned to the living room.

"Paul, Dani tells us you've been doing some renovation on the family home. Where do you find the time?" Mom asked.

Dani cringed. "Mom, don't pester Paul with questions."

"Dani, it's fine." He took a swig of beer.

"Mrs. Michaels."

"Oh, please. Don't call me Mrs. anything.

I'm Olivia, and my husband is Mason."

Paul smiled. "All right, Olivia, fire away."

Dani cringed. "Dad?"

"Sorry, honey, you know your mother." He held up his hands in a grand gesture of helplessness.

For the next ten minutes, Mom peppered Paul with questions about his family, education, friends, and job. Apparently satisfied, she smiled at Dani.

"I'm feeling a little hungry. What time did you say we're eating?"

Dani's cheeks flamed pink. "Since you're finished with your interrogation of my friend, I'd say anytime."

Paul laughed. "Don't worry, Dani. I don't scare easily."

Dad stood up. "Liv, if you're done, let's eat." He looked at Paul. "Dani's pasta carbonara is as pretty close to heaven as it gets."

"I'm reserving judgment." He winked at Dani. "Her red sauce was amazing."

Mom cocked her eyebrow. "You made red sauce?"

"Yes, Mother, I made red sauce."

"Hmm, interesting. Paul?"

"Yes?"

"You can call me Liv."

Dani did a double take as she set a large pasta bowl in the middle of the table and then a smaller bowl with greens near her mother. Paul could call her Liv. That's an interesting twist.

Dad surveyed the table. "No bread?"

"Hold your horses, Pop. It's coming." Dani placed a bread basket next to her father. "Just the way you like it, loaded with butter and garlic."

Dad rubbed his hands together and pulled back the tea towel. He selected the crusty end piece and sank his teeth in. Flakes of crust landed on his dark T-shirt. Closing his eyes, he said, "Liv, why can't you make bread like this?"

"I taught Dani everything I know, but then

she did her own thing. Heaven only knows how she tweaked my recipes."

Dani passed the basket to Paul. "You'd better take what you want now. Typically, Dad eats more bread than anything else."

Paul set two slices on this plate and accepted the salad bowl. "Thank you, Olivia."

Dani passed the pasta bowl. Paul placed a generous portion on her plate before filling his. Dani noticed Mom was keeping a close watch on Paul.

Thankfully, as the meal wore on, her parents stopped scrutinizing Paul and focused on dinner. Dad took the last slice of bread and rubbed it over his plate. He looked up.

"No sense in leaving any specks of sauce behind for the dishwasher. Your mother never makes pasta since you moved out."

Mom said, "If I made it as often as your dad would like, we'd never eat anything but pasta."

Paul grinned. "And what's wrong with pasta every day? It's my idea of good eating."

Dani was pleased to discover it was comfortable for Paul to share dinner with her parents.

Everyone was looking at Dani. "What?"

"Were you daydreaming?" Paul teased.

"No, I was just thinking about what's going on at Winnie's house."

Paul grinned. "I guess Ellie told you?"

"Of course, she did. I guess Pad told you."

"Who told who what?" Mom asked.

"Ellie and Pad are telling her parents and his aunt they want to get married in Winnie's garden this October."

"Two months from now?" Mom looked at Dani. "How will they ever get a wedding planned? Weddings take months, sometimes more than a year to plan."

"They want a small wedding with family and a few close friends. Ellie doesn't like a lot of attention and hubbub. Frankly, I agree with her. Marriage isn't about some big, fancy, expensive day. It's about the promise of love and the lifetime commitment they'll share." Dani pushed back from the table.

"Dani," Mom spoke softly. "Don't be irritated with me. I was just surprised. Ellie comes from a big family, and they seem to have many friends. I thought it would be a larger affair."

"It's fine, Mom. Just don't say anything to Ellie. It's her day, and it will be her vision."

"I won't say a word."

Dani finished clearing the table and asked, "Who wants dessert?"

"I don't know about your parents, but I saved room."

Ellie tightened her hands on the steering wheel. "Thanks for letting me drive. I'm nervous to tell everyone we've set a date and ask Winnie if we can get married at her place."

"Why? Everyone is expecting us to announce the date." Pad's voice was soothing to her jangling nerves.

"You still want to get married in October, right? Because if you've changed your mind, we can wait." Pad watched Ellie continue to chew on her lower lip.

"No. I want to get married this year, and October is beautiful in the Northeast. It'll be perfect. But will our families think we're rushing it? We've only been engaged for a few months."

"El, I've loved you from the moment I carried you up the stairs and you bled all over my favorite shirt, and if you were honest, you fell in love with me shortly thereafter. It'll be almost two years since I came back from Scotland. No one is going to think we're rushing. Relax and look forward to seeing their happy faces when we tell them the good news."

Ellie stopped the car at the bottom of Winnie's long driveway. She pulled his face to her, kissing him lightly on the lips. "I hate to tell you this, but I fell in love with you the first time you walked through the door of The Looking Glass. I never believed in love at first sight, until that moment. But you accepted me and never wanted me to be anyone else. We are perfect partners."

Pad pulled her closer and sank into the kiss until a honking horn broke their concentration.

"Hey, you two." Ray's window slid down. "Are you coming up to the house or should we have Winnie come down here?"

Heat filled Ellie's cheeks. "Right behind you."

Pad squeezed her hand. "You know they'll be as happy as we are."

"Let's get this party started, Mr. Stone."

Ellie parked in the half circle, next to her parents. Pad hopped out and ran to get her door.

"Hi, kids." Cari smiled. "I see Ellie had to drive tonight."

Pad grinned. "You have to love our little control freak."

"I do and I also know driving calms her down. I wonder…"

Cari was interrupted by Winnie floating down the walk. "Finally, you're all here. Please, come in. I have wine and a few nibbles, and then we can have a light supper if you're still hungry."

Pad gestured for Mom and Ray to go first. Giving Pad's hand a tug, Ellie wanted to skip up the walkway but was glad he kept her grounded.

Winnie escorted them to the sunroom, and as usual, she had laid out an impressive spread of food and wine and beer.

"Pad, be a dear and pour the wine, please?"

"Of course, Auntie."

Small talk floated while Ellie and Pad passed the drinks and everyone filled their plates.

"I may have gone overboard. I made a variety of everything."

Cari nibbled a tiny piece of bread with a

creamy filling on top. "Everything is delicious, Winnie."

Ellie and Pad sat side by side on the sofa. Pad cleared his throat. "I'm sure you're wondering why Ellie and I asked for us to gather tonight." He pecked her cheek.

Ellie sparkled and Pad beamed. "We've set a date for our wedding, and Aunt Winnie, we'd like to get married in your garden."

"Oh, Ellie, Pad," Cari cried. "We've been anxiously waiting for this announcement."

Winnie wiped a tear from her eye. "Of course, you can get married in the garden. Do you have a date in mind?"

Ellie chimed in. "The third Saturday in October."

Cari choked on her wine. "What year?"

Ellie giggled. "This year."

Winnie clasped her hands together and let the tears stream down her face. "This is wonderful. We must get started planning right away. There is much to be done."

Pad said, "Auntie, it's going to be a very

small wedding. Just family and a few close friends."

"It'll be under fifty guests, including all of us, of course."

"Ellie, you don't want a large wedding with everyone you and Pad know? Savoring the parties and showers leading up to the big day?" Cari was stunned.

"Mom, everyone we love will be invited."

Ellie looked between Mom and Winnie. "So. Are you up for a wedding?"

Winnie dashed out of the room. Ellie looked at Pad, who seemed as confused as she felt. She came back in with a large pad of paper and a pen.

"Okay, what are the details? Then we can make a plan." Winnie held the pen hovering above the paper.

"Winnie, we already wrote everything down. Pad?"

Pad handed his aunt and Cari a folder. "Ellie's got it all under control. Everything is in here from the guest list to flowers, food, tent rental, and tables and chairs."

Cari and Winnie opened the folders and glanced at the spreadsheet and order forms inside.

"Ellie, you did think of everything. What do you need from us?"

"Mom, I'm going to see when Kate's free, and I'd like to go dress shopping with you, Kate, Winnie, and Dani. Kate's my matron of honor and Dani isn't in the wedding, but I'd like for her to wear something special."

Winnie dabbed her eye with a cloth napkin. "You want me to go dress shopping with you?"

"I do, Winnie. If it wasn't for you, Pad and I might not have found our way back to each other."

"You were destined to be together. I just gave you a few nudges from time to time."

Pad snorted. "Auntie, I don't think sending me pictures of Ellie from your cell phone was subtle."

Winnie laughed. "And here I thought I was so subtle."

Ray stood up. "I'd like to propose a toast."

Ray waited until everyone had a glass in hand. "To Pad and Ellie. May your wedding day be filled with love and laughter, but most of all may Mother Nature smile down on you."

Ellie and Pad clinked glasses. Ellie whispered to Pad, "I don't care what the weather is, I can't wait to marry you in Winnie's magical garden."

Pad's brow arched. "Magical?"

Ellie nodded. "The first time I sat in the garden with Winnie, I knew that's where I wanted to marry you. For me, there was no turning back."

Pad entwined his arm with hers. "You know my parents got married there too."

"I remember Winnie told me the story. In a way, all the people we hold dear will be with us." She kissed his lips. "Like I said, magical."

*E*llie wandered around The Looking Glass, straightening a few items here and there. She was killing time until everyone gathered to go dress shopping. The group had grown to include her sisters-in-law, Abby and Sara. Kate was going to meet them at the wedding salon since it was halfway between Crescent Lake and Loudon. This way, she could get home easier since little Ben was in the midst of his terrible twos. He didn't take kindly to his mother being away from him for long periods of time.

She heard the back door and her mother calling her. Ellie hurried into the kitchen. Mom, Winnie, and Dani were waiting for her.

"Good morning, Ellie. Abby and Sara are right behind me. Are you ready to go?" Winnie asked.

Ellie picked up her handbag and shoes. "I'm so excited. Was everything okay at What's Perkin'?"

"Olivia has been a godsend. She volunteered to help out today and wanted me to tell you to enjoy being pampered."

A horn honked from the driveway. "The girls." Ellie grabbed her keys. "I'll drive."

Winnie looped her arm through Ellie's. "I have a little surprise for you."

"You do?"

Winnie and Ellie walked through the back door, and a shiny black limousine was parked at the end of the driveway. "I thought it might be fun if we could all ride together."

Ellie gasped. "You shouldn't have. It must have been expensive."

Winnie winked. "Don't give it a second thought. You know my art has been selling extremely well in recent years, thanks to this wonderful gallery owner I know."

Ellie hugged Winnie tightly. "Promise me this will be the last extravagance."

"Pishposh. You'll have to learn, Ellie, I spend my money the way I want to." With a wave of her hand, Winnie said, "Ladies, shall we?"

An impeccably dressed driver held the door and helped each lady inside. Once settled, they discovered there was a full bar of bottled water, soft drinks, and champagne on ice.

"Champagne?" Ellie exclaimed.

"We'll want to celebrate later today. We might as well have it on ice now."

Ellie tilted her head to one side. "Huh?"

"My dear Eleanor, we'll have to celebrate when you find the perfect dress." Winnie gave her a playful nudge.

"Oh, right," Ellie giggled.

The ride to the bridal salon was filled with laughter and stories of Ellie as a little girl. Ellie changed seats to sit next to Dani.

"I want you to find a dress today."

"I don't need anything special to wear."

"Oh, but you do. I want you to make a certain cop drool." Ellie grinned. "And then maybe you two will get back on track."

Dani whispered, "I think I'm ready for him to ask me out again."

Ellie squealed. "Why don't you ask him?"

"You're kidding. I could never!" Dani exclaimed.

"I thought you told Paul you'd let him know when you were ready to date again?"

"I did, sort of, I guess," Dani drawled.

"Then send him a text and ask him to go on a picnic. It'll be fun."

Dani hesitated and then pulled her phone out of her bag. She looked at Ellie. "Should I?"

"Go ahead." Ellie's eyes sparkled. "You know you want to."

"Since you set your wedding date, you've gotten pushy."

"Something like that, but only when I know my intended victims are right for each other."

"I'm ripping the Band-Aid off."

She typed: Interested in a late afternoon picnic tomorrow in the park?

Then before she could delete it, Ellie leaned over and tapped the send button.

"Oh, and by the way…" Ellie winked. "This is a date for two."

The limo slowed. Ellie peered out the window and shrieked, "There's Kate!"

The back door opened, and the driver was there to help each lady out of the car. Ellie thanked him and whispered to Abby and Sara, "This is pretty cool."

"Welcome to The Elegant Bride. My name is Natasha, and I will be at your service." Her sharp eye surveyed the group and zoomed in on Ellie. "You must be the bride?"

Ellie noted Natasha was dressed entirely in black. Her makeup was flawless, her hair secured in a tight bun.

Ellie's beamed. "Yes, in seven weeks."

Natasha nodded. "Lovely. I'm confident we will find you the perfect dress. In addition to your dress, who else needs gowns?"

Ellie's arm swept the group. "Everyone needs something special to wear." Ellie pushed Cari and then Kate and Winnie forward. "This is my mother, and my sister, the matron of honor, and my fiancé's aunt. In addition, we need the perfect dress for my best friend and my two sisters-in-law."

"Let me get two more stylists to assist." Natasha slipped away and Ellie twirled in place before stopping to steady herself.

"Here's the game plan. I'll choose a few dresses. Kate, I'd like you to wear burgundy, style of your choice. Mom and Winnie, anything that complements Kate and be comfortable; it's going to be quite a day. Abby, Sara, and Dani, pick out a few things and try them on. I'd like to see them, but whatever you like is fine with me, and I'm paying for everyone's dress, no argument, so price is not a consideration today."

Abby, Sara, and Dani protested. "You're not spending a penny on us."

"Ellie, if you insist, I won't buy a dress." Dani's eyes narrowed. "We are all perfectly capable of buying a dress."

Natasha returned and introduced the two women. "This is Fiona and she'll work with your sister, mother, and aunt, and Sally will assist the rest of the ladies."

"Let's try on some dresses, and we'll all show off our favorites in a bit." Ellie's voice caught in her throat. "Above all, have fun."

Ellie fingered the skirt of a gown. "This is overwhelming. I'm not sure where to begin."

"Let's start with color. You would look lovely in a soft white to pale pink. Were you thinking lace or silk, perhaps?"

"I love the idea of soft white, and the wedding is outdoors. I'd like to be comfortable and warm as the day might be cool. I don't want a long train. Classic, elegant, and it needs to make Pad's eyes pop and jaw drop."

"All right. I'll choose a couple for you, and you can model them for your family. And for a veil?"

"It needs to be short. I'm more of a minimalist."

Natasha silently slipped away, leaving Ellie to wander in the accessory department.

Natasha made several trips to the bride's

dressing room. The area was on a platform with chairs arranged in a semicircle. Just beyond the chairs, there were five floor-to-ceiling mirrors for viewing at all angles. Ellie's family gathered. "I know Ellie wanted you to choose your dresses now; however, the bride should choose her dress first. She will set the tone for the event." Natasha held the door open wide. "Ellie, if you're ready, we can begin."

"Mom?"

Cari said, "I'm ready, Pixie."

Ellie slipped into the first dress. It had long sleeves, a high scooped neckline, and was covered in lace. Ellie waited while Natasha fastened the long row of buttons. She tried not to tug on the bodice.

She stepped onto the riser where everyone was gathered around to look. All eyes were on her. Ellie squirmed.

"Ellie?" Mom said. "What do you think?"

Ellie shrugged her shoulders. "It's pretty but itchy. I don't think I would last five minutes."

Natasha said, "You must be comfortable." She gathered up the skirt and helped Ellie into the dressing room.

Dress after dress came and went. As each dress was discarded, Ellie's frustration grew. She stepped out again. Cari's hand flew to her mouth, suppressing a laugh. "I don't think this is the right dress, Ellie. It looks too matronly."

Ellie looked at her reflection and started to cry. "We've looked at millions of dresses, and I haven't had one that I love." She wailed, "We're going to have to postpone the wedding if I can't find a dress."

Natasha laid a comforting hand on Ellie's arm. "I won't give up until we find your dress."

"Seriously, do you have any dresses I haven't tried on yet?"

"Please, don't worry. We have plenty of dresses."

Natasha waved to Fiona. She pointed in a direction of the salon Ellie hadn't gone into and asked her to bring out two specific gowns.

"Ellie, let's get you out of this dress. I have a good feeling about the next one."

Natasha emptied the room of all the discarded dresses and Fiona knocked softly on the door. Natasha held up the two new selections.

"Which one shall you try on first?"

"This one." Ellie selected an ivory off-the-shoulder scalloped lace dress with a chapel length train.

Natasha nodded and unzipped the gown, allowing Ellie to step into it. She zipped up the back and then fastened the lace-covered buttons and adjusted the long lace sleeves.

Ellie watched as Natasha smoothed the sweetheart neckline. The silk lining had a blush of pink, adding just a hint of sweetness to the overall look.

Ellie sucked in a breath. Blinking back tears, she whispered, "I think this is the dress."

"One more touch." Natasha added a short veil with a floral clip to Ellie's hair. She said,

"You look beautiful. Are you ready to show your mother?"

Ellie couldn't speak. She wiped the tears from her cheeks. "I am."

Ellie stepped onto the platform. She could have heard a pin drop if the entire salon wasn't covered in plush gray carpeting.

Ellie moved slowly from side to side and then turned to look at the back of the dress. Cari stepped up and cupped Ellie's cheeks in her hands. "Is this your dress, Pixie?"

Tears clung to Ellie's lashes. "Yes, this is the dress I'm going to wear when I marry Padraic Stone."

23

Butterflies danced in Dani's stomach. For the third time, she examined the contents of the picnic cooler. What must Paul think, me asking him out?

"Dani, what time is Paul coming by to pick you up?" Mom asked.

"He said six." Dani glanced at the wall clock. "I expect him any…"

A knock on the door interrupted Dani. "Guess who?"

Mom teased, "Don't keep the young man waiting."

Dani pulled open the door. Paul was leaning against the handrail. "Well, hello there. Are you ready?"

"Hello. Right on time, as always. I need to get the cooler, and we can go."

Paul walked inside and greeted Olivia. "Hello, Liv. How goes the house hunt?"

"I put in an offer on a house this morning. We're waiting to hear if it's accepted."

"Good for you. Where is it?"

"It's out on Green Lake, a few houses down from Shane and Abby's home. Mason really loved the place when we stayed with them. It made sense to concentrate my search in the area."

"Mom, we're going to head out. You can tell Paul all about it when we get home. I don't want to miss the sunset."

"You two have fun."

Paul picked up the cooler. "Did you pack enough for an army?" Laughing, he held the door for Dani. She grabbed a sweater from the sofa and waved to her mom.

"I couldn't decide on what to pack, so I packed a little of everything."

Strolling down the sidewalk, Paul said, "I was happy to get your text."

Dani looked out of the corner of her eye. "I'm happy you said yes. Something Ellie said yesterday made me realize I needed to let you know I was ready, you know, to date."

Paul chuckled. "Texting is a good step. I'm hoping I get a lot more texts. I've had a smile on my face all day."

Dani laughed. "I hope you're looking forward to the company as well as the food."

"You know I'm a sucker for anything you cook or bake. I'm in the café often enough."

Tentatively, Paul reached out for her hand. His hand was warm. A pleasant sensation slid up her arm, and her blood began to hum.

Dani said, "Isn't the park beautiful?"

"Yes, the view is stunning." Paul's lips hovered near her ear. "You look different tonight. Did you change something?"

Dani's looked up through her long dark

lashes. She brushed back brunette curls, and said, "Why?"

"I don't know it's just… you're not wearing glasses."

Dani spread out the blanket and patted it, indicating Paul should sit down next to her.

"I don't need to wear them anymore."

"I thought you needed them to see?" Paul said.

"I'm wearing my contacts again."

"Oh." Paul's thumb caressed her cheek, trailing down her jawline. He tilted her chin up, his lips a breath away from hers.

"I get it. You won't need them ever again." Tenderly, he kissed her once and then again.

Dani whispered, "Thanks to you."

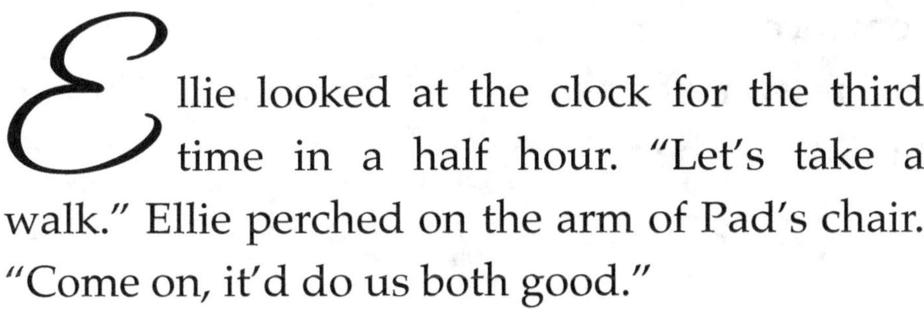

Ellie looked at the clock for the third time in a half hour. "Let's take a walk." Ellie perched on the arm of Pad's chair. "Come on, it'd do us both good."

"Ellie, we don't need to spy on them. They're adults."

"I know. But they're our friends. Don't you want to see how things are going?"

"I'm sure they're fine. Paul is the second-best guy you know, and they have feelings for each other. Frankly, the rest is up to them. There isn't anything you can do to make them fall in love."

"But Padraic Stone, you know better than most, sometimes people need a little encouragement."

"Ellie, you've pushed enough. You got Dani to text him. Now, leave it alone." Pad pulled Ellie onto his lap. "Besides, I can think of other things to do than think about our friends and their romantic date."

Ellie snuggled close. "Are you up for a little romance of our own?"

Instead of answering with words, Pad let his lips do the talking.

∞

*D*ani and Paul strolled around the pond, watching the fish jump, catching water-skimming bugs. The sun was sinking toward the horizon. "It's almost time for sunset." Paul slipped his arms around Dani and held her close.

Dani sighed. Tonight had been amazing. She was ready to embrace her future. Shivering, she pulled her sweater close.

"Are you cold?"

Dani shook her head. "No. I can't remember the last time I enjoyed the sunset this much. You know, my dad always said, 'red sky at night, sailor's delight.'"

"And it means?"

"Tomorrow's going to be another great day."

"What is your dad's saying about hoping for more than one great day?" Paul murmured in her curls.

"Hmm, I don't think he has a saying for

more than one day. We'll need to watch more sunsets to find out."

"I like how that sounds." Paul's lips traveled down the side of her face until they reached the sensitive area behind her ear. Her skin warmed under his feather-like kisses. Dani turned and slid her arms around his neck, pulling his mouth to hers. If he was surprised at the intensity of her kiss, she couldn't tell. Dani's lips demanded more, her tongue teasing and tempting.

Paul groaned and pulled away, giving himself a moment to take a much-needed gulp of air.

"Dani." His voice was hoarse. "Do you think we should stop?"

She answered him by deepening the kiss. "I don't want to stop, but we're in a public park."

He held her close and said, "Do you want to go to my place?"

Dani laid her head on his chest, listening to his heart hammer.

"I hope this doesn't sound like I'm a tease,

but would you mind if we waited? As much as, in the moment, I know exactly what I want, we both need to be sure where this might lead."

Paul cupped her face in his hands. "Dani, I'm not the love 'em and leave 'em kind of guy."

"It's not you I'm worried about, it's me. I want to be sure, for myself, when we do make love I'm not chasing away a demon."

Paul held her close. "Take all the time you need. I'm not going anywhere."

Dani reveled in the warmth his embrace held. She wanted to pour out her heart to Paul. Tell him how she was stupid to get caught up in Derek's lies and then to run and not really resolve the past before falling for him. She wanted to confess she had deep feelings for him, not as the cop who had come to her rescue, but the man who came into the shop with a lopsided grin every morning since she started working at What's Perkin, or the man who held the door for her when taking her out for the first time to a posh restaurant.

"Are you all right?"

Dani tightened her arms around him. "I'm wonderful."

~

Ellie perched on the stool in the kitchen of What's Perkin'. She was sampling cupcakes where each was slightly different than the others. She held up one. "This is the wedding cake."

Dani grinned. "Finally, champagne cake, raspberry filling, and buttercream frosting."

Ellie nodded. "We do, and Dani, you've made this so much fun. I never knew cake tasting could be this way, and Pad has loved the samples too, but truthfully, he loves everything you bake, which is why the final decision is mine."

Ellie looked around. "Is everyone gone?"

Dani smiled. "Yes, Luke left about a half

hour ago, and your mom cut out right after lunch. We have the café to ourselves."

"Good. You'd better spill the beans or I'm going to beat it out of you."

Dani pretended to wipe down the countertop. "I have no idea what you're talking about."

"Paul." Ellie grabbed the rag from her hand. "Rumor has it you've been out every night since your picnic in the park, and I'm assuming he's your date for the wedding?"

Dani sat on a stool with her elbows propped on the counter. "I had no idea what it was like to have a relationship where friendship, trust, respect, and fun were all rolled into one." She closed her eyes and sighed. "And how he can kiss."

"Do tell?"

"Ellie, where is your sense of discretion? I shouldn't be kissing and telling all the details."

Ellie laughed so hard she almost fell off the stool. "I've seen a similar look before on my sister's face. It's the look of pure bliss."

Dani held out her pinky. "I swear. If we were talking baseball, we haven't had a home run. Yet."

"Do you want to get closer?" Ellie asked.

"I think I do. He's a terrific guy, and at first, I was worried my judgment was skewed, and my feelings for him were mixed up with the kidnapping. But what's going on inside of me is something I've never felt before Paul. This is what I imagined real love is supposed to be. He accepts me exactly as I am. He never criticizes what I wear, who my friends are, or if I want some time for myself. He's just chill."

Ellie listened and said, "I'm happy for you. Maybe you'll have an announcement."

"Ellie, let's not get ahead of ourselves. I'm very happy dating a good guy."

"I've told him he won't find anyone any better than you, and he shouldn't wait too long before letting the whole world know he's a lucky guy."

Dani's cheeks flushed pink. "Thanks for the vote of confidence. We need to get back to the last of the wedding details. Your wedding is in less than a week."

Ellie twirled her engagement ring, the light sparkling off the diamonds. "Can you believe it? I thought I'd spend my life as a single girl, and now I'm on the cusp of getting married to the most amazing guy."

"Pad's a lucky guy. When do Kate and Don arrive?"

"Early Thursday. They're staying with Mom. You know she can't wait to see little Ben and spoil him rotten."

"I'm sure he's gotten big since the last time I saw him."

"My godson is adorable, but in the throes of the terrible twos. I just hope when he toddles down the aisle, he doesn't drop the rings."

"We'll tie them to the pillow, and I can have a tiny pair of scissors to snip the thread."

"Dani, you think of everything."

"What other problems need to be solved?" Dani nibbled on the second half of Ellie's cupcake. "Mmm, this is good cake."

Ellie grabbed the plate. "Get your own. From what I've been told, I'll be lucky to eat more than one bite at the wedding."

"I'll make sure to put a slice in the freezer. You can enjoy it when you return from your honeymoon. Which, by the way, you still haven't told me where you're going?"

"I don't know. Actually, I'm having trouble packing. When I asked Pad if I needed warm weather clothes or sweaters, he told me to pack both. Of course, I tried to dig deeper and told him I'd need an extra suitcase, and just to irritate me, he grinned."

"Interesting." Dani tapped her finger on the tip of her nose. "I have an idea. If you want, I'll ask Paul. I bet he'll tell me, never suspecting I'd give you a heads-up."

Ellie wrinkled her brow. "You know, I want it to be a surprise. Whatever he's planning will be wonderful, romantic, and special."

Dani tapped her heart. "Oh, you're making me choke up."

"Then let's clean up the kitchen and drive

out to Winnie's, if you're free. I'll walk through the ceremony with you again and show you where we're getting dressed."

"I'd love to go." Dani scooped up what was left of the cake and taped up a bakery box. "Share these with Pad."

"We'll see." Ellie eased up a corner and tucked a couple of plastic forks inside. "We might get hungry along the way."

Dani washed the mixing bowls and set them to air dry, covering them with a crisp white towel. "Do you guys have any plans tonight?"

Ellie pulled out her phone. "Let me check. What do you have in mind?"

"Paul and I were going to have burgers at his place. I'm sure he'd love to have you guys too."

"Sounds like fun. Let me touch base with Pad." Ellie hit two buttons on her phone.

"Hi, honey. I'm here with Dani. Is Paul with you?"

Ellie hit the speakerphone button.

"Hey, Paul. The girls are on the phone."

Dani and Ellie could hear a rustling sound.

"Hey, girls. What's going on?"

Dani beamed. "Hi, guys."

"Dani and I are headed out to Winnie's to check on a few last-minute details, and Dani mentioned getting together for dinner tonight."

Paul piped up, "A great idea. We can swing by the market and pick up a few more things and meet you at my place around six."

"Ellie, will you have enough time at Aunt Winnie's?" Pad asked. "This morning you mentioned you still had quite a bit to do before Saturday."

"Not to worry. The cake flavor has been chosen, and everything else is good. I think we deserve a normal evening."

Pad joked, "Since when is hanging out with Paul normal?"

Dani grinned at Ellie. "Paul, if you need me to bring something, shoot me a text; otherwise, we'll see you at six."

"Great, looking forward to it," Paul said.

The guys disconnected, and Ellie looked at Dani. "Any chance you've got more cake hidden somewhere? You know how our guys feel about sweets."

"I'm sure we've got something in the walk-in." Dani pulled open the doors and pulled out a small plate of brownies. "If we pick up some coffee ice cream, I can throw together mocha sundaes."

Ellie groaned. "I'm never going to fit into my dress."

Dani laughed. "You can't do much damage in the next few days, and if you're really worried, let's run an extra mile tomorrow."

"Are you offering to run with me?"

"I guess it's the least I could do since I keep tempting you."

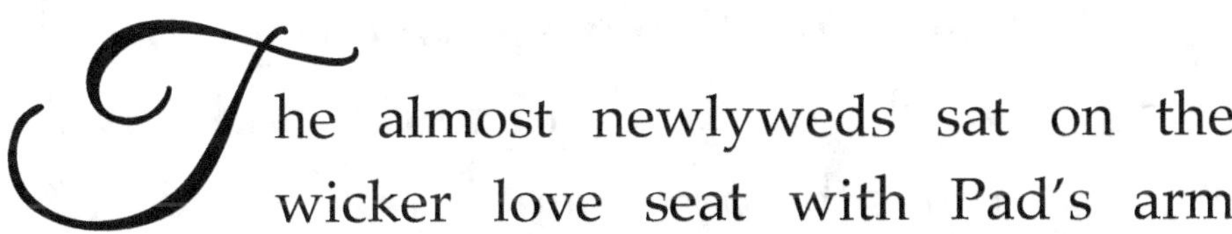

The almost newlyweds sat on the wicker love seat with Pad's arm draped around Ellie's shoulders. Dani and Paul sat on a matching sofa, not quite touching, arm to arm. A tall, wide beeswax candle glowed softly under a hurricane glass. Small plates with a few brownie crumbs lay forgotten on the wicker table.

Ellie patted her stomach. "Everything was delicious."

Pad tucked a stray lock of blond hair behind her ear. "You'll burn off all the extra calories over the next few days. Nervous energy."

Ellie pointed her index finger at Dani. "Guess who agreed to run with me?"

With a hearty chuckle, Paul said, "I'm guessing Dani has been coerced into being your running partner?"

Dani quirked an eyebrow. "Something more you didn't know about me. I used to run all the time."

"I never said you couldn't run; I'm just surprised. Ellie seems to have a way to get people to do what she'd like them to do, and having you pounding the pavement is no exception."

"Hmm." Dani smirked. "You do have a way of pushing me out of my comfort zone."

Ellie shrugged. "No need to thank me. It's a gift."

Pad laughed and pulled Ellie to a standing position. "On that note, I think we should head home. This was fun and a much-needed distraction."

Dani and Paul walked them to the front door. "Can I hitch a ride back to my place?" Dani asked.

"Dani, I'll drive you home. I thought we could sit and enjoy the evening."

Dani's heart fluttered. "Okay." She gave Ellie a quick hug. "I'll see you after work?"

"Sounds good to me. I'll pop into the café at some point."

Ellie hugged Dani again and said goodbye. Dani leaned against the doorjamb, watching Ellie and Pad stroll to the car, lost in conversation.

She sighed dand closed the door as their taillights faded into the dark. Paul took her hand and led her to the porch.

"Why the big sigh?"

"I was wondering what it would be like to be on the verge of marrying the man I love. Every girl dreams about the big day from the time she starts playing with Barbie dolls." Dani leaned into the cushions.

Paul tipped her chin up, and he lowered his mouth to hers. Softly, he said, "Do you still dream?"

"Oh, yes," she whispered, and Paul claimed her lips.

The intensity built. Dani's pulse raced. *So, this is what it's like to have a man's kiss set you on fire.* She yearned to feel his lips on her skin, to discover if the burning heat extended to more than her lips. Paul's lips found the sensitive area. His lips trailed down the hollow of her neck. She arched into him, wanting more.

His voice husky, Paul asked, "Dani, do you want to go upstairs?"

Dani's thoughts raced. "Oh." Her eyes fluttered. She looked at Paul through a haze. "Um."

He placed a finger over her lips. "You don't have to say it."

"Paul."

"I want to make love to you when you don't have a moment's hesitation. For now, I'm happy to have you in my arms and in my home."

"I'm sorry, Paul. Making out like teenagers is leading you on."

"Shh. It's good to feel like a teenager again."

"But—"

"Dani, no buts. I have strong feelings for you, and I'm not going to jeopardize our future by rushing you."

"You… You want a future with me?"

His finger traced a sprinkling of freckles over her nose. "What did you think, I was just some guy with an overactive hormone issue?"

"I didn't. Well, I wouldn't let myself think

about the future. But I really like the sound of it."

"I'm going to drive you home, and let's agree we have plans to see each other tomorrow night."

"Paul, that sounds really nice, but with the wedding this weekend, would you mind if we played it by ear? If Ellie or Cari needs something, I'd like to be available."

Paul pulled Dani into his arms. "You're the nicest person, and just to be clear, I've fallen in love with you."

Dani answered with her lips on his.

24

Dani blinked. Bright sunshine streamed through the blue-and-white-checked curtains. It took several minutes to remember Ellie asked her to spend the night at her place. It was Ellie's wedding day.

She wandered down the hallway, her footsteps muffled by the soft, plush carpet.

Tapping on Ellie's door softly, she said, "Ellie, are you awake?"

"Come in." Dani pushed open the door and discovered Ellie sitting on the window seat in her fuzzy pink bathrobe.

"How long have you been awake?"

"It seems like for hours, but in reality, maybe fifteen minutes. I really hope this day doesn't drag. I should never have said we should get married at three."

Dani plopped onto the bed. "What time is the family getting here?"

"Around ten. The hairdresser is due at eleven, and the photographer will be here at one, then out to Winnie's for pictures of the men, and we arrive promptly at two forty-five."

Dani's smile couldn't be contained. "Since it's just barely seven, are you interested in breakfast and coffee?"

"I'm not sure how much I'll eat, but coffee, absolutely." She looked out the window. "The weatherman is calling for rain. I hope it holds off until after the ceremony."

"The last thing you should worry about is rain. You're marrying the love of your life, your soul mate. Life doesn't get much better than that."

"I know but the pictures…"

"Will be stunning. All anyone is going to see is the love you have for Pad and him for you. And if it does rain, you might see a rainbow. Now that would be a magical photo-op."

Ellie slipped off the bed and danced around the room. "You're right. I don't care what the weather is today. When I go to sleep tonight, I'll be married to the most wonderful man who draws breath." She wagged a finger at Dani. "You can disagree, but Pad is perfect for me."

"Yes, he is." Arms linked, Dani and Ellie twirled. "Come on. I'll make you a cup of coffee, your last as a single woman."

It didn't take long for Ellie's house to be buzzing with women. Ellie's sister and sisters-in-law arrived. Ellie's grandmother Susan came with Cari, who, of course, brought a tray of snacks for those who were hungry.

"When is the hairdresser coming?" Ellie

paced the kitchen, glancing at the clock. Her deep-burgundy toes peeked out from under a white silk robe. "Do you think she got lost?"

Kate grabbed her hands and looked deep into her eyes. "Pixie, breathe. She'll be here and she's not late."

"Katie, I can't be late for my own wedding."

A car door slamming had Ellie dashing toward the window. She announced, "Everything's fine, she's here." Ellie opened the front door before the old brass knocker could be used. "Come in, Nell. We'll go upstairs to my bedroom."

"Hello, everyone." Nell took a look around the room. "Ellie, I hope you don't mind but I brought my cousin, Daisy, as an extra pair of hands."

"Not at all."

Dani stepped in. "Ellie, why don't you and Nell get started on your hair, and I'll show Daisy where to set up to make sure everyone gets the final primping done so we're on time."

Ellie hugged Dani. "I'm glad you're here. I turn over responsibility of all the McKenna women to you." Ellie grabbed a tote bag and ushered Nell up the front staircase. "See you shortly."

Dani surveyed the group. "Who wants to go first?"

Ellie sat on a vanity chair, looking out the window but not seeing what was in front of her. She was oblivious as Nell clipped up sections of her long blond hair and twirled it around the hot curling iron. Her thoughts drifted back to the moment Pad walked into her gallery and life. *Daddy, if you can hear me, thank you for not giving up on me. For everything you did so I wouldn't miss out on the love of a good man. And for sending him back to me. I know it was you on the moors of Scotland.*

Out of the corner of Ellie's eye, she saw the soft, filmy form of her father appear on the window seat. "Nell. Would you give me a couple of minutes? Maybe you can check on Daisy."

"I'm almost done. Would you like me to finish first?"

Ellie shook her head. "I need a few minutes."

Nell left the room.

"Hi, Daddy."

"Pixie, you look radiant. You'll give Pad quite a start when he sees you walk down the aisle."

"I wish you could give me away." Tears slipped down Ellie's cheeks.

"I'll be with you each and every step down the aisle. Your grandfather on the right and me on your left."

Ellie grabbed a box of tissues. Using one, she dabbed her eyes. "Will I see you again?"

"I don't know."

Ellie's sapphire eyes shimmered. She stood up. "Can I hug you?"

Dad opened his arms, and Ellie walked into them. All the love she had in her heart rushed out into this one comforting embrace.

"I'll always love you, little one, and I'll be

with you wherever you go. You're going to have a wonderful life with your husband."

Ellie squeezed her eyes tight. She didn't know how long she stood in her father's arms until slowly, his warmth slipped away. She looked around the room. Ellie didn't see Dad, but she wasn't alone. She finally understood, her father was a part of who she had become.

"I love you, Daddy."

The door creaked. Cari stood on the threshold.

"Ellie, is everything okay?"

Ellie wiped the tears from her cheeks. "I'm fine, Mom. Can you ask Nell to come back in? I'm ready to put on my gown and get to my wedding."

"I'll be right back."

Ellie fingered the lace on her dress. "Eleanor McKenna Stone, it has a nice ring."

ani told Cari she'd lock up before heading out to Winnie's. She was glad to have had a few moments alone. After tidying the kitchen, she put Ellie's room back in order. Dani straightened the makeup on the vanity top and peered into the mirror.

Dani turned from side to side. "So much has changed, and yet I don't look different. Well, except for getting rid of the huge glasses." Dani leaned in and took a closer look. "Ellie was right, this evergreen-green silk sheath is very flattering." She took one last look. "I wonder what Paul sees when he looks at me."

"Dani?"

Dani spun around, her heart pounding. "Mom, you scared me."

"Your dad and I were driving out to the wedding and saw your car. I thought you might want to ride with us?" Mom looked around. "Who were you talking to?"

Dani's heart rate slowly returned to normal. "You know me, always talking to myself."

Mom turned Dani around. Side by side, mother and daughter looked at their reflection in the mirror. "To answer your question, when Paul looks at you, he sees the woman he loves. A strong-willed, fiercely independent woman with a huge heart. A heart encased in a thick, almost impenetrable outer shell but at long last a heart that is free to beat again without constraints."

"Do you think it's too soon to have fallen in love, or worse, is what I feel for Paul a rebound?"

"I don't. If you're unsure, did you talk to your therapist?"

"She said I've been over Derek for a long time and what I went through wasn't my fault. In her opinion, I shouldn't hold Paul at arm's-length. We had been dating and it was fun, easy, and most of all, I wanted to be with him because he made me smile on the inside."

"Falling in love doesn't happen on a

timetable. I loved your father from the first time I saw him. Like all married couples, we bicker from time to time, but it doesn't mean I haven't loved him with all my heart, every day since we met. Follow your heart, not your head, Dani. If you do, you'll know."

"I'd love to ride to the wedding with you and Dad."

Dani stepped from the car. Her heart skipped a beat when her eyes found Paul. "Mom, will you excuse me? I want to talk to Paul."

Olivia followed her daughter's eyes. "Go. Follow your heart."

Dani ached to slip her arms around his neck and declare her love for him. *Mom's right, I do know.*

"Pad, you look very handsome."

Pad tugged on his shirt. "Have you seen Ellie?"

"I saw her when she left the house. I drove out with my parents."

Paul asked, "Will you need a lift home?"

Dani giggled. "If you're offering, I might take you up on it."

Pad looked around the tent. "I wish it was time to get started." He wiped his palms on the sides of his pant legs. "This waiting is gonna kill me."

"Bro, I think you'll survive your pre-wedding jitters," Paul joked.

Paul kissed Dani lightly on the mouth. "I need to be the dutiful best man and get Pad to the altar. Maybe you could check on Ellie and report back to us?"

"I'd be happy to." Dani stood on tiptoes and kissed Pad's cheek. "She looks stunning."

Dani entered the main living room where Ellie was posing for pictures with Winnie. "I just saw your future husband, and he's a bundle of nerves."

Ellie twisted her pearl earring. "Me too."

Winnie kissed Ellie's cheeks. "I'll see you outside, my dear."

Ellie pulled Dani in front of the fireplace. "We need our picture taken too. Smile for the photographer."

"This is your day."

"Exactly. This is the last opportunity for us to have a picture as two girls." Ellie whispered, "We'll need to redo this picture soon when you're the one wearing white."

Dani gave in and enjoyed the moment.

Breathless, Ellie said, "I'm ready to get married."

"That's my cue to get everything organized."

"Yes, I can't wait one more minute."

Dani ushered everyone but Cari, Ray, and Dave, Ellie's grandfather, out of the room. Hovering at the door, she heard Ellie say, "Ray, would you walk down the aisle with me and Grandpa?"

Ray touched a finger to his lip. "I'd be honored, Ellie."

Dani bustled about, cueing the musicians and getting the last stragglers seated. Shane accompanied Cari down the aisle and took a seat next to Abby and Devin. Jake and Sara and the triplets were on the other side of the aisle with Don. Dani cued the wedding march and slipped into an empty chair next to her mom.

Ben toddled down the aisle, stopped, and scurried back to take his mother's hand. Kate glided down the flower-strewn aisle. She was halfway to the altar when Dani turned her attention to Pad. She grabbed her camera and waited. She wanted to capture Pad's expression the moment he saw Ellie.

Clicking rapidly, Dani got the shot.

Ellie reached Pad, and he took her outstretched hand. Dave and Ray took their seats and Kate arranged the back of Ellie's short scalloped lace train. Dani thought she had never seen a more beautiful bride. A lump lodged in her throat as she listened to Pad and Ellie exchange vows and seal their marriage with a kiss. Dani's eyes locked on Paul's as Ellie and Pad made their way down the aisle amid cheers from family and friends.

Paul held out his hand to Dani. "Shall we?"

Dani slipped her hand into Paul's. He kissed the top of her head. "I need to get outside for pictures."

Dani felt the first drop of rain on her arm. She looked toward the heavy clouds, holding out her hand. Another drop.

"Oh, shoot. I'll be right back." She ran to where she had stashed a bunch of clear umbrellas and grabbed what she could. Paul was right behind her. "Here, let me help."

Dani grew weak in the knees. "I can always count on you."

"Yes, you can." Paul flicked one open and held it over Dani. "Let's pass these out to the family, but first to Mr. and Mrs. Stone."

Paul opened a second umbrella when they reached Pad, who was holding his jacket over Ellie. "Pad."

Ellie's eyes widened. "I can't believe you have umbrellas."

"While someone I know was focused on food, I was keeping an eye on the weather. Go get your picture taken."

Ellie and Pad strolled away with the photographer trailing them. The remainder of the guests took cover under the large tent where the reception was to be held.

Paul and Dani stood closely, their bodies barely touching, hands interlocked.

"Paul?"

"Have I said you smell intoxicating?"

Heat flushed her cheeks. "I need to tell you something."

His finger lightly followed her jawline and slid over her lips. "I'm listening."

Her breath caught. "I can't think when you do…"

"I know." His finger trailed over her freckles.

"This morning, I had an epiphany."

"And?"

"I'm ready."

Paul's eyes searched hers "Are you saying what I've been longing to hear?"

With her face upturned, Dani said, "I am."

Paul dropped to one knee and reached into his pocket. He pulled out a small box, the velvet worn on the corners. "Dani. I have waited to find the woman I'd love for the rest of my life." He flipped open the top of the box. Nestled inside was a single solitary diamond ring. "I bought this ring two years ago, after the first moment I laid eyes on you at What's Perkin'. I've been carrying it with me ever since."

Dani gasped, clutching her heart. "For two years?"

"You captured my heart the moment I looked into your clear blue eyes and now, if you'll agree, I'm asking you to share the rest of my life."

Dani put her hands on his face and pulled him up to her lips. She whispered, "Oh, yes, I'll marry you."

The sun broke through the clouds as a rainbow curved above the rose garden.

If you loved Magic in the Rain help other readers find this book: **Please leave a review now!**

Bookbub
Goodreads

Are you ready to read more? Enjoy a sneak peek at **Breathe**, Book 1
in the Price Family Romance Series.

Also don't forget to sign up for my newsletter for a free download at www.lucindarace.com/ newletter

or

A FREE STORY FOR YOU

Have you enjoyed Magic in the Rain? Not ready to stop reading yet? If you sign up for my newsletter at www.lucindarace.com/news letter you will received Blends, the love story of Sam and Sherry, right away as my thank-you gift for choosing to get my newsletter.

Can two hearts blend together for a life long love..

His mother's final illness waylaid Sam Price's college dreams, but he's content working in his family's vineyard in a small town in upstate New York. When he finds a woman with a flat tire on a vineyard road, he's stunned to discover it's the girl he'd had a crush on in high school. He'd never been confident enough to ask her out back then. He'd been a farm kid. Her daddy was the bank president. Way out of his league.

Sherry Jones is tired of her parents' ambitious plans for her life. She'll finish her college accounting degree like they want, but how can she tell them about her real love: working with growing things? Then a flat tire and a neglected garden offer her an unexpected opportunity, with the added bonus of a tall, gorgeous guy with eyes that set her senses tingling.

What does a guy with dirt under his nails and calluses on his hands have to offer a woman like Sherry? It will take courage for her to defy her parents and claim her own dreams. Sam and Sherry's lives took different paths, but a winding vineyard road has brought them back together. Are they willing to take a chance to create the perfect blend for a lifelong love?

Blends is only available by signing up for my newsletter – sign up for it here at <u>www.lucin darace.com/newsletter</u>

LOVE TO READ?

Cowboys of River Junction

<u>Stars Over Montana</u>
The cowboy broke her heart but he never stopped loving her. Now she's back ready to run her grandfather's ranch…

Hiding in Montana

Orchard Brides Series
<u>Apple Blossoms in Montana</u>
Twenty years later Renee and Hank are back where

they fell in love but reality is like a spring frost and is a long-distance relationship their only option for their second chance?

The Sandy Bay Series
<u>Sundaes on Sunday</u>

A widowed school teacher and the airline pilot whose little girl is determined to bring her daddy and the lady from the ice cream shop together for a second chance at love.

Last Man Standing/Always a Bridesmaid
<u>Barrett</u>

Has the last man standing finally met his match?

<u>Marie</u> *May 2023*

Career focused city girl discovers small town charm can lead to love.

The Crescent Lake Winery Series
<u>Breathe</u>

Her dream come true may be the end of his...
Crush

The first time they met was fleeting, the second time restarted her heart.

<u>Blush</u>

He's always loved her but he left and now he's back…the question, does she still love him?

<u>Vintage</u>

He's an unexpected distraction, she gets his engine running…

<u>Bouquet</u>

Sweet second chances for a widow and the handsome billionaire…

Holiday Romance

<u>The Sugar Plum Inn</u>

The chef and the restaurant critic are about to come face to face.

Last Chance Beach

<u>Shamrocks are a Girl's Best Friend</u>

Will a bit of Irish luck and a matchmaking uncle give Kelly and Tric a chance to find love?

A Dickens Holiday Romance

<u>Holiday Heart Wishes</u>

change three sisters lives forever as they fulfill their grandmothers last request try on the dress.

<u>Borrowed</u>

He's just a borrowed boyfriend. He might also be her true love.

<u>Blue</u>

Will an enchanted wedding dress work its magic one more time?

The Loudon Series

<u>Between Here and Heaven</u>

Ten years of heaven on earth dissolved in an instant for Cari McKenna when her husband Ben died.

<u>Lost and Found</u>

Love never ends... A widow who talks to her late husband and her handsome single neighbor who has secretly loved her for years.

<u>The Journey Home</u>

Where do you go to heal your heart? You make the journey home...

<u>The Last First Kiss</u>

When life handed Kate lemons, she baked.

<u>Ready to Soar</u>

Kate will fight for love, won't she?
<u>Love in the Looking Glass</u>
Will Ellie's first love be her last or will she become a ghost like her father?
<u>Magic in the Rain</u>
Dani's plan of hiding in plain sight may not have been the best idea.

Cozy Mystery Books

A Bookstore Cozy Mystery Series
<u>Books & Bribes</u>
It was an ordinary day until the book of Practical Magic conked Lily on the head causing her to see stars. And then she discovered her cat, Milo, could talk.

Catnip & Crimes May 2023
The fun continues as Lily practices her magic and needs to investigate another murder.

Tea & Trouble August 2023
A fall festival and reading tea leaves and just

enough to propel Lily into a new murder investigation.

Scares & Dares October 2023
A haunted house and Halloween, what could go wrong in the small town of Pembroke Cove?

SOCIAL MEDIA

Follow Me on Social Media

Like my Facebook page
Join Lucinda's Heart Racer's Reader Group on
Facebook
Twitter @lucindarace
Instagram @lucindraceauthor
BookBub
Goodreads
Pinterest

ABOUT THE AUTHOR

Award-winning and best-selling author Lucinda Race is a lifelong fan of reading. As a young girl, she spent hours reading novels and getting lost in the fun and hope they represent. While her friends dreamed of becoming doctors and engineers, her dreams were to become a writer—a novelist.

As life twisted and turned, she found herself writing nonfiction but longed to turn to her true passion. After developing the storyline for A McKenna Family Romance, it was time to start living her dream. Her fingers practically fly over computer keys as she weaves stories of mystery and romance.

Lucinda lives with her two little dogs, a miniature long hair dachshund and a shih tzu mix rescue, in the rolling hills of western Massachusetts. When she's not at her day job, she's immersed in her fictional worlds. And if she's not writing romance or cozy mystery novels, she's reading everything she can get her hands on.